Windsong

Published in the UK in 2023 by Cool Clear Press

Copyright © Rosalie James 2023

First edition published 2023

Rosalie James has asserted their right under
the Copyright, Designs and Patents Act, 1988,
to be identified as the author of this work.

Paperback ISBN 978-1-7399780-2-0
eBook ISBN 978-1-7399780-4-4

Cover design and typeset by SpiffingCovers

for the latest information visit:
rosaliejamesauthor.com

Windsong

ROSALIE JAMES

'If it is true that there are as many minds as there are heads, then there are as many kinds of love, as there are hearts.'

Leo Tolstoy

SPRING 1986

LYDIA

'One day I turned my back on the life I had always known and walked away. I never intended to look back'. Lydia put down her pen and sighed. In the last half an hour, she had only managed these few words. Her therapist told her that writing about her feelings would help her make sense of the last five years, but every time she started, the task overwhelmed her.

Since finding the courage to leave her family home and move away, Lydia was still quite reliant on Jane. Over several sessions, Jane helped Lydia to see that as a child and even a young adult, her mother had tried to mould her into a young version of herself. Juniper had also relied on her daughter emotionally, in a way that she should not have.

'It may be,' Jane suggested, 'that your mother believed she could wipe the slate of her own life clean. Perhaps she couldn't see that in doing so, she was sublimating your life to hers.'

Lydia was surprised at this assessment of her mother. 'You see Lydia, it is the adult who takes responsibility here, not the child. Your task is to come to terms with how it has made you feel.' Jane paused, allowing her words to hang in the air. After a while Lydia broke the silence.

'I feel guilty,' she said, 'as if I'm being disloyal speaking about Mum like this. Letting her down, when she only had my best interests at heart.' Jane sat quietly, waiting for Lydia to say more. After a while, she said, 'Most children don't like the idea of boarding school, but when I was sent away, I was relieved. I didn't want Mum to know I felt like that.'

'You mean you felt disloyal, wanting to go away?'

'I suppose I did. I was afraid Mum would think I didn't want to be with her anymore if she knew I was looking forward to it.'

'Is there any reason she might have thought that?'

'She was very insecure. With Dad away all the time, she only had me.'

'You have a brother, don't you?' Jane asked gently. 'Roger, isn't it?'

'Yes, but he lives in France. He and Mum don't get on all that well.'

'Did you believe that your mother's happiness was your responsibility?'

'Yes, I think I did.' There was a silence while Jane waited for Lydia to elaborate, but she didn't.

'What about your own happiness?' asked Jane.

'My own happiness?' asked Lydia, surprised. 'I've never thought about it.' There was a silence while Lydia reflected on this, then she said. 'I suppose I was too busy coping, to think of being happy. Mum got so depressed after Alice died. They'd become close and Mum began to rely on her. She said Alice was the only true friend she'd ever had. I don't think anyone else realised, about the depression I mean. I was the only one who saw it.'

'Lydia, you were barely more than a child yourself. Was there anyone you could have told, perhaps turned to for help?'

'Who could I tell?' she said. 'Dad was never there.' Lydia looked at the floor, following the swirls on the carpet, trying to block the memory. The feeling that she was responsible for Juniper, the fear that she might do something terrible. It still weighed heavily on her.

'You said a moment ago that you were too busy coping. Would you like to say more about that?'

Lydia's voice began to shake, 'It was just life. I was coping with living, trying to be normal with the other kids; while at home, nothing was normal. Even school became impossible in the end.' She wiped away a tear. 'There was constant pressure to be slim, to be witty and to be liked. I just didn't know how to deal with it.'

'Is that when you stopped eating?'

'Look, I don't want to talk about this,' Lydia burst out. 'You know what happened, we've talked about it before. My mother didn't even notice I had bulimia, she just sent me away again. If she hadn't, she might have had to stop thinking about herself. She might have done something to help me for once.'

'You sound as if you are angry about that, Lydia.' Lydia began to cry then and Jane pushed a box of tissues towards her.

'Mum sent me to Aunt Alice. I'd always loved her. She was undemanding and I felt I could tell her anything. In the end, it was Alice who saw that I needed help. Mum and I went to family counselling together. For the first time, I felt seen, heard and understood for who I am, and for what I was feeling. Unfortunately, my relationship with Mum became a casualty of the process.'

'How did that play out?' asked Jane.

'I think she was just so shocked to find that she had been at fault, it honestly hadn't occurred to her. For a while, we got on much better. Mum showed me more kindness and understanding. She treated me with a new respect. She even admitted once, that counselling had helped her as much as it had me.'

'So did you feel your mother was beginning to take some responsibility, at that stage?'

'I don't know, but I do remember her saying, "Nobody teaches you how to be a mother you know, Lydia. It is very hard, nobody realises that. Being an adult is hard as well. All I can say is that I've done my best and I'm sorry if I have let you down." Mum cried then, trying to make me feel guilty.'

'Did you feel guilty?'

'Yes, I did, but I fought it. Our family therapist likened our worries and feelings to monkeys. She said that each person should look after their own. I was able to see that this was Mum's monkey, and I was determined not to take it on.'

'That sounds like good advice, did you succeed?'

'It was hard, there was always the guilt, the feeling that I was responsible for her. But I kept reminding myself of our therapist's words. She said that when we take responsibility for our own feelings, we can meet each other in the middle, with equanimity and understanding. I kept reminding Mum of that, but she didn't want to hear it. Over time, no matter what her intention, Mum slowly reverted to type. Perhaps it was the death of Aunt Alice that derailed her, followed by the divorce from my father.

'So, despite the family counselling, living with Mum became as difficult as it had ever been. More so, because I knew things could be different. I began to question the way Mum was, instead of blindly accepting it.'

'In what ways, specifically, did she become more difficult?'

asked Jane.

'Mum was always needy, she expected me to become a counsellor and support her. It was as if she was the child and I was the parent. Sometimes it became too much, and I would escape by walking across the park. There was a library just the other side of it, where I could step into another world and lose myself.'

'Are books important to you?'

'They make me feel safe and they give me escape routes, so yes, they are very important. It's why I work in a library.'

'Have you ever considered keeping a diary?' asked Jane. 'Writing about how you feel can be helpful.'

'I've kept one for years,' said Lydia. 'It's full of frustration and anger, mostly.'

'Is there anything positive in it?' asked Jane.

Lydia thought for a moment and then she said, 'Not much, if I'm honest. Life's been pretty unfair.' She studied the swirls on the carpet again, as the silence lengthened. Eventually, she took a deep breath and looked up at Jane. 'I want things to be different from now on.'

Jane glanced at her watch, 'Well done Lydia, I feel we've had a bit of a breakthrough today. You've made real progress.' Lydia stood up.

'Thank you. I need to get back to work now. I'll see you next week.'

THE LIBRARY

The library had wide, high windows above the bookshelves. Shafts of bright sunlight sliced into the gloom as Lydia pushed the trolley around. She stopped now and again to replace a book, taking pleasure in the neatly ordered rows and the monotony of her task. As she did her rounds, she was looking for a book called, 'A Night to Remember' by Walter Lord.

The recent discovery of the wreckage of the Titanic, off the coast of Newfoundland, captured Lydia's imagination. She found herself wondering how it must have felt to be suspended in deep water, spiralling down and down to certain death. Lord's book was said to be the best account of the sinking, documenting the testimonies of some of the survivors.

As she moved through the aisles, she noticed a slightly built man perusing the reference books. He turned briefly towards her as she passed, but returned his attention to the shelves, as she continued on her way. After that, she noticed him at the library often. He would sit at one of the tables to take a few notes, then replace his book and leave. She wondered whether other people found sanctuary in the library as she did. For Lydia, it was a place of safety, like a quiet cocoon.

Juniper's lifelong influence continued to press at the edges of Lydia's being, bleeding into the blank canvas of her life. She felt both responsible for her mother's happiness and yet, desperate to free herself.

When she eventually found the courage to leave home, two years after her parents' divorce, it was Grandmère Clémence who provided Lydia with a small allowance and the use of a modest flat on the south coast. 'Lydia darling, the time has come for you to strike out on your own. I promise you; your mother will be alright. She needs to find her own way in life, as you do.'

Lydia cut herself off from her mother when she moved. Juniper didn't know where she lived, nor did she have her number. It felt cruel, but it was the only hope Lydia had of breaking free and finally learning to live as an independent adult.

At first, the move was everything Lydia dreamed it would be. It was only when she was without the responsibility of her mother, that she saw how all-consuming it had been. It was a relief to be alone, to be herself. She had a view of the beach and the sea and could fall asleep to the sound of the waves. She could eat when she felt like it, and best of all, she was free of her mother's constant observations of her shortcomings. Lydia knew they were well meant, but they chipped away at her self-esteem, like the relentless drip of a leaking tap.

It took Lydia no time at all to find the job at the local library. Her experience and love of books convinced them that she would be an ideal replacement for one of their staff, who was about to retire. The work engaged Lydia's mind just enough to stop her from thinking too much. The environment was cordial rather than friendly, so Lydia could keep herself to herself, no questions asked.

At the end of her working day, she walked the short distance home to her flat. The building was separated from the beach by a wide road and a low wall. Seagulls swooped and called as she rummaged for her keys, her nostrils full of the fresh salty air. She often walked across the road in the early evening to feed the seagulls, taking some old bread for them, rather than throwing it away. They were company of sorts, she supposed. She pushed the front door open and climbed the stairs to the first floor.

Once inside her flat, she looped her coat onto the hook in the hall and pressed the button to play back her messages. The clipped tones of her mother's voice filled the room, 'Lydia, it's me. It's been so long since we spoke. Why are you hiding from us all, darling? I do miss you. Please write to tell me how you are.' The colour drained from Lydia's face. How had her mother found her number? For a moment her carefully constructed, independent world, collided with the girl she had once been; the girl from another lifetime who was never good enough – still wasn't good enough.

She closed her eyes and gripped the edge of the hall table as she swayed, taking deep breaths to steady herself. After a moment, she went directly to the fridge and opened a bottle of wine. She poured herself a large glass of it to steady her nerves, downing it quickly. Then she topped it up, drinking it more slowly this time. She walked over to sit near the long window, to watch darkness falling. The dark made her anxious these days. There was a time when she might have sat by the open window all evening, listening to the waves. It didn't occur to her then, that she could be seen from outside.

It was an evening like this, soon after moving into her flat, that it had happened. She blamed herself, and she blamed the wine. So why was she still drinking so much of it? She pulled the curtains together smartly, to shut out her concerns. By the time she had finished her third glass of wine, her worries had evaporated, giving way to intense loneliness. So she topped her glass up once again, to chase it away.

Alcohol had become her secret, her way of coping with the knocks life kept throwing her way. She almost always drank alone, not wanting to admit, even to herself, how dependent she had become. Who would she drink with anyway? She didn't know anyone. Each morning as she plied herself with hangover remedies before work, she swore she would cut down. By the evening, as she walked back home, her overriding thought was her first sip.

The memory of what happened that night was eating away at her. It was getting worse as time passed, and it threatened to derail her. It was an evening much like this one. She had just secured a job at the library and was celebrating alone. She wished she had some friends, a boyfriend, anyone really, just to share the moment with. By 9 p.m., the wine bottle was empty and she·was unsteady on her feet. She'd eaten a few nuts, but had forgotten to make a meal for herself. It wasn't the first time.

The doorbell rang, which was odd, she didn't know anyone. She walked unsteadily to the door and peered through the peephole. It was a balding man in his fifties, did he live upstairs? With hindsight, she should never have opened the door, but at the time she'd been desperate for company and the wine made her reckless. She put her head in her hands, trying to block out the memory.

She slept deeply that night and, in the morning, instead of taking hangover pills, she pulled on her swimsuit and walked out to the beach for her first sea swim. The initial contact with the icy water made her wince, but she ploughed on, determined to go in. She dived forward into a wave, shrieking and gasping with shock as she emerged. Her skin became numb, and her fingers and toes experienced actual pain from the cold as she tried to steady her gasping breath. The shock sent her into survival mode, her mind and body instantly uniting in their quest to preserve life. She held her hands out of the water to ease the icy pain of it, before slowly lowering them in again.

After a painful few minutes, her body began to tingle and come alive, then her breathing slowed. The water began to cradle her like a cold, comfortable compress and she relaxed. She experienced an unexpected moment of pure bliss, suddenly understanding what it meant to be at one with herself, for the first time ever. As she floated in the cold water, slowly acclimatising to the temperature, she was wrapped in an overwhelming feeling of calm and well-being. It was as if the sea was holding her in its arms, rocking her, telling her that everything would be alright. She felt her face and jaw soften and her mouth relaxed into a smile.

Wow! What had just happened? Could it be that the sea was showing her the way to a new future? If it was, she knew then, that she held the key in her hand. After she had showered and dressed for work, Lydia poured the remaining wine from her fridge down the sink. On her way home she would buy some proper food, some soft drinks, fresh lemons and ice cubes to enjoy after work. She set off with a new purpose, still enjoying a deep feeling of calm. She could do this. Hadn't she seen a notice at the library for a new sewing group? Perhaps she would muster the courage to join. What did she have to lose?

VIDDY

The last thing he remembered, was the old piece of frayed ribbon he kept in his pocket; rubbing his grubby fingers along its length, as he fell into an uneasy sleep. He was hunkered down for the night in a sheltered doorway out of the wind. The smell of alcohol and piss wormed its way into his consciousness as he closed his eyes.

It must have been much later when he felt the first punch to the side of his head, and then relentless kicks to his torso, then nothing at all. Later, he became aware of bouncing and swaying, as if he was in a cradle. A wailing siren wrapped itself around him, as he sunk into a bed more comfortable than anywhere he had slept for a long time. The pain had gone and he was floating.

He drifted along in the softness and warmth, as it lulled him back into oblivion. At the back of his eyes, musical notes danced like fireflies, merging until their great collective light dazzled him. He felt himself drawn into the light, dancing with a freedom he had never known. He felt infinite, overwhelming joy until he was jolted back. It was much later that he understood he had come close to death.

When the ambulance arrived, Sarah rushed outside with the team. A thin unshaven man lay on the stretcher, his eyes closed, a dark lock of greasy hair falling across his face. His bony hands hung over the top of the bed cover, and a ring, ingrained with dirt, clung to his finger. He was dressed in filthy old clothes, and the stench swam up around them as they lifted the rolling bed from the ambulance.

His eyes opened then, just briefly, blinking in the dawn light, before doors opened like a mouth and swallowed him. He was wheeled along the throaty white corridors of an alien landscape, voices and lights echoing into his mind, pulling him this way and that. An elongated sun shone on him and then it was gone, shone again and was gone. The voices chatted on, echoing and receding in his mind, 'attacked', 'homeless', 'harmless'. Finally, there was a jolt and he was still; the light faded, the voices went quiet and he was alone.

Sarah quickly completed the admission papers. She was tired, nearing the end of a ten-hour shift. She headed for the canteen where doctors and other staff sat around eating, drinking and gazing vacantly into the crowd. The smell of food, heat and stale air greeted her as she pushed through the double swing doors. The early morning sun was beginning to slant through the windows, illuminating tired faces and the grey linoleum floor of the canteen.

Sarah asked for some hot buttered toast. Clutching a mug of strong tea, she went to sit by the window, to look out at the misty morning. Beads of moisture glinted on the grass, and birds cocked their heads before plunging their beaks into the earth in search of worms. She was impatient to be outside.

Sustained by food and a hot drink, Sarah made her way towards the staff room. She pulled on her walking boots and coat. She would head home through the woods, then along the path towards the sea. She pushed through the revolving doors, leaving the heat of the foyer, and was quickly enveloped by the chilly morning air. She strode across the car park to join the path to the village, sighing a long, relieved breath into the morning air. Her shoulders dropped, her jaw relaxed and a smile played about her lips. She loved this time of day. It felt quiet, fresh and new after the intense environment of the hospital. It was still too early for most people to be out and Sarah relished her time alone on the walk home.

As she walked, her mind drifted back to the patient. How could that young man have been brought so low? Sunlight flashed through the trees, as she stepped through shadows playing across her path. Two breathless runners emerged suddenly from the woods, chatting as they flew past her, their voices trailing ghost-like, as they ran out of sight.

Eventually, Sarah reached the clearing that heralded the ascent to the cliff path. Seagulls swooped overhead, their white bodies catching shafts of sunlight through the mist. Higher and higher she climbed, her steps releasing the rich loamy smell of freshly dug earth. When she finally reached the top, she stopped to gaze at the view. The sea, far below her, sparkled at the base of white cliffs, rising vertically into a blue sky. She sat down on a rock for a moment to catch her breath, her mind wandering back to the hospital and the unconscious man. Who was he?

Before her shift began the next morning, Sarah went to look in on him. His old clothes had been taken away and, in their place, a faded hospital gown swamped his thin body. He lay bathed and shaved in the only available bed, at the far end of the ward. His shoulder-length hair, now clean, lay across his pillow. His face was gaunt, pale and badly bruised, and his lips were gently parted in sleep. The dirt on his hands had been carefully scrubbed away by a diligent nurse, and his ring carefully washed and placed on the locker by his bed.

Sarah had a brief word with the nurse on duty, to try to find out more. 'He seems to have no idea who or where he is,' said Anna. 'He just gazes vacantly about him. If anyone is in his line of vision, it's as if he can't see them. Otherwise, he sleeps.'

'Such a shame,' said Sarah. 'I wonder who he is?'

'Me too,' said Anna. 'I bet he was handsome once upon a time, have you seen those eyelashes?' Sarah smiled.

'OK, thanks,' she said. 'I'll pop in again tomorrow.'

The next day there was some progress. Anna reported that he had eaten hungrily of everything offered, before falling again into a heavy sleep. He was able to walk unsteadily to the bathroom to relieve himself, before returning to bed, trembling with the effort. Anna said that tears ran down his face as he lay back against the pillows, and she tried to speak to him.

'He just closed his eyes, as if he wanted to shut me out. "Tell me your name," I said to him. I didn't want to walk away, I couldn't. He seemed so very sad and lonely. So I persisted, I told him my name is Anna and that I wouldn't take no for an answer. I can't bear to think of him having no family, and being handed over to social services. He looks so delicate somehow, as if a puff of wind might blow him away. Do you know what I mean?'

Sarah did know, he had an other-worldly look, almost ethereal. It was how she might have pictured Christ on the cross. A plan formed in her mind. She wasn't sure why, but she wanted to help this young man, to get him back on his feet again. She and

Andrew could share their little bungalow, nestling in the downs. He could recuperate by helping in the garden while benefitting from the healing sea air. Her husband would say she was soft in the head, and maybe she was, but she knew in the end he would smile and agree.

On the ward, the man in the bed struggled to hear the concerned voice of the nurse, who looked in on him every now and again. A pretty girl brought her face close to his, her mouth was moving but no sound emerged. She seemed to be trying to tell him something but he couldn't say what. He could still hear the gentle melody of shining, musical notes in his mind. The beauty of the sweet sound dazzled him, as it rose and fell about the room. Arms reached out to touch him, then slid away. He felt tears on his face, salt ran into his mouth, down his chin and into the crevices of his neck. His fingers moved over the sheets and then were still. He saw the face of his mother gazing gently into his own, her skin the colour of pale olives, her fine curly hair swinging forward as she willed him to live. A thread of strength insinuated itself into his heart then, and it pulled him gently back. He could hear himself mumbling as he reached out to touch her face.

'There you are,' said Anna. 'That wasn't so hard, was it? So, your name is Viddy, I haven't heard that one before. How about I pour you a nice glass of water.'

THE SEWING GROUP - SPRING

Anya looked around the light, airy space, pleased with what she had created. Wide glass doors looked over a dewy lawn, and the first blossoms of spring adorned her small apple tree.

Inside, black and white floral floor tiles were offset by two azure blue sofas and a couple of armchairs. These were arranged in a large, open circle at one end of the spacious room. At the other end, a wide sewing table was surrounded by six chairs. Anya's paintings and other art she had collected over the years, hung haphazardly around the studio walls, interspersed with colourful patchwork and appliqué canvases, each with its own memory of a particular time in her life. The overall effect conspired to make the room look warm, comfortable and welcoming.

Her first sewing group took place on a sunny Saturday morning. There was still a chill in the air, but the sky was clear blue and the first daffodils were nodding in the breeze. Anya glanced at her watch as she heard footsteps approaching. A flamboyantly dressed young man was making his way up the wide steps, to the studio door. He wore silver trousers with a red belt, knee-length flat boots and a white ruffled shirt. Over this, he wore a navy, military-style jacket, its lapels lined with gold brocade. The jacket had wide scarlet cuffs, overlaid with gold stripes. His long curly hair was held back in a loose ponytail. Anya's face broke into a smile as she beckoned him in, 'Come on in!' she said, opening the door. 'You must be Jonathan.'

'I am,' he said, 'how did you guess? Don't answer that,' he said laughing. 'I expect I'm the only man.'

'I believe you are,' said Anya. 'You are very welcome! Lovely to have you here.' Just then, a willowy girl in a long skirt and skinny rib jumper stepped inside. She had long dark hair, an anxious face and round glasses.

'Am I in the right place for the sewing group?' she said uncertainly.

'Yes, come on in,' said Anya smiling. 'I am Anya and this is Jonathan.'

'I'm Lydia,' she said smiling.

'There is a row of hooks for your coats over there, make yourselves at home,' said Anya, turning to greet two more people who had arrived together. Anya recognised Maggie, who explained she was pregnant when she enrolled. Beside her was the final attendee who must, therefore, be Sarah, the local nurse.

'Maggie and Sarah, welcome!' said Anya. The two women looked at one another surprised and then broke into smiles.

Maggie wore a round neck knitted dress that clung to her large belly and she looked hot. Her wispy hair escaped from clips designed to hold it off her face. 'I carn understand it,' she said loudly, 'It's nowhere near summer and yet I feel as if I'm permanently in some kinda sauna.'

'Come on in, Maggie,' said Anya. 'There's a seat for you over here, let me get you a glass of water.'

'Thanks,' she said gratefully, 'just what I need.'

'Sarah, you can hang your coat over there,' said Anya, pointing to the hooks.

'Thank you,' said Sarah breezily, 'will do!'

Jonathan and Lydia sat down on the larger sofa, Maggie on the small one and Sarah in one of the armchairs. Anya came back with some water for Maggie and then joined them in the remaining armchair.

'Welcome everyone!' said Anya. 'This is the first of several sewing circles I'm planning over the coming year. I want it to be a place we can come together for friendship, enjoyment and to learn new skills.'

'Christ, I 'spect you lot'll run rings round me,' stated Maggie. 'I don't know one end of a needle from the other!'

'Well, that's why we're here,' said Anya. 'No prior knowledge expected, but equally, if any of you are experienced sewers, I can advise on more advanced work too. We will each progress at our own pace.

'I want to share with you the deep calm, and pleasure that a love of sewing, or any other quiet skill for that matter, can bring. Let's start by introducing ourselves and maybe you could each say briefly why you decided to come here today. Who'd like to start?'

Maggie and Jonathan began to speak at the same time, and then both stopped and laughed. 'Go on Jonathan, you begin,' said Anya.

'OK, well, as you heard, I'm Jonathan. I'm a final year fashion student. I can already sew, reasonably well, and I design my own clothes.' There were collective 'oohs' and 'aahs' as the others smiled.

'Told ya,' burst out Maggie. 'I don't stand a chance with you lot!' Then she laughed raucously before beginning to cough and splutter. A sip of water calmed her throat, as Jonathan continued.

'The reason I've joined is to find some space to plan my final show. I want my ideas to flow unhindered by all the other planning that goes on around me at college. I've got some great ideas, but they need refining. I'm thinking of gold embroidered embellishments. I need some help with that, learning how to do it I mean. It's the detail that gets me every time.' He stopped, pushing an escaped tendril of his long hair back over his shoulder. Then he looked around at everyone and smiled, leaning back into the sofa, his silver-coloured legs and boots stretched out in front of him.

'Thank you, Jonathan.' The others murmured and smiled as Anya added, 'Would you like to go next, Maggie?'

'I've gone all shy,' she said, her eyes downcast. 'Just for you though, can I be honest?'

'Of course,' said Anya, smiling.

'I've come 'ere for some peace and quiet. Me old man won't leave me alone. He knows I'm preggers, but it don't stop 'im wanting 'is lunch on time, 'is dinner on time, the fridge full of 'is favourite foods. 'E goes mad if I forget something. What's 'e gonna be like when the baby comes, that's what I'd like to know.' She paused, sighing in defeat, fiddling with her jewellery, as the group looked on, unsure what to say.

'Did you have something in mind you would like to make, Maggie? Have you done any sewing before?' asked Anya.

'It was years ago now, I used to sew with me Nan,' she said wistfully. 'They were really 'appy times.' She paused, then said, 'I was actually thinking of making one of them baby blankets, you know with a bit of patchwork in the middle, maybe a rabbit, or summat like that.'

'That sounds lovely,' said Sarah encouragingly, speaking for the first time and looking at Maggie with concern.

'It does,' said Anya, 'I'd love to help you with that.' She paused for a moment and smiled, 'Now, Sarah, why don't you go next?'

'I'm a nurse at the hospital,' she said. 'As you can imagine, some days can be harrowing and some just plain exhausting. I happened to see the flyer in the library, on my way home from a difficult shift. It was the word 'calm' that attracted me. I think it's time for me to try to regain some balance and build in some me time. I can't sew though,' she said, 'but I'm willing to learn.' She looked at Anya with a grin and shrugged her shoulders.

'I think you said you work at the library, Lydia?' asked Anya.

'Yes, I do, I've always loved books. I've started sea swimming recently too.'

'Sea swimmin'? Are you outa ya bleedin' mind?' said Maggie.

They all laughed then and Sarah said, 'I hear it can be really good for you. Did you enjoy it?'

'It was freezing to start with but after a while, it felt amazing.' Lydia couldn't believe she'd said so much and went quiet. She wanted to hug her sea experience to herself, like a secret; fearful that in sharing it, some of the joy might be lost. Sarah made a mental note to suggest Viddy take it up, it would do him good to get out of the house.

Then Anya asked her, 'Have you done any sewing before, Lydia?'

'A bit,' she said. 'I've got a family of felt mouse characters. I used to make outfits for them as a child. It probably sounds silly, but I enjoyed it.'

'That sounds fun,' said Anya. 'Good,' she said, looking round at them all. 'It's been really helpful to get an understanding of where you are all starting from.'

An hour later, when decisions had been made about what they would all work on in the coming classes, Anya stood up. 'Let's have a break there. Who would like some coffee and cake?' she said, moving into a small kitchen beside the studio. They all sat around chatting for a while, discussing ideas and enjoying Anya's cake.

'Is everyone clear on what they need to bring next time?' asked Anya. 'If you have any queries just give me a call, my number is on

THE SEWING GROUP - SPRING

this card.' She handed one to each of them.

'Thanks Anya,' said Sarah. Then they gathered their things ready to leave. 'See you next week. Which way is everyone going?' asked Sarah. 'I've got my car, so I can offer a lift towards the hospital.'

'I'm goin' that way,' said Maggie.

'Hop in then,' said Sarah. 'Anyone else?' Jonathan and Lydia looked at one another.

'I'm heading back towards the library,' said Lydia.

'Me too,' said Jonathan. 'I live near the park, it's on the way.' They set off together, and Lydia found herself tongue-tied. Jonathan didn't seem to notice, he chatted about plans for his end-of-year fashion show, a party he was attending at the weekend and his love of outlandish clothes. When there was a silence, she tried to think of something interesting to say, but he started on another topic. It was a bit like listening to a lively radio broadcast. Then, when there was another silence he turned to Lydia and said, 'So, you work at the library. How long have you been there?'

'It's the only job I've ever had, it must be a few months now,' she said. She could feel her cheeks growing warm, uncomfortable being the focus of his attention. She told him about the children's book circle she'd started on Friday mornings, and began to relax.

Soon they came to a neat row of Victorian houses, and Jonathan said, 'This is me.' He pulled open the gate and stepped onto a tiled path leading to a blue front door. A dog started to bark inside. He turned and smiled, 'That's Tilly. Do you like dogs?' Without waiting for an answer, he unlocked the door and a little white dog came bowling out of the house, its whole body wagging in excitement at Jonathan's return. Lydia's face broke into a delighted smile, her shyness forgotten. She closed the gate behind her and bent down to stroke the little dog.

'You are adorable,' she said, laughing.

'I know she is; I'm lumbered with her while my parents are away.'

'She's so sweet,' said Lydia. 'How long will they be away?'

'Oh, it's been a while,' he said. 'They're usually gone for a few months. They'll be back in a month or so.'

'Well, if you ever want someone to walk her for you, I'd be

glad to. I love dogs. The library is just around the corner.'

'Do you mean it?' he said. 'That would be the most fantastic help. My sister usually does it during the day, but even she's about to go away for a couple of weeks.'

'Definitely,' said Lydia. 'Just let me know. Here's my number, I don't live far from here.'

On the way home, Lydia could hardly believe her own boldness. Jonathan was gorgeous, not that he'd be interested in her, obviously. Still, she'd love to help out with his dog. Anya was nice too. Why couldn't her own mother be homey and welcoming like that? She smiled, glad she'd made the effort to go along to the group. She wondered whether Anya was the kind of person she might be able to confide in.

JUNIPER

Juniper pulled on a jacket and strode purposefully out into the morning air. Her walks along the River Thames calmed her, bringing routine to days she might otherwise have struggled to fill. The sun shone brightly in a crisp blue sky, as she walked along the well-trodden path to the riverside.

Her divorce from Étienne two years ago, even though she had feared it, was ultimately a relief. She was finally free from a life lived in the background of his affairs. Over the years, Juniper learned to turn a blind eye, and Étienne trusted that she would. It resulted in a toxic relationship, rotting slowly from its heart.

It was only after the divorce, when the uncertainty fell away, that Juniper realised how much it was affecting her. She was so young when they married, and Étienne, ten years older, had taken advantage of her youth and malleability.

Nothing changed for him. He continued to live his life much as he had before their wedding, she could see that now. She realised with the clarity of hindsight, that she'd been a pawn in a game designed to please Clémence, his exacting French mother.

It hardly mattered anymore, she sighed as she strode along. There was something liberating in the knowledge that it was all behind her. Her beautiful home in Richmond Park was hers, she had grown up there. Thankfully, her parents had the foresight to ensure her sole ownership, in what seemed at the time, the unlikely event of her divorce. She found great comfort in her home. She smiled to herself; life was good.

It was a glorious morning, the mist was burning off and it was beginning to feel warm. She would stop at her favourite waterside café, near Teddington Lock, to watch the boats come and go. Even in the spring, it was surprising how often the weather was pleasant enough to be outside.

The waitress raised her hand to Juniper as she approached, and offered her a table in the sun, near the water. Juniper sat down and leaned back, closing her eyes for a moment, enjoying the feeling of the warmth on her face. A few minutes later, a steaming cup of coffee was put in front of her.

'Thank you,' she said smiling at the waitress. She took a long sip and sighed, feeling so lucky to have this small pleasure in her life. As she reached out to take another sip of her coffee, a long shadow fell across the table. She looked up in surprise, as a man of about her own age leaned over.

'Excuse me, is this chair free?'

Couldn't he see that this was her table? She looked up at him with what she hoped was a discouraging look, as he continued, 'It's just that the other tables are either occupied, or in the shade. I thought you might not mind sharing.'

What on earth had given him that idea, she thought, trying to hide her surprise. He sat down, quite unperturbed by her lack of welcome and raised his hand for the waitress. Juniper recovered her composure and said belatedly, 'Of course, yes, please do.' She turned back to her coffee and continued surveying the river and the nearby tables, as if he wasn't there. She could see his arm out of the corner of her eye, resting on the table. It was broad and tanned with blonde hair, surrounding a heavy wristwatch. He wore light beige loose cotton trousers and she could see the pale blue cuff of a fine cotton shirt. As he looked up to order his coffee, she saw he had a tanned face, with heavy lines around blue eyes. His thick blonde hair was streaked with grey, and he wore an unlikely pale denim baseball cap.

His was not the uniform of an ambler along a muddy towpath nor that of a dog walker. As he had already invaded her space, she decided she might as well make the best of it.

'Are you here on holiday?' she asked awkwardly.

'Not really,' he said. 'I'm here to get a repair done to my boat. Although, I always feel a little as if I'm on holiday when I'm near the water.' He leaned back and smiled at her, relaxed and unhurried. 'How about you?'

'I live a couple of miles along the river, in Richmond,' she said. 'I walk along the Thames most days. I find the water calming; it clears my head. This little café is a favourite stop-off.'

They sat in silence for a while, and Juniper continued to look out across the water, sipping her coffee. She felt him watching her, and sensed a faintly amused smile on his face. When the waitress arrived with his coffee and distracted him, Juniper rummaged in her bag and pulled out a large compact. It was set with colourful mosaic stones, a gift from her flamboyant friend, Hermione. Juniper felt self-conscious using it, particularly as the man was now glancing in her direction again. He seemed to have all the time in the world, as he thoughtfully sipped his coffee, leaning back in his seat in leisurely contemplation of her.

Juniper thought him rather rude. He must have sensed her awkwardness and appeared to be doing his best to make her uncomfortable. She glanced briefly into the mirror, dabbing the corners of her mouth with her napkin, then clicked the compact shut and stood up. 'Well, I must be going, it was nice to meet you.' She paused, realising she didn't know his name.

'Jed,' he volunteered, 'likewise.' He tipped his fingers up to the peak of his baseball cap, as she turned to walk away. 'You didn't tell me yours,' he called. She turned back and he smiled, 'Your name,' he said.

'Juniper. It's Juniper, goodbye!'

Juniper walked back towards home. That was unexpected, she thought, unsure whether the man had annoyed or intrigued her. She was used to spending full days without speaking to a soul, always observing, rarely interacting. Jed had taken her by surprise, just sitting down at her table like that. Normally one look from Juniper would be enough to deter any unwelcome company.

Far from being intimidated, Jed had seemed faintly amused. His affable, and yes, she had to admit, handsome face was rather agreeable. His blue eyes crinkled as he looked directly at her, eyelids relaxed and slightly hooded as he studied her. She felt a flush creeping up her neck as she pictured it. Did he say he was waiting for his boat? She thought he had. It probably explained why his face was so tanned, no doubt from hours spent on board. Why had she been so unfriendly? She sighed, conversation seemed to come so easily to some people. Why was she so awkward and self-conscious? She couldn't deny that the encounter had unsettled her.

She let herself in through the gate on the lane in Richmond

Park, bolting it behind her, and then ambled through the garden. The blossom trees were abundant at this time of year and she stopped for a moment to take long, calming breaths. She listened to the birdsong as she followed the trail of pale pink petals, along the path to the garden door. As she turned the key, she heard the phone ringing in the house. She hurried inside and picked it up, 'Hello,' she said breathlessly.

'Hello, is that Juniper?' said a man's voice.

'Yes, it is. Who is that speaking?' she said, more stiffly than she intended.

'This is Jed, from the waterside café. You dropped your purse.'

'My purse?' said Juniper, hastily opening her bag, confirming that her small change purse had indeed fallen out.

'I hope you don't mind,' he said, 'I took the liberty of opening it, in the hope of finding a contact number for you.'

There was a silence. Juniper certainly hadn't expected to see the man again, let alone hear from him as soon as she arrived home. Before she could speak, he continued, 'Tell you what, how about we meet at the café again tomorrow and I'll buy you lunch. Can you manage without your purse until then?'

'I really don't know what to say,' she said, completely taken aback. 'How kind of you to retrieve my purse. There is no hurry for it to be returned.' Then she thought for a moment as he waited, and she decided to throw caution to the wind. 'Alright, I'll meet you at the café tomorrow.'

'Shall we say 12.30?' he said.

'Yes, I'll see you then,' said Juniper.

As she put the phone down, she caught sight of herself in the mirror. Her eyes were bright and her cheeks pink. She was being given another chance.

The next day she went to a little more trouble than usual, before setting out on her walk. Perhaps, after all, it was time to move forward into the next phase of her life. She was a child when she married Étienne, dazzled by his urbane charm and good looks. She was sure his fortune had played its part too, how could it not? Not that she had ever been in want of luxury herself. Her life, as the pampered only daughter of Claudia and Charles de Montfort, had given her everything she could possibly wish for, materially.

As for the rest of it, she had become a dysfunctional adult and let everybody down.

A few minutes later she found herself approaching the café and Jed raised his hand in greeting. 'Well, this is unexpected,' she said to him.

'I call it fate,' he replied. 'Short of following you home, I might not have seen you again. You are an interesting woman Juniper, and I'd like to get to know you better.'

'There is nothing interesting to know about me. I have a flawed character and I've made lots of mistakes. I'm making my way through life as best I can.'

'You're not the only one,' he said. 'Now, come and sit down. How about a glass of wine? Salmon salad is today's special. I made enquiries before you arrived.'

'That sounds perfect,' said Juniper. 'Thank you.' While Jed disappeared to order their food, Juniper slid her jacket off her shoulders. She leaned back in her chair and relaxed in the sunshine. A few minutes later, Jed came back carrying two glasses of rosé, and a bottle of mineral water, which he'd tucked under his arm.

'Here's to new friends,' he said, raising his glass to her.

THE CRUISE

It didn't take long for Juniper to feel glad she had come. Sitting beside the river, drinking a glass of chilled rosé, she was relaxed and happy in Jed's company. In fact, she wondered why she had been happy alone for as long as she had. She looked at Jed and said, 'Have they repaired your boat yet?'

'As a matter of fact, they have. I'm going to collect her after lunch. If you like, I could take you for a short river cruise this afternoon.'

'How lovely,' said Juniper. 'I'd like that.'

'So, tell me more about you; do you have children?' asked Jed.

'I do, but it's a sore subject,' she replied. 'I've made a bit of a mess of things with them really. For different reasons, I hardly see them. They are adults now, with their own lives.' Her words hung in the air, she didn't want to say more. Just then the waitress appeared with two plates of poached salmon, accompanied by baby new potatoes and a green salad.

'This looks delicious,' said Juniper. 'In all the years I have been coming here, it has only ever been for coffee at mid-morning. I had no idea they did lunch, and such a nice one too.' They ate in silence for a while, distracted by a yacht as it sailed slowly past them. Two children on board were causing a commotion, briefly shattering the tranquillity, until they sailed out of earshot. Then Juniper said, 'Do you have children?' Somehow, asking about children seemed less of a leading question, than asking if he was married. She certainly didn't want to get involved with a married man, even as a friend.

'There's not much to tell really. I'm divorced, quite happily, and we had no children. I spend most of my time on my boat. When I'm not sailing, I'm either at my house on the south coast or my home, not far from here.'

'What happened? With your wife, I mean, or is that too personal a question? Tell me to mind my own business if you like.'

'I don't mind you asking. She was young and beautiful; a party girl with a very expensive lifestyle. I think, in the end, she found me dull. She went off with a younger man, younger than me, anyway.' He laughed as he said it. 'I think it was for the best. I don't think I could ever have made her happy. Unfortunately for me, I realised that too late.'

'Well, aren't we the battle-weary pair,' said Juniper.

'Yes, I suppose we are,' he said, smiling back at her in that laid-back way he had.

'Do you ever wonder what it would be like to go back to being young again, but with all the wisdom gained through experience?' said Juniper.

Jed gazed into the distance, reflecting on her words. Then he said, 'If I'm honest, no. I don't think I'd have the energy to do it all over again. As it is, I am content with my life. I have the luxury of time on my hands and today, I'm having lunch with a beautiful woman.'

'You flatter me,' said Juniper, 'but thank you. The compliment is noted and appreciated.'

'Now,' he said, 'how do you feel about a stroll, a little further along the river? We can pick up my boat, and I'll take you for a short cruise.'

Ten minutes later, they approached the marina repair shop and Jed pointed out a small motor cruiser.

'There she is,' he said, turning to Juniper with a grin. Twenty minutes later they were cruising slowly along the Thames. Juniper sat beside Jed as he steered the wide stretch of river, passing industrial barges and vast willow trees, trailing into the water. Soon the banks opened up to reveal discreetly elegant mansions, their lawns sweeping down to meet the water. In one garden, an artist sat outside a summer house near the water's edge.

'What a beautiful place to paint,' said Juniper.

'Do you paint?' he asked her.

'No, but my son does.'

'Do you have other children?' asked Jed.

'Yes, I have a daughter, Lydia,' she said.

'You said earlier you don't see much of them?'

'Sadly no. Roger lives in France with his partner and I haven't seen Lydia for well over a year.'

'That's too bad. You must miss them,' said Jed.

'I do miss them, but not as much as you might think. Lately, I have tried to be more self-sufficient, emotionally I mean. I was never much of a role model for Lydia, as she was growing up. I imagine she looked, but couldn't find it in me. It was her Aunt Alice who seemed always to find just the right thing to say to her. Lydia adored her.'

'Hold that thought,' said Jed, as he steered the boat towards a small jetty, a short distance away. 'When we arrive, do you think you could jump off?' he asked her. 'I'll get as near as I can, then once you're off, I'll throw you the rope.'

'Where are we going?' said Juniper. 'Where is this?'

'It's my home,' said Jed. 'I thought you might like to join me for a cup of tea in the garden.'

'I didn't realise it was quite as near as this,' said Juniper. 'You are full of surprises.'

As they passed by a large weeping willow, the full extent of Jed's beautiful home came into view. Neatly manicured lawns swept up to a low, white house. In front of the house, a wide terrace led to steps giving access to the lawn. Juniper was about to say something when he called, 'Juniper, are you ready?' Quite suddenly, the boat came alongside the jetty and Juniper was able to step off easily with the rope. 'That's it,' he said. 'Now loop it once around the bollard and pass it back to me. I'll pass you another rope from the front.'

Once the boat was securely tethered, Jed led the way up to the house. He stopped for a minute to take off his deck shoes, and continued barefoot through the springy grass. As they climbed the steps to a large terrace, Juniper could see a swimming pool, surrounded by tubs of flowers. To the left of it, a round table and comfortable chairs were arranged in the shade of a cherry tree.

The central part of the terrace opened into the house, where full-width glass doors were folded back. Inside, two armchairs faced the river. 'Why don't you take a seat,' said Jed, indicating the chairs. 'I'll go and organise some tea for us.'

'Thank you,' she said. 'Do you mind if I freshen up?'

'Of course,' he said. 'I should have thought. There is a bathroom just along the corridor.' He pointed to a doorway, off to the right of the large room. When Juniper returned, Jed was sitting in one of the armchairs, long legs stretched out in front of him. A tray of tea was set on a small table, between the chairs. Juniper sighed as she sat down.

'Ah, a lovely cup of tea. I always find the prospect so soothing. Is that so very English of me?'

'I suppose you are a little like an English rose, now I come to think of it.' He grinned at her. 'One lump or two?' he said.

'Now I know you are mocking me. Shame on you.' Juniper grinned back at him. She was beginning to enjoy his company. He picked up the teapot and poured their tea into two matching mugs, and handed one to her. Then he looked at her more seriously.

'I interrupted you on the boat. I felt you were in the middle of telling me something important. Will you go on?' he asked her.

'Oh, it was nothing really. I was talking about my children, Lydia in particular. I was saying that I haven't been much of a role model for her.' She paused. 'You see, I never found someone to trust and guide me as I was growing up, my own mother let me down badly.'

'How so?' he asked.

'Oh, I can't talk about it Jed. It's all in the past now, but in light of that, it was probably unrealistic for me to imagine that I could be that person for Lydia. For the moment we are estranged, Lydia lives her own life. I do worry about her, but I am ever hopeful that things will change.'

'I think we could all tell stories a little similar to that. The trouble is, we grow up believing our parents are infallible, that they know everything. They are the framework through which we view the world. It's a shock when we discover that they are human, after all, with their own uncertainties and heartaches.'

'What about your son? Do you see much of him?' Juniper went quiet, gazing towards the river and the willow tree.

'That's a longer and more difficult story, maybe for another day.'

'Sorry Juniper, I haven't meant to pry, it's none of my business.' He paused. 'Come on, why don't we have a walk around the garden.'

'I'd love that,' she said.

She followed him past the swimming pool, and along a paved path meandering over the lawn. As they approached a wide, trellis fence covered with early flowering clematis, he led her to one side of it. They emerged in a small kitchen garden, enclosed by a stone wall. Old stone potagers brimmed with herbs and the first signs of vegetables. A weathered greenhouse soaked up the sunshine. 'How lovely,' said Juniper.

'It's one of my favourite places,' he said. 'The smell of new tomato leaves in summer, the beauty of the courgettes flowering.' His voice trailed off, as if he was reliving the experience. 'The peace I find here makes me happy.' He looked at Juniper and smiled. 'Do you enjoy your garden?'

'Yes, I do,' she said. 'Unfortunately, I didn't discover the joy in nature until much later in my life.'

'Well, it's never too late,' he said. 'Do you see that old wooden bench, against the wall?' She looked across at it, bathed in the late afternoon sunshine. 'Most afternoons, this is where I can be found. I just sit and contemplate, soaking up the tranquillity of the garden. Would you like to sit with me for a minute?' Juniper looked over at the inviting seat in the sun, and a vision of herself and Jed sitting there as a contented older couple, came unbidden into her mind. She stared at the bench for a while and sighed. What was she thinking? She had only just met the man.

'Thank you, but I ought to go,' she said, more abruptly than she intended. 'I've really enjoyed the day. Thank you so much, Jed.' He looked surprised but said nothing, and they made their way slowly back to the house. When they reached the two armchairs just inside, the tea tray had been cleared away, and Juniper's jacket was neatly folded over the arm of the chair.

'Let me drive you back,' he said.

'No, please don't trouble yourself. I can call a taxi.'

'Juniper, I don't mind at all. The least I can do is drive you home.'

'No really,' she said, 'I'd rather get a taxi, but thank you.' All of a sudden, she needed to be alone, to think. She was beginning to feel a sense of rightness about being with Jed. The vision she'd had of them sitting together on that sunlit bench, quiet and comfortable in each other's company, had both confused and unnerved her.

'Well, if you are sure,' he said, 'I'll make a phone call.' A few minutes later, he watched the taxi drive away and sighed. What had made her run away like that? He would call her again when he was back from France.

LYDIA

Flat 3, Sea Rd
Seahaven
Sussex

Ma Chère Grandmère
  Thank you for your letter. Life at Windsong sounds as idyllic as ever. I know you enjoy the warmth and your precious sunsets. I am sad that Grandpère Simmy is no longer there to share it with you. Somehow, I always picture you together, out on the deck, watching the sun go down.
  You will be pleased to hear that life is finally improving for me! I know you have been urging me to get out and meet people, but it doesn't come easily. However, I took a big step forward last week and joined a sewing group. I saw a notice for it in the library. I was feeling particularly low in spirit, and decided I had nothing to lose. You are probably thinking that I can't really sew, but I can a bit. Do you remember those mice I used to make clothes for, when I was little?
  Anyway, I have so much to tell you! The lady running it, Anya, was really welcoming, she's probably Mum's age. There was a pregnant lady who seemed to have a bit of a hard life, (Maggie I think). Then there was a nurse, called Sarah.
  Best of all, there was a young, good-looking man! It was the last thing I expected! If you can picture Bon Jovi, (you probably can't, he's a pop star Grandmère) he looked like that!
  After the class, we walked back to his house together; it was on the way home for me, and not far from the library where I work. He lives there with his sister and the family dog.
  Their parents are abroad at the moment. I've offered to walk the dog sometimes when neither of them can get home to do it. His name is Jonathan by the way, and his sister is Berry. She seemed nice, probably a couple of years younger

than me. She's creative, she was painting a huge canvas in the conservatory when we got there. Jonathan said he'd pop over with the dog one day next week, so that I can get to know her.

My other piece of news is this. Do you remember I told you I go swimming in the sea sometimes? It has become quite a routine for me, and although it is absolutely freezing, it seems to have a positive effect on my whole day. My energy fizzes and zings afterwards. It has actually become quite addictive. Don't worry though, I wear a bright swimming cap and have a funny balloon thing, attached to my waist. That's so that I can be seen, in case there is ever a problem; not that there will be.

Usually the beach is deserted. I go early, before work as it's just across the road from the flat. I say beach, but actually, it's thick shingle, sloping steeply down to the water's edge. Do you remember those steep shelves of sand at the Baie des Anges, in Nice? It's like that. One step forward and suddenly, you're in. It's probably for the best, because you can't dither and change your mind.

Anyway, the other day, as I was swimming towards the shore, I realised that there was someone else in the water too. A really thin man, quite young, but good-looking. He had olive skin, longish hair and thick eyelashes. We got up onto the beach at the same time, and he smiled at me. He looked vaguely familiar, but I couldn't place him.

We ended up chatting for half an hour, he had a lovely, European accent. He said I should call him Viddy. He seemed nice, so I asked him up to the flat for a hot drink. It was strange, he walked up the stairs really slowly, and by the time we got inside he was breathless. He said he's been ill, but he didn't say more.

He admired my plants and while I was making our drinks, he started tending to them, pulling off the dead leaves, topping up their water and so on. He did it almost without thinking. When I caught sight of him, he seemed peaceful and absorbed in his task. That's when I noticed his ring, which was unusual. My eyes were drawn to it as it was so heavy on his finger. It had a lion on it, standing up on its hind legs.

As I stepped out of the kitchen with our drinks, he jumped, as if he had forgotten where he was. It was only when he picked up a book, that I remembered where I had seen him. He comes to the library often and spends ages in the gardening section. He recognised me on the beach, and assumed I had also recognised him. He's offered to come and help me get the back garden tidied up, he said he loves gardening, so I said yes.

By the way, I had a telephone message from Mum the other day. She says she misses me. I'm not sure how she got my number but I wondered whether it was you Grandmère, trying to build bridges? Maybe it's time.

Anyway, enough from me. I send you lots and lots of love, and I look forward to your news when you next have time to write.

Bises, Lydia xxxx

THE GARDEN

It was the weekend and Lydia was up early. Viddy was coming over for coffee with her, and they were going to discuss the garden.

The doorbell buzzed soon after 10 a.m. Lydia glanced quickly into the mirror, before letting him in. He was wearing more functional clothes this morning; old khaki shorts that came to his knees, stout socks and a pair of well-used, lace-up gardening boots. He wore a loose, checked shirt over a white t-shirt and his hair was pulled back into a ponytail. He smiled a shy smile as he came into the living room, seeming more robust than on his last visit.

'Shall we have a look at the garden?' said Lydia. 'Then I could bring some coffee down. We could sit out in the sunshine if you like.' She led the way to a door that opened onto a small balcony. A metal staircase led down to the square of lawn below. The garden was shared with the flat on the ground floor, but so far there had been no sign of her neighbour. There was an overgrown patio at the far end with two rusting chairs and a small table on it. Overgrown flower beds flanked the sides of the grass, with last year's forlorn flowers, withering on their stems. Lydia's heart sank.

They stood together on the lawn, in the sunshine. Viddy said nothing, apparently quite content in the silence, as he took it all in. Lydia, for some reason, felt the need to fill it. Nerves probably. 'To be honest, it has never crossed my mind to come down here until now. I'm not sure why. Probably because I'm not much of a garden person. It looks like a bit of a no man's land, doesn't it?' She paused and looked at him. He was leaning on his fork, a peaceful smile on his face, as he surveyed the scene.

'It has possibilities,' he said quietly.

Lydia smiled at him and said, 'Thank you for coming over. I don't really see many people. It's kind of you.'

By the time Lydia came down with their coffee and two cushions, Viddy had pulled the grass and weeds out from between the paving stones and neatly edged the patio with his spade. 'What a difference!' said Lydia. 'You work fast.' He smiled and took the cushion she proffered. They both sat down on the flimsy chairs to enjoy their coffee. 'It's so warm!' said Lydia. 'To think, I have missed so many opportunities to sit outside.'

They sat in companionable silence and after a while, Lydia picked up their cups and headed back inside. 'I won't be long,' she said over her shoulder.

Viddy sat for a moment, enjoying the tranquillity of the garden. He could hear the sea in the background, rising and falling over the shingle. He was glad Sarah had suggested swimming. Apparently, cold water swimming was especially helpful in recovery, where mental health was part of the problem. It had certainly helped him gain more equilibrium, but he knew he needed to take things slowly.

Just then, the garden door at the top of the stairs flew open, and a little white Westie came bounding down and almost leapt up onto his knee. Her little tail wagged furiously, as she ran around in circles at his feet. His face broke into a smile and he leaned down to fuss the dog, its silky warm fur sliding under his hands. His vision blurred as he was overcome with emotion, and then he looked up in surprise, to see a shadow looming over him. Long legs in silver trousers, momentarily blocked out the sun. Viddy swiftly wiped his face with the sleeve of his shirt before sitting up in his chair.

'Hi, I'm Jonathan,' said the man. 'I hope Tilly didn't scare you, she flew out of the house before I could grab her!'

'It's no problem, I love dogs. I'm Viddy,' he said, standing up and reaching out to shake Jonathan's hand.

'Well, aren't you the star of the show,' said Jonathan. 'How did Lydia manage to rope you into this?' Despite the nonchalance of Viddy's words, the hasty wipe of his cheek with his shirt sleeve, had not been lost on Jonathan. He watched Viddy carefully as he replied.

'I don't mind,' he said quietly. 'I love gardening.' There was a silence. 'I'll get on,' said Viddy, and picked up his fork.

'I'll leave you in peace then,' said Jonathan. 'Come on Tilly, let's go up!' Tilly went scampering up the fire escape, and soon afterwards, the door at the top shut behind them.

'Who is that?' said Jonathon when he got inside. 'He's certainly a man of few words, seems sensitive too.'

'I know, it takes a bit of getting used to,' said Lydia. 'He seems so peaceful most of the time, I'd love to be like that. I think he's been ill, he's quite weak. I met him at the beach, when I was swimming the other morning.'

'So, how did he end up doing your garden?' said Jonathan.

'I invited him up for a coffee, and he started tending to my plants, as if he couldn't help himself. Then he offered to come back and help clear the garden.'

'Lucky you,' he said.

'Now you're here, why don't you stay for a sandwich in the garden?' said Lydia. 'I've got hummus or tuna and cucumber.'

Jonathan was curious, intrigued even, by the man in the garden. This would be an opportunity to find out more. 'Thanks,' he said. 'Why not.'

As they munched sandwiches, in the dappled shade of a small willow tree, Viddy began to open up to them. 'I really appreciate this, Lydia. I've been through a difficult time. It's not something I can talk about yet, but I ended up in hospital with nowhere to live. One of the nurses took pity on me and invited me to stay. She said I could help in the garden when I felt like it, and otherwise rest and recuperate. I'm not sure what I would have done if she hadn't offered.' He felt himself become emotional again and he looked away.

Jonathan looked at Lydia, wanting to divert attention from Viddy, who seemed overcome. 'Great sandwiches Lydia, thanks. Really good.'

'You're welcome,' she said. 'I've lived here for ages, and I've never really made friends. All of a sudden, I have the two of you.' She raised her glass of elderflower to them. 'Here's to new friends.'

Viddy smiled, lifting his glass in their direction, before taking a sip. Jonathan looked at him thoughtfully, and then said, 'Do you like walking Viddy, or maybe cycling? There are some great trails in the woods around here. I often go, I'd be glad to take you, if you feel up to it. I don't wear silver trousers for that, obviously.' They all laughed.

'I don't have a bike,' said Viddy, 'I'd love to if I had.'

'I think we've got one at the back of the shed,' said Jonathan. 'It needs sprucing up a bit. Why not pop over next week, and let's see what we can do.'

Viddy's face lit up in a smile, the first they had seen. 'I'd like that, thank you.'

Jonathan left soon after that, and Viddy spent the rest of the afternoon working in the garden. As they enjoyed a final cup of tea together, in the cooling afternoon, Lydia saw his progress. He had cut back all the dead leaves and twigs from last year's flowers, revealing fresh green shoots pushing their way through at the base of the plants.

'You have made such a difference, Viddy. Thank you so much! I owe you dinner, are you free this evening?'

'That is so kind, but I need to go home. I'll probably have an early night. Thank you though.'

Soon after that, he was gone and Lydia felt deflated. She had probably talked too much and frightened him off. Normally, she lived quietly, hardly saying a word to anyone. It was probably nerves that had made her do it. Deep down, she saw herself as boring and imagined that this was how she came across. So she'd over-compensated, said more than she intended, and where had it got her? It was Viddy Jonathan had invited to cycle in the woods. Why not her? Not that she even liked cycling, but still, he didn't know that. It would have been nice to be asked.

She looked at herself in the full-length mirror, trying to see herself as they might have seen her. Studious was the first word that came to mind. Tall and skinny, she wore owl-like glasses, with beige, unremarkable clothes. Her hair hung lank and lifeless about her shoulders. Hardly surprising then, all things considered. She sighed, resolving to give herself a bit of a makeover.

THE RED DRESS

Clémence read Lydia's letter with interest, delighted she was finding her feet at last; making some new friends. So, Juniper had tried to call her daughter. Good, it was a start.

There was something else niggling at the back of her mind, and she couldn't quite put her finger on it. With a mild sense of unease, she called out to Alberta.

'Alberta, could you bring in the last few copies of Le Figaro for me? I need to look for an article. I think it was a couple of weeks ago.'

'Of course, Mz d'Apidae,' she said, appearing shortly afterwards with the newspapers in a neat pile. 'Is there anythin' else you need?'

'Not for now. Thank you, Alberta.'

Clémence had the French newspapers flown in regularly from Paris so that she could keep up with news and events. Despite living the most idyllic and isolated life on Captiva Island, her mind was active and she enjoyed following the lives of old friends. She settled down in a comfortable chair and spread the papers out on a low ottoman in front of her. She slowly turned the pages, stopping every now and again to glance briefly at something, until eventually, she found what she was looking for. She smoothed the paper open carefully and began to read. When she had finished, she smiled with satisfaction, folded the paper, and went to sit at her writing desk.

Pulling out a sheet of writing paper, she picked up her fountain pen and wrote a letter to her old friend, Christine de Courcy. Elegantly written words, in light turquoise ink, looped effortlessly over the page. When the letter was finished, she addressed it to the Château de Courcy in France, and returned to her chair.

Alberta came into the room again, a few minutes later. 'I will be leaving shortly Mz d'Apidae, would you like some tea before I go?'

'Yes please, I would,' said Clémence. 'Thank you.' Soon

afterwards, Alberta returned with a delicate china pot and matching cup and saucer. Beside them on the tray, was a tiny plate of lemon slices and another of wafer-thin biscuits.

'I sliced the lemons fine, the way you like 'em Mam. There are some homemade, key lime cookies for you too.'

'Thank you, Alberta, you are a treasure. There is an important letter on my desk, could you please post it for me this afternoon, on your way home?'

'Of course, Mz d'Apidae.' She paused for a moment, and then said, 'Mam, I just want to make sure you remembered, I won't be comin' in tomorrow.'

'Yes, I had. Thank you, Alberta. Enjoy your day with your family and I'll see you the day after.'

Once the house was quiet, Clémence sat back in her chair. She really ought to go and lie down on her bed, she was a little out of sorts today. Perhaps a nap after tea would do her good, there was plenty of time. For now, her eyes were drawn to the wall at the far end of the great room. A portrait[1] of a little girl in a red dress, dominated the space, lit up by the late afternoon sun.

Clémence's face relaxed into a nostalgic smile as she gazed at it. She'd been about six when it was painted. Her father told her much later, that he met the artist, Robert Henri, on a business trip to the Netherlands. Henri was known for his portraits of children, many of them painted in Ireland. On this occasion, he was in the Netherlands studying the work of Frans Hals, in particular his portraits of laughing children.

Julien d'Apidae managed to persuade Henri to make a detour to Paris to paint his daughter's portrait, before flying home to New York. So, when his business in the Netherlands came to an end, Henri arrived at the family apartment on The Avenue George V, and stayed for almost two weeks.

Each day Clémence was dressed in a formal, dark navy day dress for the sitting. Her dark hair was neatly brushed and unadorned. As soon as her father left them with a maid, Henri would tip the maid to slide a sleeveless red linen smock over the top of Clémence's day dress, mess up her hair a little, and then place a red ribbon around it. Henri referred to her as Clemeen, she

1   Please see notes at the end of the book

never did know why, nor why the maid went along with it. Even now, she remembered the delicious sense of freedom it gave her.

The red smock was roughly pleated and folded into a gathered collar of bright scarlet linen, giving way to shades of orange in its folds. In the portrait, Clemeen is facing the artist, her impish face dominating the canvas. Her head is turned slightly away, but her large brown eyes look sideways towards Henri. Her cheeks are glowing pink, and her dark eyes are full of mischief.

Her full lips are softly closed together, turned up at the corners in the slightest of smiles. She looks for all the world as if she had been caught stealing apples and didn't mind at all.

It was always a mystery to Clémence, that her loveless and austere father, who had so dominated their lives, favoured this picture as he did. It hung in his study in Paris from the day it was finished, until the day, not so many years ago, when Clémence brought it to Captiva.

She spent her whole life trying, and failing to please him. Yet this painting represented the opposite of what he wanted her to be. It was as unlike any image of her real childhood, as she could possibly imagine. The day she unpacked the painting, she noticed for the first time, that a small note was taped to the back of it. It was brown at the edges and faded with age.

The artist had written 'Clemeen' on the back of the painting, before signing and dating it. This was another thing Clémence had never known. The painting hung in her father's study, for as long as she could remember. Even after he died, it was never moved, until it came to Captiva.

She held the note in her hand now, but she didn't need to look at it. She knew and treasured every word. It was unlike anything he had ever said to her, during his lifetime.

My darling Clemeen,

I treasure this painting. Henri has not only seen, but managed to reveal the true essence of you. I think of you now as my Clemeen, and it gladdens my heart. It brings to mind the formidable spirit of you, my dear daughter.

I know not why courage fails me in matters of love, but I struggle to show my heart.

> *Stern rigour, as my own father showed to me, is all I know.*
> *Forgive me Clemeen, for what I am. Please know that you*
> *are so very much loved.*
> *Your loving Papa,*
> *Julien d'Apidae.*

Clémence allowed his words to fill her mind. Her brow relaxed and her lips formed a gentle smile, as she found comfort in the knowledge that she had, after all, been loved. She felt a lightness as she became that impish little girl once again, her red smock flying about her in the wind. She laughed as she ran through fields of blossom, then out of sight, as the evening sun slid slowly away from the painting.

SUMMER

THE SEWING GROUP - SUMMER

By the time their third session came around, it was early summer. The group were relaxed and comfortable in each other's company. 'What you lot been up to this week then?' asked Maggie. Her belly was larger than ever as she leaned back, rubbing her palms into the small of her back.

While Jonathan lamented the responsibility of the family dog, Sarah told them she had started a vegetable garden with the help of her new lodger. 'S'alright for some,' said Maggie, 'I ain't got a garden. I'd love one, 'specially when the baby comes. Not keen on dogs though. Forever need ya to clean up after 'em don't they?'

'Tell me about it,' said Jonathan.

Once around the sewing table, Anya moved slowly around the group, spending unhurried time with each of them. She loved the hum of industry and promise around her table. They were learning new skills, and coming together, to create a community of friends. No doubt they were all dealing with life's problems, as she had at their age. She enjoyed their company and took pleasure in sharing her experience.

Last week, she was concerned about Lydia, she'd seemed anxious and withdrawn. Today, she seemed better, but Anya's intuition told her there was something wrong. As the session came to a close, Lydia surprised her by offering to help clear up.

'I'd love some help, thanks, Lydia. Bye,' she called to the others as they left, one by one. 'See you next week!'

Once they were alone, Anya asked brightly, 'So, are you still sea swimming?'

'Yes, I love it, I'm surprised how much I enjoy it,' she said. 'Have you ever tried it?'

'When I was younger, I swam a lot, but I was in India then. It was warmer. I'm not sure I'd have the courage to swim in the English sea. What made you decide to try it?'

'Oh, it's a bit of a long story. I've had a few problems lately. I mostly seem to bring them on myself.'

'Oh?' said Anya, pausing, hoping Lydia might say more. When the silence lengthened, Anya continued, 'Is there anything I can do to help?'

'Not really,' she said. 'I just need to look after myself better. I probably shouldn't say this, but part of the problem is I've been drinking too much.'

'What do you think makes you do that?' said Anya kindly.

'I don't know. Maybe it gives me the courage I wish I had, and it helps me forget some of the bad stuff.' She hesitated, and then added, 'If I'd been more in control . . . ' there was another pause, 'certain things might not have happened. Anyway, that's how I came to start sea swimming.

'I woke up one morning, at rock bottom, hung over again and hating myself. I just wanted to walk into the water and drown. It's hard to believe now, but at that moment, I didn't care if I never came out.'

'Oh, my dear,' said Anya. 'So, what happened?'

'I'll tell you what happened,' she paused. 'The sea saved me; it took me by surprise.'

'What do you mean, the sea saved you?'

'It's a strange thing, but the cold water had an unbelievable effect on me. It shocked me and jolted me out of myself. It woke me up if you like. There was a brief moment, when I first experienced the freezing cold of it, that my life flashed before my eyes. It made me see that a better life is worth fighting for.' Lydia looked at Anya, 'Can you understand that?'

'Life of any kind is worth fighting for,' said Anya. 'I am sorry that you felt so very low in spirit that you doubted it was.'

'I had a kind of epiphany in the sea that day. It was the last thing I expected, but it changed my life. I suddenly realised that it was up to me, that the key to a better life was in my own hands. When I got out of the water, I walked up to my flat, poured all my wine down the sink and decided to start afresh. I haven't touched a drop since.'

'Lydia, that is amazing!' said Anya. 'Well done you. Come here and give me a hug.' Lydia stepped into her outstretched arms and leaned against her shoulder, breathing a huge sigh of relief. It felt so good to be held. Anya's hair smelt of spices and herbs, and her plump skin was soft. Just for a moment, she could imagine that she was cared for.

'I don't seem to have much luck with relationships either,' she added. 'The only person I'm close to is my Grandmère Clémence, and she lives overseas.'

'Well, I have an idea,' said Anya. 'Why don't you come along to a meditation group I go to on Sunday afternoons? You might enjoy it. You'll probably benefit from some calm, quiet time. When I lived in India, meditation was part of each day, it was as natural as breathing. We all felt better for it. What do you think?'

'I suppose I could,' said Lydia, glad to have the chance to spend more time in Anya's company.

'Perfect. Why don't you meet me here on Sunday then, and we'll go together?'

When they arrived at Floral House, Anya led the way along a curved gravel path that wound its way past flower beds, a wood store and eventually, a small pond. Lydia stopped for a moment, her attention caught by flashes of orange, as fish meandered through the water, before disappearing among the plants below. When she looked up, she saw that there was a large white house on the far side of the garden.

'Is that where we are going?' she asked, reminded for a moment of her family home in Richmond.

'No,' said Anya. 'We are going to the yurt, on the other side of the garden, you'll see it in a minute. It's very welcoming, you can just relax and leave your concerns at the door.'

The yurt sat like a majestic old lady, rooted into the earth. Trails of lichen climbed the faded white of its sides, and a jaunty red awning fluttered in the breeze. The low wooden doorway was propped open over a narrow deck, which had the look of a drawbridge about it.

Anya stepped confidently onto the deck and dipped her head, before stepping through the low doorway. Lydia followed her into the dimly lit, circular space, illuminated by a multitude of candles. The ceiling swept up high in the centre, like a circus tent, with twinkling candles inside colourful lanterns, hanging from the beams above.

As her eyes became accustomed to the light, Lydia saw that people were seated around the edges of the circle, on large cushions. Several raised a hand to welcome her, others put their hands together as if in prayer, bowing their heads in her direction. She raised her hand awkwardly in return, and followed Anya to the far side of the circle, where two large cushions awaited them. Gentle music, with an Indian rhythm, filled the air and incense wafted around them. Lydia was soothed by the atmosphere and fascinated to discover what would take place here.

After a while, someone pulled the door closed, and the atmosphere changed. The walls of the yurt became quiet and womb-like, holding them in an intimate circle; then someone began to speak.

'Welcome to our yurt, especially the new faces here today. I'm Natasha.' Everyone put their palms together and bowed their heads towards her. 'Let's open our circle today with three chants of Ohm. Hold your palms together, like this,' she demonstrated, 'thumbs against your chest as you breathe in. Then, as we breathe out, we will chant the sacred sound of Ohm together.' Natasha sat down and put her hands together in prayer. 'Now, all together, breathe in and we will bring the sacred sound of the universe into our circle.'

Lydia took a deep breath, formed her lips into an O, and then she allowed her outward breath to carry her voice into the wave of sound around her. As it built to a crescendo, the powerful vibration of their voices moved around the walls of the circular space, washing over and through her. She could feel the sound resonating inside her body, as it travelled from her chest through to her thumbs. As the first Ohm faded, Lydia took another deep breath, and closed her eyes. As she chanted 'Ohm' again, she felt her trapped emotions take flight, as if they were finally being given voice. She didn't hold back. The power of her own outpouring, blended as it was with so many others, made her feel free, and yet connected to so much more than herself.

As silence finally fell, a silent tear worked its way from the outer corner of Lydia's eye, and she was grateful for the dim light. She felt Anya take her hand and give it a gentle squeeze, as someone walked among them, chiming delicate little bells. When the bells completed their circle, the meditation began.

Lydia followed Anya's lead, placing the backs of her hands on her knees, palms open, the tips of her thumbs and index fingers touching.

'Make yourselves comfortable on your cushions, just relax and follow your breath,' said Natasha. 'Let your thoughts float away, like clouds in a blue sky.' Her soothing voice continued its lulling rhythm, to the backdrop of gentle music.

Much later, Lydia became aware of the delicate sound of bells again, indicating that the meditation had come to an end. It took her a while to come back from what had been like a sleep, with full awareness. She began to move her fingers and toes, before allowing her eyes to flutter open and rest on the flickering candlelight in front of her.

When the circle came to an end, they stood up and made quiet gestures of farewell to each other, nobody wanting to break the spell. When the door was eventually pushed open, Lydia and Anya stepped out into the fading afternoon light.

'Thank you so much for bringing me here, Anya,' said Lydia quietly. 'My heart is full of peace.' Anya smiled, as they made their way slowly back to the car.

THE BIKE RIDE

Jonathan and Viddy loaded their bikes onto the back of the family car, and headed onto the coast road. As they left the town behind, wide open countryside spread out before them. They passed swathes of undulating green and straw-coloured fields, dotted with sheep. In the distance, against a blue sky, a lighthouse clung to the clifftop overlooking a sparkling sea. 'This is breath-taking,' said Viddy quietly.

'Is it the first time you've seen the coast from up here?' asked Jonathan.

'Yes, it is. I had no idea it was this beautiful.' The road began to descend, eventually passing through a small village where a pub nestled on the green, and flint-finished houses lined the road. As the car climbed again, leaving the village behind, they passed an old church tucked among trees, beside a small pond. Two walkers ambled along the narrow lane beside it, eventually disappearing into the shadows, towards the cliff path.

As the car continued along the coast road, woodland on one side and the downs and sea on the other, a magnificent view of wide flatlands opened out between white craggy cliffs. A blue, snakelike river, wound its way in from the sea in long loops that curved back on themselves as they came inland. Viddy could make out a cluster of kayaks on one of the river bends, and the white backs of swans gliding slowly through the water. 'This must be one of the most beautiful places in the world,' said Viddy quietly.

'Isn't it,' said Jonathan, slowing the car, as traffic began to build.

Soon afterwards, he turned right into a narrow lane, leaving the coast road behind. Half a mile further on, he swung the car in through a wide gate. A rough circular track formed the woodland car park, and Jonathan manoeuvred into a spot under the trees.

'Here we are,' he said, turning to look at Viddy. It took a moment for their eyes to adjust to the light. After the bright blue sky and sunshine, the dimly lit wood had an eerie and almost magical quality to it. The sunlight filtered through the canopy of trees, illuminating pathways through the woods in all directions. 'Abbey Woods has always been one of my favourite places, we used to come here as a family in the school holidays. We'd have walks and picnics, bike rides too, of course,' said Jonathan. 'At this time of year, the thing I remember most, are the bluebells.' He looked across at Viddy, 'I think you're going to love it.'

Jonathan wasn't sure why, but he felt protective of his new friend. He sensed a fragility in him, that Viddy tried hard to hide. He said, 'The trails are mostly quite flat and easy, they head off in all directions. We probably won't go too far this time; we can build up to longer rides.' Viddy looked at him gratefully. 'Come on, let's get the bikes unloaded.'

Once the bikes were off the car, Jonathan swung a small rucksack onto his back. 'Are you ready? OK, let's go.' Soon they were bumping along the trail among the trees. The bluebells stretched out in swathes as far as they could see, their purply-blues illuminated by sunlight, piercing the gloom of the woods. Birdsong rang in their ears as they rode in companionable silence. Viddy felt the wind rush through his hair and fresh air fill his lungs. It brought a sense of freedom and exhilaration he hadn't felt for a long time.

They had been riding for almost half an hour, when Jonathan slowed his bike and pointed to a narrow path off to the right. 'There's a pond along there, why don't we stop and have some lunch?' Viddy gave him a thumbs up and they turned slowly off the trail and dismounted, pushing their bikes in single file along the narrow footpath. Soon they emerged into a sunny clearing with a pond, surrounded by grassy banks and graceful trees.

'How did you know this was here?' asked Viddy.

'I've always known it,' said Jonathan, throwing his bike onto the ground. He sat down on the grass and began to unpack a picnic from his rucksack.

'We used to picnic here with Mum and Dad. Later, as teenagers, we came to smoke weed. Have you ever smoked it?'

'I used to grow it actually,' said Viddy, 'with a friend. My parents thought we were watering the tomatoes, which we were, but we diversified.' He looked at Jonathan and grinned. 'There was a time when I don't think I could have got through the day without it.'

'Really?' said Jonathan, surprised.

'Yes,' said Viddy. 'The glasshouse was my refuge, and smoking weed became part of that. The warm, sharp scent of tomato leaves, and a few puffs of weed, made me believe that everything was alright in my world.'

'It sounds idyllic,' said Jonathan. 'Where is your glasshouse and why did you leave it?'

'It's a long story,' said Viddy, 'maybe for another day.' This was the closest he'd come to talking about it, but he couldn't go on. Not today, anyway. There was something about Jonathan that made him feel he could confide in him. He sighed and lay back on the picnic rug, gazing up into the canopy of the tree, memories of home flooding his mind. 'It's in France, in the Loire valley.' He said it so quietly, that Jonathan almost missed it. For some reason, he sensed that this was difficult for Viddy, so Jonathan remained silent. He reached out for Viddy's hand in quiet support and Viddy turned his head to look at him with gratitude.

Jonathan didn't mention it again, but they went on regular bike rides after that, discovering the many woodland trails and coastal paths in the area. Viddy grew tanned and stronger after lunches in sunny pub gardens and the occasional picnic under a tree.

One day, as they overlooked the myriad blues of the English Channel, offset by white cliffs and wheeling seagulls, Viddy turned to Jonathan and said, 'I will always remember our time together, Jonny. I'm beginning to feel so much stronger and so hopeful. You have made me believe that there is nothing I can't do, if I really want to.'

'You make it sound as if it's coming to an end,' said Jonathan.

Viddy pressed his lips together in a sad, half-smile, and said, 'All I have ever wanted, is to live a simple life. I love the countryside, animals and nature, especially my plants.' He paused, and Jonathan waited for him to continue.

'I can be truly myself in your company, without fear of being judged. The way things have become between us, feels so natural to me.' He paused and looked into Jonathan's face and for a long moment, he met Viddy's gaze. 'Do you understand what I'm saying, Jonny?'

'You know I do,' he replied. 'I'm right here, by your side.' A silence stretched between them as they contemplated the sea. Then Jonathan said, 'So, do you feel ready to tell me what happened? Why you left France?'

Viddy sighed, continuing to look out to sea, then he said, 'It's a long story. There was a boy around my own age, Philippe. His family used to help my parents in the grounds of the Château. We grew up together and always shared a love of plants. The glasshouse was not only my favourite place; it was his as well. We would spend hours in there. The early mornings were the best, we had a kind of silent communion with the plants, and with each other. We would walk out over the dewy grass, the sun still low in the sky, as it spread a warm, peachy light over the walls of the Château. I would stand gazing at the honeyed stone; sensing my parents, my grandparents and their parents before them, standing beside me, rooted solidly in the land I loved.

'One part of the Château is built across the river Cher, supported by a series of arches. It houses a long and beautiful ballroom with windows on both sides, looking along the length of the river. They light up like fire in the early morning, as the rising sunlight bounces off the glass. It has always been my favourite time of day, while everything is quiet and still.'

'So, what made you leave?' asked Jonathan.

'One day, I realised that my feelings for Philippe were beginning to change. I was confused, it wasn't what I was supposed to feel. We were both around fifteen by then. I dared not broach the subject with him, in case he hated me for it. You see, I would have done anything to make sure he stayed by my side. So I hid it from him, and from everyone else. An awkwardness rose between us after that, and I think he sensed it too.

'A year or so later, I remember it was late afternoon, we were checking to see which seedlings were ready to be planted out the next day. Our hands accidentally touched over one of the plants, and he looked up at me. He gazed into my eyes for what seemed like an eternity, and then he pulled me to him and kissed me. It was a long slow kiss, and my heart felt as if it would burst with happiness. I returned his kiss with all the love I had buried within me, for so long. Unfortunately for us, at that moment, his father walked into the glasshouse and found us.' Viddy stopped and sighed.

'So what happened?' asked Jonathan.

'In less than a week, the whole family moved away. They had been with us for as long as I could remember. My mother never understood why they left us so suddenly, after a lifetime of loyal service. Philippe's father swore me to secrecy and I was only too happy to comply. They told my mother they had to return to the south of France, for family reasons. It nearly broke my heart to see them go.'

'Is that what made you leave?' asked Jonathan.

'No, but it was the reason I became so dependent on weed. I couldn't stand the pain of being without Philippe, after what had finally happened between us. I know now that it was a life lesson for me. It helped me to understand and begin to accept, who I really was. Soon after that, we heard that my brother, Louis, had been killed, and everything fell apart.'

'What was your brother like?' asked Jonathan.

'I adored him,' said Viddy, 'but he betrayed my trust and my loyalty. He broke my heart. My mother has no idea, he was always her golden boy,' he said bitterly. 'I've been grieving for him twofold, first when he was alive and again, now he is dead. I feel such terrible guilt for the way I began to hate him.'

Jonathan reached out to touch Viddy's hand, 'You don't need to say any more if you'd rather not,' he said. 'I'm just so sorry.'

'I'll have to go back in the end,' said Viddy, 'but I can't bear to live a lie. My mother is hellbent on finding a wife for me, so that we can live happily ever after in the Château. She expects me to somehow restore its fortunes. I have no idea how she thinks I can do that. She can't do it alone either. I feel so helpless.'

They cycled home in silence, Viddy in despair and Jonathan silently trying to come up with a plan.

CHRISTINE

Juniper was sipping the last of her coffee, reflecting on a recent conversation with her daughter. Why on earth were things so complicated with Lydia? She tried, she really did, to create an amicable adult relationship with her, but Lydia insisted on clinging to old grievances, that Juniper had never fully understood. She sighed, and was about to telephone to leave her a conciliatory message when the doorbell rang.

Juniper looked at her watch, it was almost midday, and she certainly wasn't expecting anyone. She stood up and smoothed her hair, walking through the elegant drawing room into a large light hallway. Shafts of sunshine slanted through blue glass, on either side of the door, creating slices of iridescent light over the flagstone floor. Juniper glanced into the mirror and then opened the door.

To her surprise, she saw a limousine pulling away and an elegant woman standing on her doorstep, vanity case in hand and a fur coat over her arm. Beside her, stood a larger matching suitcase.

'Hello,' said Juniper. 'May I help you?'

The woman smiled hesitantly and said with a French accent, 'Good morning, my name is Christine de Courcy, are you Mrs Juniper d'Apidae?'

'Yes, at least I was. I am known as Juniper de Montfort now. Should I know you Madame de Courcy?'

'No, of course not,' she said gently. 'I'm so sorry to intrude. Clémence told me that you would be expecting me.'

'I am sorry,' said Juniper, 'I'm forgetting my manners, please come in. Let's go through to the drawing room.' Juniper indicated a chair as she led the way into a light-filled room. 'Please do sit down.' The French woman sank gratefully into an armchair, placing her vanity case carefully on the floor by her side.

'Thank you, I am so relieved to be here.' She sighed and closed her eyes, leaning back into the chair.

Juniper looked on, mystified. She had not heard from Clémence for several months, and now she had apparently sent this unknown woman to her home; but why? 'May I offer you a drink, Madame de Courcy?' she said kindly. 'I have sherry, martini or perhaps a cup of coffee?'

'Thank you, a small sherry would be lovely, and please, call me Christine.' Juniper walked over to the cocktail cabinet and poured them each, a generous schooner of sherry. She handed the elegant glass to Christine, and it caught the light as she raised it to her lips. 'Aah, that feels better, thank you. May I call you Juniper?'

'Of course, please do.' She raised her glass to Christine and took a sip, before leaning back in her chair. 'Now Christine, please tell me how you think I can be of help to you.'

Christine sighed again, apparently uncertain where to begin. Then, she put her glass down on the small table beside her, and took a deep breath. She straightened herself in the chair, before beginning to speak quietly.

'My son is missing,' she said simply. 'I haven't seen him for over three months.'

'Oh dear, I'm so sorry to hear that. How is it you think I can help you with this?'

'I understand your confusion Juniper, me turning up unexpectedly on your doorstep like this. I am so sorry. I can't think why Clémence didn't write to you, as she promised she would. It really is most unlike her. Please let me try to explain. Clémence and my mother were at finishing school together in Switzerland, many years ago. Our families have kept in touch through cards each year. We exchange brief news of our offspring and the big events in our lives, nothing more than that. This year was no different, except that soon after New Year, my youngest son disappeared.'

'How old is your son?' asked Juniper.

'He is twenty-one, not so young, but Daveed is a sensitive boy, and this is very unlike him. At first, I thought he had just gone away for a few days. We have all been through the most dreadful time you see. My eldest son, Louis, was killed in a sailing accident last year. The pressure on us all since then has been intolerable.'

'How dreadful, I am so sorry,' said Juniper.

'There was nothing we could do to curb Louis' daredevil

lifestyle. His father despaired of him. Louis was to have taken on the Château on the death of my husband, but he told us he was not ready to settle down. One more race, he said, one more summer, and then he would come home. Daveed worshipped him, looked up to him. He was everything Daveed wished to be, and he seemed to love him for it. He was devastated when Louis died, it was a tragedy that none of us were prepared for.'

'And your husband?' asked Juniper.

'He was quite a lot older than I was when we married, he died three years ago. To spare Louis what he saw as his fate, I have been doing my best to run the Château alone. Each year I hoped he would finally come home and face his responsibility, but now it will never be.'

Christine rummaged in her handbag for a handkerchief and dabbed her eyes, apparently exhausted. 'I'm so sorry,' she said quietly. 'I have disturbed you long enough Juniper, perhaps you can recommend a hotel nearby.'

'I won't hear of it,' said Juniper. 'You must stay here as long as you need to. Let me show you upstairs to our guest suite, we can talk some more later. In the meantime, I will ask Louise to bring a light lunch to your room, and you can get some rest.'

'You are very kind,' she said, standing up. 'Thank you so much, Juniper. It is true, I am very tired. I know you must have many questions, as you say, we will speak later.'

When Christine came down just after 6 p.m., she looked rested. She had changed into a pair of wide-leg navy trousers, with a white ribbed top that skimmed her elegant form. Its round neckline was offset by a fine gold chain and small pearl drop earrings. 'Juniper, thank you. I feel so much better after a sleep and a lovely bath.' Christine's English was flawless, with a charming French accent.

'It's no trouble,' said Juniper, standing up and smiling. 'If I'm honest, I am pleased to have some company. Louise has prepared a light supper for us in the kitchen. Shall we go downstairs and pour ourselves a glass of wine?' They had the house to themselves, now that Louise had left for the day.

Lately, Juniper had been more relaxed in the kitchen, than in any other part of the house. It was a far cry from the old days, when she barely knew what it looked like. She reflected with sadness on the moments she had missed, as Lydia and Roger were growing up. Jack and Rosa, their housekeeper and gardener, were like grandparents to them, listening to their stories from school, making their meals and putting plasters on their knees. Inevitably, Juniper would be out at a lunch party, or in the drawing room reading a magazine.

'This is cosy,' said Christine, as they stepped into the warmth of the large kitchen. The floors were of light grey stone, surrounded by wooden kitchen units of hyacinth blue, these offset by pale marble worktops. Two large windows overlooked the garden and the fading evening light. Juniper flicked a switch and the outside lights came on, illuminating two bronze statues. One was a pair of boxing hares and the other, a young girl looking down at her feet, as if searching for something. 'How lovely,' said Christine, as she gazed out of the window. 'You even have a pretty parterre outside the kitchen.' Juniper looked at her and smiled.

'I know; I love it down here. It wasn't always that way, but that's a story for another day. Let's just say I'm not the woman I once was.' She gazed into the garden, remembering a day when Rosa brought her a cup of tea and a piece of cherry cake, just when she was at her lowest ebb. 'Dear Rosa,' she said quietly, surprised that she had spoken it aloud. Then she turned to find Christine gazing at her sympathetically, not wanting to intrude on her thoughts. 'Sorry, I was daydreaming,' said Juniper. 'Please, do sit down.'

She indicated two comfortably upholstered bar chairs at the marble-topped island, and opened the fridge to take out a bottle of white wine. 'I have red, if you prefer,' said Juniper.

'No, white would be lovely, thank you,' said Christine.

'So,' said Juniper, once they were settled. 'Tell me more about what brings you here.'

Christine pulled an envelope out of her handbag and handed it to Juniper. 'Do you read French?'

'Yes, I do,' she replied.

'I received this from Clémence a few days ago. When you read it, you will understand why I came.' Juniper took the letter from her, immediately recognising Clémence's neat, looping handwriting and the unusual colour of the ink she used. She opened out the cream paper and began to read.

Windsong
Captiva Island,
Florida

My Dear Christine,
   It has been a while since we were last in touch. I send this to you in the hope that you are managing to remain hopeful and positive at this difficult time. I read about the distressing disappearance of your son and my heart goes out to you. How very difficult, coming so soon after the tragic death of your eldest boy in a sailing accident.
   Christine, I do not want to falsely raise your hopes, but I heard some news yesterday that made me wonder whether your son may be on the south coast of England. My granddaughter, Lydia, writes to me regularly with her news. Her latest letter mentions two young men who have recently come into her circle. (She lives in Seahaven, near Brighton). They sound like many other young men of their generation, but there is something that caught my attention.
   Lydia describes one of them as wearing a ring, with a shield-like shape bearing a lion, standing up on its hind legs. Christine, my dear, I have long known this to be your family crest. Your mother and I spent two years together at finishing school in Switzerland. It was emblazoned upon several of her belongings, as mine was, on my own. Such were those halcyon days.
   I imagine you will want to leave immediately for England. When you arrive, please make yourself known to Juniper d'Apidae, you will find her address at the bottom of this letter, along with Lydia's on the South coast. Lydia works at the local library, should you be unable to reach her at home.
   Juniper was my daughter-in-law before her divorce from the errant Étienne, and I am inordinately fond of her. I believe she has been estranged from Lydia for a while, which is a dreadful shame. I would like nothing more than to see them make their peace. So you see, I hope this may kill two birds with one stone.
   I will end this in haste, so that I can post it to you

immediately. I will follow it in the morning with a letter to Juniper, so that she will be expecting you. I hope she will be able to offer you some support in your quest, and that through this, you and Juniper might become friends.

My dear, I wish you the very best of luck in your search for Daveed. For better or worse, our children are our very lifeblood, aren't they?

With kindest love
Clémence d'Apidae

JUNIPER

Juniper put the letter aside, lost in thought for a moment. 'I'm sorry, Juniper,' said Christine. 'Some of this is quite personal to you, and none of my business.'

'Not at all,' she said. 'To be perfectly honest, it will be good to talk about it. Especially with someone who understands what it is to have things unsettled with one's children. That is not to say that I am comparing my rift with Lydia, to the disappearance and unknown whereabouts of your son. That really is a dreadful thing.'

'What has caused your rift with Lydia?'

'I just didn't know how to be a mother. I thought I did, but really I was still a child when she was born, and a selfish one at that. I was spoilt and indulged most of my life and I just carried on as if I didn't have children. Rosa and Jack did most of the work, while I spent my time helping on charity committees and looking at magazines. My idea of a day out with Lydia was to take her to Harrods for the latest fashions, and dress her up like a doll. It was only when we attended family counselling, when Lydia suffered from an eating disorder at boarding school that it all came out.'

'What came out?' asked Christine.

'The way Lydia felt about me. The kind of mother she saw me as. I always assumed she loved me, as all children love their parents. It was a shock to see myself through her eyes.'

'I'm sure she loves you, Juniper.'

'Yes, I'm sure she does in her way; but she has made it clear that she feels stifled around me. She said she needs space to develop into the person she is meant to be. Apparently, she can't do that with me in her life.'

'You just need to give her time,' said Christine. 'Is that why she is living on the south coast?'

'You knew more than I did until I read this letter. Lydia hasn't wanted me to know where she is living. I've had to respect that. It has all been so dreadfully hurtful, but I am doing my best to move forward, in a positive way.'

'How difficult for you.'

'It really has been. It is one thing not to know where your child is, but quite another to be told you are not wanted in their life. I have had to take a long hard look at myself. It just leaves me with more questions, to which I wish I had answers.' She looked at Christine and smiled ruefully.

'Some things just don't have answers,' said Christine. 'That is quite hard to accept. Daveed and I were always so close. I didn't notice the exact moment he began to grow away from me. It was almost imperceptible, but one day, I realised that he was awkward around me. He had always been such an open child, with a serene and loving countenance. I can't tell you how much it hurt, but I don't need to, do I? You already know. I'm so sorry, Juniper.'

'Oh, don't be,' she said. 'I'm coping as best I can. I have done a lot of soul-searching, actually. I know deep down, that I am to blame for so much of what Lydia feels. I have a lot to thank Alice for; she was Étienne's late cousin, for the way I have learned to look at the world.

'Ours was a short but blessed friendship, and it changed me more than I could ever have imagined. She was so brave as she faced an early death, so generous in spirit and so very kind to me, right to the end. I can hardly believe I harboured such jealousy towards her, for so many years.' Juniper smiled ruefully. 'If only I had seen, much sooner, that she had the power to show me the way out of my misery.'

'She sounds like a wonderful person.'

'She was, and Lydia adored her. The children spent every moment they could with her when we were in France. Anyway, enough about all that, tell me more about Daveed.'

As Juniper set out a small cheese plate for them, Christine said, 'Daveed was at his happiest among plants and animals. It was when our caretaking family at the Château left suddenly, a few summers ago, that he became very withdrawn. You see, he and Philippe, their son, grew up together. They were like brothers really, inseparable. They shared a love of plants and the garden and were always in the glasshouse planting seeds and nurturing cuttings. In a funny sort of way, I think they loved each other too.'

She paused, 'I know that may seem a strange thing to say, but I think I always knew he would follow a different path. That is what makes this especially sad.'

'What do you mean?' asked Juniper.

'Well, he won't be able to choose now,' said Christine. 'With Louis dead, the responsibility of the Château will rest on Daveed's shoulders, for the rest of his life.'

'I see,' said Juniper.

'I have held things together for as long as I can,' said Christine, 'spurred on by the long line of strong women in the Château's history, but I am not getting any younger. I don't know how much longer I can manage, without the fresh energy and enthusiasm of the next generation.'

'Do you think it's why Daveed ran away?'

'Partly, yes. Most of all though, he was devastated by the death of his brother. He lost his best friend with Philippe's departure, and I think Louis' death was the last straw. That, and the knowledge that he would now bear the burden of the Château as well.'

'That is difficult,' said Juniper, 'both for you and for him. I do hope that when we find him, you can smooth things over.'

'I can't thank you enough for your support Juniper, I have felt so alone with this.'

'Well, there are two of us now,' she said. 'Let's have an early night and in the morning we will decide what to do.' Once Christine had gone up to bed, Juniper put away the last of the supper things as she turned the situation over in her mind.

She finally knew where Lydia was, it was a huge step forward. Would she have the courage to go and see her? This person Lydia had met, surely couldn't be Christine's son, could it? Supposing Clémence's hunch was just a wild goose chase?

Whatever the truth of it, this was the chance Juniper had been waiting for, to make things right with Lydia. Hadn't Jed said he knew the south coast? Her thoughts swirled in her head, it all felt like too much to contemplate. She was tired.

She would call Jed in the morning; he would know what to do. She had tried to call him a couple of times since their afternoon out on the water, but both times, an answering machine picked up the call. She wanted to make things right with him too, he must have thought her rude when she rushed away, after his kind hospitality. She sighed as she climbed the stairs slowly to her bedroom.

Over breakfast Juniper told Christine about Jed, 'I've come to rather like him,' she said. 'He's very easy to be with, kind and relaxed. He's too easy to be with really.'

'How can someone be too easy to be with?' asked Christine.

'Oh, I don't know. He lulled me into such a sense of security, that I found myself daydreaming about having a life with him.'

'What's wrong with that?' asked Christine. 'He sounds nice. After all, you are on your own,' she added.

'I'm quite happy on my own,' said Juniper, a little defensively.

Then Christine said, 'We all need love, Juniper. I was so lonely after Marc died, I missed him dreadfully; but now I have someone else. Alain has been such a comfort to me. I don't think I love him, at least not in the way I loved Marc, but I need him. I need to feel his arms around me, loving me, whispering to me in the darkness. It makes me feel less alone.'

There was a silence, as Juniper reflected on Christine's words. She continued, 'You shouldn't resist Jed if you like him. Life is so short; it goes by in the blink of an eye. You should make the best of every moment you have.' Christine was beginning to sound like Alice once had. She continued, 'I know you miss Lydia and you feel you have unfinished business with her, but if you have a fulfilling life of your own, it will all take on a new perspective.'

'You are so kind. They are wise words,' said Juniper slowly, gazing out into the garden. 'I have always found it difficult to follow my heart, I think that's because I struggle to truly know it. What I do know is fear, fear of being hurt again. I thought I had become better at it, but I've taken a retrograde step since Lydia left.'

'Things have a way of working out. Sometimes we just have to let things take their natural course,' said Christine.

'I behaved badly when I last saw Jed,' said Juniper suddenly. 'I had a vision of us growing old together and it frightened me. I've only just met him.' She paused and looked up at Christine as she said more quietly, 'I don't want to get hurt again.'

Christine reached out to put her hand over the top of Juniper's and patted it, 'Juniper, you need to have more faith in yourself.' She paused for a moment, 'Now, you said you have an idea, tell me.'

'Yes, I have,' said Juniper. 'I'm going to call Jed to see if he can help us. He spends a lot of time on the south coast; perhaps he will have a suggestion.' After breakfast, she picked up the phone and dialled Jed's number. To her surprise, he picked up after a couple of rings.

'Juniper, what a wonderful surprise.'

'Jed, I'm so sorry for the way I behaved last time I saw you. You gave me such a lovely afternoon. I shouldn't have rushed off the way I did.'

'Nonsense,' he said. 'Don't give it another thought. I did wonder whether I said something to frighten you off, but here you are on the telephone, so I'm a happy man.' Juniper smiled with relief.

'Actually, I'm calling to invite you over for lunch. I have a friend here from France, and we have a bit of a mystery on our hands. We were hoping to ask for your advice.'

'I'd love to,' he said. 'What time would you like me there?'

THE SUSSEX COAST

Over lunch with Juniper and Christine, Jed was swift to offer his help.

'I'll tell you what,' he said. 'I will drive you down to Sussex myself. I love a mystery.'

'Would you, Jed? How very kind,' said Juniper.

'Not only will I drive you, but I can offer you my home at the marina, as a base. It will be my pleasure to help.'

'Thank you, Jed,' said Christine. 'This is far more than I could have hoped for.' Juniper breathed a sigh of relief, glad to hand the situation over to Jed, it felt so good to have his support.

The next day, settled comfortably into Jed's Mercedes, they made the journey from London to the South coast. They travelled alongside hordes of other traffic, in drizzling rain.

'I can hardly believe that this time yesterday, we were relaxing over lunch in a sunny garden,' said Juniper, feeling a need to fill the anxious silence. Christine smiled in acknowledgement, but said nothing, no doubt reflecting on the fact that the journey might come to nothing for her.

Finally, as they approached the Sussex coast, glimmers of sunlight began to illuminate the ragged landscape. The road wound its way through downland and cliffs, giving way to a panorama of sea, luminescent in shades of blue and turquoise. Ahead, the fields were dotted with blurs of creamy sheep as they grazed, and beyond them, a lighthouse stood proudly on the headland.

'What beauty,' said Christine as she took in the scene.

'That's the Belle Tout Lighthouse,' said Jed. 'It's been there since 1832. When they built the new one at the foot of the cliffs at Beachy Head, it was decommissioned. The BBC owns it now. I've heard they're making a film there.'

'How interesting,' said Christine. 'How long have you lived in the area, Jed?' she asked.

'I bought my house five years ago, so that I can split my time between here and London. I keep a yacht at the marina. I enjoy sailing here; even occasionally, across the channel to France. The location is not only convenient, but quite beautiful, as you say.' They fell into a comfortable silence then, and Juniper felt her eyelids getting heavy. 'Not far now,' said Jed. The car slowed at the top of a hill on the coast road, before descending towards the town. Seahaven lay below them predominated by lush trees and white buildings, flanked by a sparkling sea.

'The marina is about two miles away, you can see it over there in the distance, beyond the town,' said Jed.

When they reached the marina, they turned into a small cul-de-sac. Jed's house was at the far end of it, facing the water. It was three stories high with American-style white-board cladding. The window frames were turquoise blue and the roof was tiled in pale grey slate. A plump, smiling woman came out to greet them as Jed pulled up on the drive. 'I'm just leaving, Mr Carruthers. I've stocked up the fridge for you and all three bedrooms are made up. It's set to be a lovely weekend.'

'You are a marvel, Mrs Baxter,' said Jed. 'We really appreciate it, thank you. Come on ladies, let me show you around.' He lifted their cases from the car and led the way through the door. It was a spacious house; the front door opened onto a long wide hallway with a huge room at the far end. There was a large open-plan kitchen, with a breakfast bar, which separated it from the deeply carpeted living space. At either end of the room, full-length glass doors opened onto balconies, overlooking the marina and the bobbing yachts.

'What a lovely light space,' said Juniper.

'Isn't it,' said Jed. 'There are several restaurants nearby, beside the water. I like nothing better than to stroll out in the evening to eat. Sometimes, I just sit on the balcony, watching the world go by.'

'Oh, the joy of being by the sea,' said Juniper. 'I can't remember the last time I saw it; I have suddenly realised what I've been missing.'

Jed led them up deeply carpeted stairs to the first floor, where two double bedrooms, each with a bathroom, had views of the sea from their balconies. 'These are your bedrooms,' said Jed. 'I hope you will be comfortable. At the end here, there is a small sitting room as well. Please, make yourselves at home.'

'How lovely! Jed, this is so kind of you,' said Juniper. Another staircase drew her gaze upwards.

'My bedroom and study are upstairs, I'm happy to show you if you like.' He smiled, looking at Juniper, and she found herself blushing. What was wrong with her? She was acting like a teenager with her first crush. Christine came to her rescue.

'Jed, you must allow me to take you both out to dinner this evening. You have been so very kind.'

'I would love that,' he said. 'You might enjoy the new French bistro; it is an easy stroll from here. Shall I book a table?'

'Yes please,' said Christine. Jed looked at Juniper,

'How does 7.30 sound?' There were murmurs of assent, and then he said, 'I'll leave you ladies to unpack now. When you come down, I'll pour some drinks. You probably want to discuss your strategy for tomorrow.'

As they watched the sun go down over the marina, drinks in hand, Jed raised his glass to them both. 'To new beginnings,' he said. The French bistro did not disappoint. Over a dinner of foie gras with fig marmalade, followed by fresh fish with samphire, they chatted about their plans for the coming days.

It was decided that Christine would call Lydia's number the next morning to introduce herself, explain her connection with Clémence, and the letter she had received from her. At Juniper's insistence, Christine would not mention her for now, but prioritise the search for her son.

Juniper wanted to bide her time, and perhaps contact Lydia in the next few days. One possibility was that she might simply go and knock on Lydia's door and surprise her, since Clémence had also provided Christine with the address.

As she sipped her dessert wine and reflected on it, Roger came into her mind. Things have never been the same with her son since the débacle that night, five years ago, in Paris. He said he had forgiven her, but she sensed a distance between them, on the rare occasions they spoke. She really had made a mess of her life; in particular, her relationships with her children. Juniper began to feel the panic of overthinking rising, and she looked up to find Jed watching her with concern. 'Are you alright, Juniper?' he asked.

'Just my thoughts running away with me,' she said. 'I'm fine. I just need to take some deep breaths and it will pass,' she said, trying to bring a serene smile to her face. She would discuss it all with Jed, and they would make a plan, but for now, Christine would make the first move.

The next morning shone bright and blue outside her window. Juniper stepped onto the balcony of her bedroom, marvelling at the joy it brought her to be here. She slept deeply and comfortably in the generous bed, surprising, given her anxiety the evening before. She leaned on the balcony and watched the little boats bobbing about, their flags fluttering in the breeze, taking deep breaths of the deliciously salty air. Upstairs, Jed, who had been sitting on his own balcony, heard Juniper's doors open. He was about to call out to her, when he saw her. She took his breath away, her creamy shoulders and sloping back emerged from a peachy silk negligée and her chestnut brown hair, mussed from sleep, fell around her shoulders. He was ready to play the long game for this captivating woman, the last thing he wanted to do was frighten her away. She was anxious, reticent and seemed unaware of her beauty, but he knew he was falling in love with her.

A woman friend told him once that when you are born beautiful, you don't think about it. She told him that for her, there were times when her beauty was a burden. He struggled to comprehend it at the time, but it came back to him now as he watched Juniper's unguarded pleasure at the scene before her. He would tread very carefully and slowly. He was about to make himself known when she turned and went inside.

By the time Juniper emerged from her room half an hour later, Christine was drinking strong coffee and smoking on the kitchen balcony. She seemed to be in her own world.

'Good morning,' said Juniper, stepping outside to join her. 'Isn't this beautiful?'

Christine started, hastily stubbing out her cigarette in the ashtray. 'Oh Juniper, you've caught me smoking. I haven't done that since my days in Paris, as a young girl. Back then, black coffee and a Gauloise was my standard start to each day. I suppose I thought it helped me to stay slim.' She smiled at Juniper, 'Today it's pure nerves.' Juniper stepped forward and embraced her, a kiss on each cheek.

'How did you sleep?' asked Juniper.

'Like the dead,' she said. 'I was exhausted. I still can't get over the kindness of your friend, driving us down and allowing us to stay. It has made such a difference.'

'Jed really is turning out to be a sweetie,' said Juniper. 'I slept well too, it must be the sea air.'

'Did I hear my name?' said Jed, stepping out onto the balcony to join them. 'Good morning ladies, how are you both this morning?'

'Just saying how well we slept. Thank you so much, Jed,' said Juniper.

'It is my pleasure,' he said. 'Can I interest you both in breakfast by the water? There is a café a short stroll from here, with tables outside in the sun.'

'I would love that,' said Juniper. 'Christine, what do you think?'

'It is a lovely idea, but please do go ahead without me. I want to make my phone call to Lydia this morning, and it is probably best I am alone.'

'Of course,' said Jed. 'If you change your mind, come down and join us.' Once they left the house, Christine took a deep breath and went to sit down beside the telephone. She dialled Lydia's number and was surprised when it was picked up almost immediately, by a breathless girl.

'Hello,' said the voice. There was a silence during which Lydia almost replaced the receiver, and then she heard the tentative voice of a woman with a French accent.

'Good morning, am I speaking to Lydia d'Apidae?'

'Yes, you are.' The woman at the other end let out a sigh of relief.

'Ah Lydia, thank goodness.' There was a pause, Lydia was mystified. The woman continued, 'My name is Christine de Courcy, you don't know me, but I know your grandmother very well. Clémence and my mother were at finishing school together.'

'Oh, I see,' said Lydia. 'How can I help you, Madame de Courcy? I'm actually late for work, so I haven't got long. I've just come up from the beach, I've been swimming you see and I need to change for work.'

'Of course, my dear. I will get straight to the point then. Clémence believes that you may know the whereabouts of my missing son, Daveed de Courcy.'

'I'm sorry,' said Lydia. 'I don't know anyone of that name.'

'Oh,' said Christine, deflated.

'It's just that Clémence told me you made a new friend. She said you met him at the beach, and I thought it might be Daveed.' Why on earth would she think that, thought Lydia. She wanted to bring the call to a close, but the woman persisted. 'Does he wear a heavy signet ring?'

'I'm sorry, Mme de Courcy, do you mind if we continue this conversation later? I really must get ready for work.'

'Wait, my dear,' said Christine, 'You have no idea how important this is to me. Please, tell me about his ring.' Lydia looked at her watch.

'Yes, he does wear a ring; it looks as if there is a lion or something like that on it.' There was a silence at the other end of the telephone.

'Thank you so much my dear, I must let you get to work. May I telephone you this evening?'

'Yes, that's fine,' said Lydia. 'I must go, bye for now,' and she put the phone down. How had this woman got her number? Then she remembered, the woman had mentioned Grandmère Clémence. She would ask her about that later.

Christine's hand was shaking as she put down the receiver. She took a deep breath, as she wiped away a tear. She rummaged in her bag for a handkerchief and dabbed her nose, before reaching for the telephone directory.

'Hello, is that the Grand Hotel? Yes, my name is Christine de Courcy. Do you by any chance have a suite available for a week or so?' There was a pause, and then she said, 'Thank you, yes, that's right. Good. Please reserve it for me. I will be with you this afternoon.'

Christine put the phone down decisively. She needed to be alone with a private space to meet Daveed – if indeed it turned out to be him. She had imposed long enough on Jed and Juniper.

JED

Having helped Christine with her luggage, and waved her off in a taxi to the Grand Hotel, Jed turned to Juniper. 'Now I have you all to myself, do you feel like a stroll along the promenade?'

'I'd love to Jed, but there is something I need to do first,' she paused. 'Actually, I'm in rather a tricky situation.'

'Is it something I can help with?' he asked.

'It might be,' she said.

'Come and sit down. Tell me about it,' said Jed. 'If you want to, that is. I'm here to help if I can.'

'Alright,' said Juniper. 'You may recall the connection between Lydia, and the young man who may, or may not be Christine's son?'

'I do, from the letter,' he said.

'Well, now that Christine has moved to the Grand Hotel, and will soon have the contact information for the young man's lodgings, I have been thinking about getting in touch with Lydia. It's coming up to two years since I last saw her. I am longing to see her, but I can't afford to get it wrong. I want to tell her that I know I made mistakes. She is so precious to me. I'm only sorry that I did so little to show it, as she was growing up.'

'It can't be that bad,' said Jed. 'I think all young people need to strike out on their own, just to prove that they can. Do you think you may have taken it all too personally?'

'Yes, perhaps,' said Juniper. She was comforted and calmed by Jed's familiar presence. He made her feel protected. With him by her side, everything took on a new perspective.

'Well, there's no time like the present,' he said. 'Come on, why don't I drive you over there?'

Half an hour later, they pulled up in Seaview Road. Juniper took a piece of paper out of her bag and looked at the address. 'Lydia lives at number three,' she said. 'She should be at home, it's Saturday.'

Jed looked at his watch, 11 a.m., not too early. He could see Juniper was anxious, and he reached out for her hand.

'Look at me, Juniper. Relax your shoulders, and take a deep breath; then smile.' After a few moments, her eyes became serene and she smiled at him.

'Thank you, Jed. I've been imagining this moment for so long, I really don't want to get it wrong.'

'You won't,' he said. 'Just be yourself. Tell Lydia how you feel; tell her you love her.'

Juniper pulled the flap of the car mirror down to check her lipstick and her hair. Satisfied, she said, 'Alright, it's now or never.'

'Would you like me to come with you?' asked Jed.

'Thank you, Jed, but I need to do this alone.' He reached out to squeeze her hand, and then she opened the car door and got out.

Jed watched her walk slowly along the road, looking at the numbers on the front doors. She stopped in front of an elegant, white building, with stone steps to an imposing front door. The flats had large floor-to-ceiling windows, probably with panoramic views of the sea, Jed imagined, as he looked up at the building.

Juniper walked up the steps and pressed the buzzer marked 'd'Apidae'. Her heart was in her mouth as she waited for Lydia to answer. Would she be pleased to see her? Perhaps she should have telephoned first. As these thoughts rushed through her mind, she looked back along the road, and was reassured to see Jed's car waiting for her.

She wondered whether she should press the buzzer again. As she deliberated, the door opened and a scruffy man in his fifties came out. 'I don't suppose you know my daughter?' she asked. 'Lydia d'Apidae?'

'Oh, that's 'er name is it,' he said. 'I know 'er rather well, as it 'appens.'

'Do you know whether she's at home?'

'Well it ain't much good asking me that,' he said. 'I wouldn't know. Norman's the name, by the way,' he said, reaching out to shake hands. Juniper recoiled as his calloused hand made contact with her own. She tried to pull her hand back, but he held on. Juniper began to shrink away from him, wondering what Lydia could possibly have to do with this objectionable man. 'What's a pretty lady like you, doing here on your own?' he said, a lascivious look on his face.

Jed, who saw the whole thing, read Juniper's body language and jumped out of the car. He called Juniper's name, as he walked quickly towards her. The man looked up in shock and dropped her hand, as Jed approached the steps. Then he pushed roughly past her and hurried away in the opposite direction. 'Are you alright, Juniper?' asked Jed. 'What happened?'

'All I did was ask him whether he knew Lydia. Then he got hold of my hand and wouldn't let go,' she said, shaken.

'Does he live here?' asked Jed.

'It seems he does,' said Juniper. 'Anyway, there's no reply from Lydia. Let's go, Jed.'

On Monday, despite her ordeal at Lydia's door, Juniper was ready to try again. This time, Jed drove her to the local library, where they thought Lydia might be about to take a lunch break. Juniper checked the mirror again, before stepping out of the car and walking inside. It seemed easier, somehow, to come into this public place, than to arrive on Lydia's doorstep again, unannounced.

'Hello, can I help you?' asked the receptionist, as Juniper walked towards her.

'I'm looking for Lydia d'Apidae,' said Juniper.

'I'm afraid you've just missed her. She's left for an early lunch break. She's walking a friend's dog this week. Would you like to leave a message for her?'

'No, thank you,' said Juniper. 'I'll try again another day.' Juniper returned to the car deflated.

'Any luck?' asked Jed.

'She's already left,' said Juniper. 'Perhaps this isn't meant to be. I probably need to accept that.'

'Why not put it out of your mind for now,' said Jed. 'Let's take the car back home and go for a stroll along the promenade. I'll take you for a late lunch somewhere.'

'Why not,' she replied. 'I just need to change my shoes and collect my sunglasses.'

The walk took them around the marina, dotted with interesting boutiques and little restaurants, then out towards the wide promenade, along the beach. Colourful wooden beach huts stood in neat rows facing the sea, and on the shingle beach, a few upturned rowing boats lay in the sun among ragged clumps of seagrass. There was a wildness to it, and Juniper was surprised. 'What a contrast to the marina,' she said. 'I expected there to be lots of people.'

'The busiest time is over now,' said Jed. 'It's very different in high summer. These beach huts aren't really used at this time of year, unless it's exceptionally warm. The other end of the beach, towards the pier, is busier and tends to be like that for most of the year.'

They had been strolling for twenty minutes or so, when the open skyline gave way to elegant white buildings flanking the road. In the distance, the pier reached out into the blue sea, its white domes curving up to the sky.

A sea breeze ruffled Juniper's hair and in spite of her recent disappointment, she felt herself relax. Being with Jed seemed to have this effect on her. It wasn't anything he said or did, but there was something calming about his presence. It made her drop her guard, a guard she only realised she maintained, when it fell away. It was so much easier, she realised, just to let go and enjoy each moment for what it was.

She wondered when she had drifted away from the meditation and yoga that Alice taught her, before she died. It was so gradual, she hardly noticed and now, her heart began to welcome back those feelings, like long-lost friends. Jed reached out to take her hand, and she smiled.

'A penny for your thoughts,' he said.

'Oh, I was just remembering an old friend. She had a very calming influence on me.' She paused. 'I realise that is how you make me feel too.' He squeezed her hand, as seagulls swooped low over their heads, wheeling and calling. 'You probably don't want to talk about this,' said Juniper, 'but it's hard for me to believe that your wife left you.'

'Oh, it's not that hard really. I'm a bit of a bookish person; I enjoy a quiet life and find pleasure in small things. Anastasia was a party girl. When I met her, the attraction was instant. Fireworks of joy seemed to pop constantly around her and as a young man, leading a fairly solitary life, I was smitten. She made me question the quiet life I had enjoyed before I met her. She encouraged me to buy fashionable clothes and took me to parties. She dazzled everyone around her, while I stood on the side lines, trying and failing to fit in.'

'That must have been difficult,' said Juniper. 'Although, there is something rather thrilling about a room full of strangers. Nobody has any prior expectations of you; you can almost become someone else.' She paused as they strolled on, as if she was considering whether to say more. Then she said, 'I went to a party once in the guise of another person. I had reached a low point in my marriage and I was desperate for an adventure. I dressed in a daring mini skirt, long before they became mainstream and had too much to drink. Unfortunately, I also did something very stupid. In the end, it changed the course of my life.'

'It sounds serious,' said Jed.

'It was. I hid what happened that night for years. It's a long story, which I will share with you one day. Suffice it to say that I ended up making a mess of my relationships with my children as well.' She paused. 'Sorry Jed, I interrupted your flow about Anastasia, please tell me more.'

'There is not much more to say really, except that our ideas of marriage were very different. Anastasia didn't have a quiet side, her life swept her up in a whirlwind and she loved it. In the end, I found it exhausting, so she carried on partying and I excused myself. Inevitably, she began to have affairs; before long our marriage hit the rocks. When it was over, I found I was relieved. I realised that the enjoyment of books, reading as well as writing, was where my contentment lay. I was glad not to have to apologise any more for being myself.'

'No, we should never do that,' said Juniper. 'It's a lesson I'm still trying to learn.'

'Tell me more about your children, if you want to. I know when we last touched on it, you preferred not to. Please know that if ever you do, I am here to listen and help if I can.'

She reached for his hand and they paused. Jed looked down into Juniper's face and leaned towards her, he was about to kiss her, when they heard a shriek.

'Mum! It can't be!' Juniper looked up and saw a lanky girl

with a scruffy white dog, sauntering towards them.

'I don't believe it! It's Lydia,' said Juniper. For a moment, she was rooted to the spot. Then, recovering herself, she rushed forward and put her arms around her daughter, but Lydia pulled away.

'What are you doing here, Mum? I thought you were in London.'

'Actually I came down with some friends,' said Juniper. 'This is Jed Carruthers.' She gestured towards Jed who was now standing beside her.

'I am very pleased to meet you, young lady,' said Jed, shaking Lydia's hand.

'Likewise,' said Lydia.

'This is such a surprise,' said Juniper. 'I was just telling Jed how much I would like to see you, and here you are. Darling, do let me take you to lunch. Jed tells me there is a lovely restaurant called the Mirabelle, at the Grand Hotel.'

'Mum, why does everything always have to be so posh with you? Why can't we be like normal people and have a sandwich by the beach?' Her tone was accusatory and combative, but it sounded as if she was agreeing to lunch.

'Tell you what,' said Jed, 'There is a little cafe a bit further along the promenade. They do sandwiches, soup and so on. Why don't you go there? I have some work to do, so should probably get back.' This was kind of Jed, thought Juniper, and looked at Lydia to ascertain her reaction.

'Do you want to do that, Mum?' asked Lydia.

'Yes, I would love to,' said Juniper. 'You can tell me all about your canine friend and we can have a catch up. Thank you, Jed,' she said, turning to him before he walked away. 'I'll see you later.'

'Who's he?' asked Lydia, still with accusation in her voice.

'He's just a friend,' said Juniper. 'He's been very kind as it happens.'

The cafe was in a sheltered inlet at the far end of the promenade. Palm trees cast flickering shadows over an otherwise sunny terrace, with blue metal tables and chairs. Over freshly made sandwiches and a pot of tea, Lydia began to relax.

'It really is good to see you, Mum. I had a letter from Grandmère the other day, I know she wants us to see more of each other. She actually said how fond she has always been of you.'

'Did she really?' said Juniper.

'I think Clémence is much more understanding than you give her credit for. She must have known what Dad was like, Mum.' Now, Juniper really was surprised. She thought Étienne could do no wrong in Lydia's eyes. 'Let's face it,' Lydia continued, 'you made one mistake, whereas he had a string of affairs and got away with it. How can that be fair?' Juniper's confidence was growing.

'It was so different in the fifties Lydia; women didn't stand up for themselves the way you do today.'

'We don't though, do we?' said Lydia angrily, as a deep dark memory stirred within her. Juniper saw her shudder before jumping up from the table and hurrying inside.

'I won't be a minute,' she called, 'I need the loo.' Juniper reached down to stroke the little white dog, who was looking up at her, wagging his stumpy tail. The feel of the dog's soft fur calmed her. Why had Lydia reacted like that? It occurred to Juniper then, for the first time, that this was not all about her, and her wish to reconcile with Lydia. It was about Lydia, and what she might want.

What was her daughter feeling? Perhaps she had problems Juniper knew nothing about. She needed to show, albeit belatedly, that she could be a mother to her daughter. When Lydia returned from the bathroom, Juniper said, 'Darling, I don't think I have ever told you how proud you make me.' Lydia looked astonished.

'Proud?' she asked. 'In what way?'

'Well look at you, you have made an independent life for yourself. You have a job at the library. Yes, Clémence does write to me sometimes.' She paused. 'You see, I never had the chance to be independent. It never occurred to me. I lived in an ivory tower of wealth and privilege and it was all I ever knew. It was Alice who made me see the world differently. It must have been very hard for you when she died, Lydia. I know you two were close.'

'The truth is,' said Lydia, 'I have always felt rather untethered in the world. If I'm honest with you Mum, I have felt unwanted. I was always in your way as a child, and I had the feeling that you preferred it when I wasn't around. Then, after the divorce, it went from one extreme to the other. You leaned on me big time, as if I didn't have enough of my own to deal with.'

Juniper felt a pang of guilt as the accuracy of Lydia's words hit home. She had been a different person back then, self-absorbed and desperately seeking the love she craved, from her absent husband.

Juniper sighed. 'Oh Lydia, I know I have let you down badly. I was so young when I married, I was still a child in so many ways. Nobody teaches you how to be a parent, or even a wife for that matter. Things were difficult for your father and me.'

'His affairs, you mean? Don't think I didn't know, Mum. Roger used to go round with his eyes shut half the time.'

'Lydia, it wasn't entirely your father's fault. Our personal life was,' she paused, 'difficult. You see, I was not the kind of wife he had the right to expect.'

'What do you mean by that?' asked Lydia. It was like listening to something from the dark ages.

'I suffered hidden abuse as a child, and it affected me for most of my early married life.'

'What do you mean, hidden abuse, Mum?'

'Oh Lydia, please don't make me spell it out to you. It was an uncle of mine; he was a dirty old man. Do you understand? For years I convinced myself that I must have deserved it, that it was all I was worth.' Lydia swallowed and her face flushed, as she tried to prevent a tear from falling. Her mother's story struck that dark chord again, hard. 'Even my mother didn't or couldn't save me from it.'

'Sometimes no one can save you,' said Lydia, staring out to sea.

'I'm over it now,' said Juniper. 'I just didn't think it was right for your father to take all the blame. Things improved between us eventually, but in the end, it wasn't enough.' Juniper hadn't noticed that Lydia's mind was elsewhere. Soon afterwards, Lydia stood up and said she needed to get the dog home. They hugged and said their goodbyes, promising to get together again soon. Then they walked off in opposite directions.

JUNIPER

When Juniper got back to the house, she walked around the back and in through the kitchen door. She didn't want to disturb Jed, thinking he may be working. Instead, she walked quietly up the stairs to her room.

The meeting with Lydia was fortuitous, she thought, reflecting on it. It saved her the worry of trying to find the best way forward with her daughter. Now, they had broken the ice, and a few honest words had been spoken.

How very kind of Jed to be as sensitive as he was, and leave them to it. He was turning out to be a very special man. Juniper decided she would risk disturbing him after all and go up the next flight of stairs to his study. She wanted to thank him for today, it had meant a great deal to her.

Still in her bare feet, when she reached the top, she could see Jed at his desk, apparently dozing in his chair. She smiled, and turned to go, but a creak of the stairs woke him and he swivelled the chair to face her. 'Juniper,' he said. 'How good it is to see you. How did the lunch go?' He stood up then, and she moved towards him, arms outstretched.

'You dear man,' she said. 'You were so thoughtful today.' Jed took her into his arms and held her close. She laid her head against his shoulder; it felt warm and comfortable. When she looked up at him, he took her face gently between his hands. As he gazed into her eyes, he ran his thumb gently along the line of her brow, then over her cheek and finally, oh so gently, along the soft skin of her lower lip. Juniper's lips parted and she sighed, as he lowered his head to kiss her. When she felt the soft, warm pressure of his lips on hers, it was as if her whole body was sighing with the rightness of it. Her small hand moved to the back of his neck, as their kiss deepened. She wanted it to go on for ever.

'Oh Juniper, I have wanted to kiss you for so long,' he whispered.

'So why haven't you?' she murmured into his mouth, as their lips played together.

'I was afraid of frightening you away,' he whispered, not wanting to break the spell. When they eventually pulled apart, Jed looked into her eyes and said, 'Juniper, I'm in love with you.'

Then, without saying a word, Juniper took Jed by the hand and led him into the bedroom. She didn't take her eyes off him, as she began to undress, very slowly, taking her time.

'Juniper, you are making me crazy,' he said hoarsely. 'This is like waking up in my wildest dream.'

When, eventually, she stood naked before him, she began to undo the buttons of his shirt. She felt his heart rate rise as she leaned into him, feeling the heat of his body radiating over her bare skin.

Finally, when they stood naked together, he swept her up and began to kiss her eyelids and her neck. He placed her gently onto the white sheets of his bed, and knelt down on the floor beside her, drinking in the beauty of her body, running his hand over every inch of her soft skin, exploring her. 'Such beauty,' he murmured.

He kissed her mouth again then, moving his tongue slowly over her chin and then her chest until his mouth found her breast. His soft lips played around her nipple for a while, licking and teasing her. Then he took her soft flesh into his mouth and began to suck and lick her soft, yielding skin. He focused intently on his task, the delectable shape of her moulding to his mouth, as his hot breath warmed her skin. When he ran his tongue over her belly and gently separated her thighs with his large hands, she arched her back to meet his thumbs, as they slid rhythmically over her moist warm, flesh.

'Oh Jed,' she gasped, as her breathing began to come faster. He moved into bed beside her then and kissing her deeply once more, he rolled her on top of him. As she lay along his body, their tongues and lips locked in a deep kiss, her thighs fell open, and he slid inside her. She gasped once more, sucking the air from Jed's mouth as he thrust gently, their hot breath mingling in their own world of bliss. When Juniper's head filled with stars and her body shuddered in ecstasy, Jed cried out too, amazed, and they both laughed with pleasure.

By the time they began to emerge from their cocoon, it was getting dark. Their bodies were warm and woven together among the sheets, and Jed pulled Juniper to him once more and kissed her. She opened her eyes and kissed him back, her lips parting as she smiled at him. 'I love you, Jed,' she whispered, pulling the sheet away so that their skin was touching again.

He felt the warm welcome of her body and began to rise against her. Their lovemaking was slow and sensual this time. Jed gazed into the depths of Juniper's eyes, as they moved and flowed as one. 'I never imagined I could be this happy,' she whispered, as her breath began to quicken, warm over his face and neck. He felt himself pulled deeper inside her, as if she was drawing him to her, closer and closer, her face etched with ecstasy and love. Then her eyes became pools of light – as if she had slipped for a moment into another world.

Much later, as Jed opened a bottle of wine for them to share, they were languid and relaxed. Juniper explored the fridge, to see what they might have to eat. 'Shall I make us a mushroom fettuccini?' she asked

'Sounds good, my darling,' he said, handing her a glass of wine. 'To us,' he said, raising his glass.

'To us,' said Juniper. She felt soft and full of love for Jed. After taking a sip of wine, she walked over to him, wrapping her arms around him and laying her head against his chest. 'Today has been a good day,' she said, looking up at him.

'You have made me a very happy man,' he said, smiling down at her.

While Juniper chopped mushrooms and garlic, Jed put a heavy frying pan on the stove to warm. 'I think this calls for some buttery indulgence,' he said, deftly cutting a cube from the packet and watching it melt slowly in the pan.

Juniper stirred in the garlic and mushrooms, coating them nicely in the melted butter, before leaving them to simmer. Once the pasta was boiling, they sat down with their glasses of wine.

'Tell me something unusual and important to you,' said Jed. 'To give me an insight into the woman I am in love with.' Juniper looked into her glass, considering for a moment and then at Jed.

'Alright then,' she said. 'There was a tall pine tree, outside my bedroom window at our home in Normandy, it had long, soft needles. When the wind blew through the tree, it sang a deep and yearning song.' She looked at Jed. 'It was a high, sighing sound, like a lament of longing. Yet it was gentle and filled with love.' She paused as Jed waited, transfixed. 'The sound touched me in a deep place in my heart, and drew me to it, like an unsolved mystery. I would lie there, still and calm, mesmerised and soothed by it.' She paused. 'I came to think of that sound as the song of my heart.' She looked at Jed and smiled, 'Today, with you, I heard the sigh of the breeze through that pine again. For the first time in a very long time, I heard the song in my heart.'

'My darling,' said Jed, standing up and moving to hold her. 'Thank you for honouring me with those precious words.' He kissed the top of her head, 'I'm going to struggle to equal that one.' She smiled at him and then stood up.

'On that note, I think dinner is ready,' she said, laughing. She drained the pasta, and then stirred some crème fraiche into the mushrooms, adding pepper and salt. When she had transferred just enough pasta into the frying pan, she stirred it carefully until it was coated with the creamy mushroom mixture, then served it into nicely warmed, white china bowls.

'Delicious,' said Jed.

'Do you enjoy cooking?' she asked him.

'Actually, I do,' he said. 'My repertoire is quite limited, but I enjoy the process. It relaxes me.'

'I feel the same,' she said. 'I came to it quite late. I always thought of cooking as a bit of a chore and could never imagine myself being any good at it, but here we are,' she said, taking another mouthful. There was a pause, as they ate in silence for a while, comfortable in each other's company. Then Juniper said, 'It's your turn now, Jed. Will you tell me something deep about yourself?'

'Are you sure you want to hear it?' he asked, smiling.

'Of course I do,' she said.

'Alright.' He paused thoughtfully, reflecting on his words, unsure whether he was quite ready to reveal something so close to his heart. Then he said quietly, 'I have become rather religious lately. I find myself reflecting on some of the deeper questions of life; the idea of God, at the centre of everything.'

He paused, while Juniper waited, watching him, with quiet attention. 'When I am in my garden,' he continued, 'I find myself following the intricate swirls and lines of a leaf, the delicate colours in the petals of a flower. The contemplation of these things takes me to a very peaceful place, in my mind and in my heart. Sometimes, it feels like a union, with the divine.'

'That is beautiful,' said Juniper, quite in awe of him.

'Do you remember the old bench in my garden, at the house in Richmond? It is one of the reasons I love sitting there at the end of each day.' Juniper smiled and reached for his hand, remembering the fleeting vision that came to her that day, about growing old with Jed.

'Do you miss your garden when you are here?' she asked.

'In a way I do, but when I'm on the coast, I find the same pleasure in contemplating the sea – the ever-changing colour and flow of it, the vastness of it. At times, I'm truly humbled by nature.' He paused and smiled at her, and they both reflected on his words. Then he said, 'On that note, talking of the sea, why don't we go sailing tomorrow? I thought we might go along the coast and then find somewhere for lunch.'

'I'd love to,' said Juniper.

It would be ten days before they finally made their way back to London.

AUTUMN

THE SEWING GROUP - AUTUMN

'Welcome back everyone,' said Anya. 'I want to start this session with each of you taking a turn to tell us what you are working on, and how it's going.' Murmurs and grins went around the table, as they pulled out their work and placed it in front of them.

'I don't mind starting,' said Jonathan. He held up a purple jacket. 'This is one of my own designs,' he said. 'The only thing I felt was missing, was some raised gold embroidery!' he said with a flourish. There was a ripple of appreciative laughter, as he continued. 'It's been a challenge, but thanks to Anya, I've done it.'

'Do you want to explain to the others how you did it?' asked Anya.

'I wanted to create a half-inch wide, raised embellishment, with a curving point at each end,' said Jonathan.

'So, how did you do it?' asked Sarah.

'I had to pad out the design before I could embroider over it, to give a raised effect. To do that, I wound string around my open fingers, to form a multi-stranded circle. Then I cut it open and pulled the strings through this block of beeswax. Once they were coated in the wax, I shaped them into a column and stitched it into position with loops of thread. To form the finer, pointed ends, Anya showed me how to lift the tails of the string up at each end, and trim the ones underneath, so that they graduate into a nice fine point. Finally, I stitched over the top of it with gold thread.' Jonathan laid his jacket in the middle of the large table, so that they could look at the design.

'That looks beautiful,' said Sarah. 'A lot of work though.'

'Sewing is all about the process and being relaxed as you do it,' said Anya. 'I like to think of it as a kind of meditation.'

'Wos that when it's at 'ome?' said Maggie, breaking the serious mood around the table. They all laughed.

'It is a way of calming your mind, and finding peace within yourself,' said Anya.

'Sounds like a good idea to me,' said Sarah.

Suddenly, Maggie stood up and shrieked, before doubling over in pain. Sarah jumped up, 'Maggie what is it?'

'I reckon the baby's comin,' said Maggie, breathing hard. The pain passed and she stood up, both hands on the edge of the table. Sarah helped her over to a chair.

'Sit here for a minute,' said Sarah. 'I'll get our coats and drive you straight to the hospital.' Anya passed her a glass of water.

'Have a sip of this, Maggie. Were you expecting to go into labour as soon as this?' With that, Maggie started to pant again and clutch her stomach.

When the contraction passed, she said, 'It's comin' a bit early; I thought I had another couple a weeks yet.'

'Come on, Maggie,' said Sarah, helping her up, 'Let's get you to the car before the next contraction comes.'

'Do you need any help?' asked Jonathan.

'Yes, could you hold Maggie's arm on the other side, just in case she gets another contraction on the way to the car?'

'Oh Christ,' moaned Maggie, as they helped her down the steps, 'Now I've gone and friggin wet meself.'

'That's just your waters breaking, Maggie, nothing to worry about,' said Sarah, business-like; she wanted to get Maggie into the car as soon as possible. Anya rushed forward with two towels and folded them onto the seat of Sarah's car, and then they helped Maggie in.

'Maggie, would you like us to let your husband know?' said Anya.

'E's probably in the bettin' shop in town,' she said. 'You could try there,' said Maggie. She winced in pain, as another contraction overwhelmed her.

'Do you need any of us to come with you, Sarah?' asked Anya.

'No need,' she said. 'I've phoned ahead and the hospital is expecting us.'

'Good luck, Maggie,' called Lydia, waving as the car pulled away.

'Who would have believed my sewing prowess was enough to send someone into labour?' said Jonathan, as they stepped back into the studio. Lydia turned an adoring gaze his way, and laughed.

'Well, I don't know about you two, but I think we need a coffee. Danish pastry anyone?' said Anya.

'Ooh, yes please,' said Lydia.

'Likewise,' said Jonathan. 'If you don't mind me using the phone Anya, I'll try to contact Maggie's husband, to let him know what's happened. I expect he'll want to get straight over to the hospital.'

'Of course,' she said. 'It's in here.' He followed her into the hall and called directory enquiries. There was only one betting shop in town, as far as he knew. Fortunately, Maggie was right. Bill Banks was in the betting shop. He didn't sound concerned when he heard his wife had gone into labour. He assured Jonathan, over the noise of the crowded shop that he would leave for the hospital just as soon as the morning's racing was over. Jonathan replaced the receiver; there was nothing more he could do.

A short time later, Anya came in with a tray, bearing three mugs of coffee, Danish pastries and a folded copy of the local paper. 'Did you manage to speak to Maggie's husband?' she asked Jonathan.

'I did,' he said. 'He didn't sound in the least concerned and said he'd go over to the hospital later.' Anya sighed.

'Well, she's in good hands. Thankfully Sarah acted quickly.' Anya set the tray down on the low table near the sofas. 'Let's sit here,' she said, sinking into the comfort of an armchair. 'What a morning!'

'Those look delicious,' said Lydia, helping herself to a small pastry. They all sipped their coffee, as Anya unfolded the newspaper. 'There's going to be a craft fair in town next week, I thought some of you might be interested in going.' She opened it out to look at the details. As Lydia caught sight of the picture on the front page, her blood ran cold. Staring out at her was a face she would never forget. The headline ran 'Local Man Arrested'.

The colour drained from Lydia's face. 'Sorry Anya, I need to go,' she said, jumping up as if she had been scalded. Anya looked up from the paper, surprised.

'Are you alright, Lydia? You've gone awfully pale.'

'I'm fine,' she said. 'Sorry, but I've got to go. See you next week.' With that she opened the door and left.

Jonathan and Anya looked at each other, 'What just happened?' said Anya.

'No idea,' said Jonathan, 'but it's been a crazy day. Perhaps it's a delayed reaction to what happened with Maggie. I should probably get going as well, I'm meeting a friend. I'll try and catch up with Lydia, to make sure she's alright.' He picked up his canvas bag, pushed his things into it and left, calling over his shoulder, 'Bye Anya, thanks for the pastries and coffee. See you next time.'

SEVEN SISTERS

'I've been thinking,' said Jonathan as the car bumped its way along the track up to South Barn.

'About what?' asked Viddy.

'About your situation; France and so on.'

'What about it?'

'I think there may be a way to move things forward for you, with your mother I mean.'

'Really?'

'Yes, but first, I'm going to show you one of the best views in England.' Jonathan parked the car in a small car park, high up on the downs. They set off along a narrow path with wide open fields on either side of them. To the left, the fields fell away to the Cuckmere River, snaking its way over a wide, flat valley towards the sea.

'Wow,' said Viddy. 'This is beautiful.'

'It is,' said Jonathan, 'but the best is yet to come. Follow me.' They forged ahead and the path widened. Scraggy trees and undergrowth created a leafy tunnel, eventually opening onto wide, flat grassland. As they rounded a bend in the hill, a magnificent wall of white cliffs rose from the sea, stretching out to their left, as far as the eye could see.

'This is what I wanted to show you,' said Jonathan, as they stood gazing at the majestic sight. Viddy was transfixed and his heart was flooded with love for his friend. How could he know how much this sight would mean to him?

'These cliffs are called the Seven Sisters. Do you remember we walked over them a few weeks ago?' Viddy would never forget the intensity of those short, steep hills, followed almost immediately by a steep descent and then another hill. They started the walk at Birling Gap, its wide shingle beaches below high chalk cliffs and finished by descending to the flat valley of the River Cuckmere at Exceat, just below them.

'I do,' Viddy said, grinning.

'Of course we couldn't see the cliff faces then; they were below us. The best possible vantage point is from here; it's one of my favourite views. The cliffs flank the left side of the Cuckmere River, and we are on the headland to the right of it.'

'It reminds me of how I felt when I first saw the cliffs at Étretat,' said Viddy. 'I was a young teenager at the time.' Philippe was there too, but Viddy kept that part to himself. 'Do you know Étretat?' he asked Jonathan. 'The cliffs were immortalised by Monet in so many of his paintings. They are off the coast of Normandy.'

'I do,' said Jonathan. 'I went there years ago, with my parents. They took us there after seeing a Monet exhibition in Paris. After that, they took me to see where Christian Dior grew up, in Granville. They always seemed to understand, that fashion design was my first love, and that art was Berry's.'

They continued to stroll along the path, the sea was a pale turquoise colour in the afternoon light. The late sunshine threw the cliffs into sharp relief, making art out of every crag and undulation. The chalk took on a peachy hue, giving way to gold and then deep beige and grey, as they dipped into the shadows.

'You see the coastguard cottages in front of us, on the headland?' said Jonathan. He pointed to a row of houses on the edge of the cliffs. Viddy looked. The cottages were whitewashed with grey slate rooves, their four chimneys silhouetted against the sea and cliffs beyond.

'They look idyllic,' said Viddy.

'They are,' said Jonathan. 'Can you believe that one of them was almost mine?'

'What do you mean?' said Viddy, gazing towards them.

'We knew the family who owned them, quite well. We used to visit them for tea. I'd forage for sea lettuce and fish for prawns, while the adults chatted. One day, Bob told Dad he wanted to leave the cottage to me, for when I was grown up. They didn't have any children of their own, and I was just a boy. I suppose they thought of me as a surrogate son.'

'It sounds like the kind of childhood you read about in a storybook,' said Viddy. 'So what happened?'

'Dad didn't want to feel under an obligation to Bob, so he said no.' Jonathan looked wistfully at the house, 'It would have made a perfect studio. Can you imagine having all that inspiration outside your window every day?'

'~~They are very close to the edge~~ though,' said Viddy. 'Is it likely the cliffs will erode, over time?'

'They already have. It is a real concern for local people. One day, if nothing is done, I suppose those cottages will fall into the sea.'

'That would be awful,' said Viddy. They walked towards the cottages to have a closer look and then moved on past them, where the path descended steeply to the shingle beach below, and the mouth of the river.

'Do you want to swim?' said Viddy.

'Why not,' said Jonathan. 'There's nobody down there that I can see.' They threw their small rucksacks onto the shingle and let their clothes fall in a heap.

'I'll race you!' shouted Viddy, running effortlessly over the stones, while Jonathan hobbled behind, his feet unaccustomed to the pain of the pebbles.

'Christ,' he said breathlessly, as he plunged into the chilly water beside Viddy. 'How do you do that?'

'It's easy when you know how,' said Viddy laughing. Their eyes met and they gazed at one another for a long moment, the pearly white of their skin glimmering in the low sun. Then Viddy's face became serious, and he whispered 'What are you doing to me, Jonny?'

Jonny moved closer and pulled Viddy towards him, 'I think you know,' he whispered hoarsely, leaning forward to lick the salt from around Viddy's mouth. Viddy closed his eyes, enjoying the warmth of Jonny's tongue against his cold skin. Then he sighed, giving himself up to the sensation and leaned into Jonny's arms. They began to kiss, slowly at first, taking their time. They licked each other's mouths, the tips of their tongues found each other and played until finally, their lips closed together in a deep kiss.

Weak with love, they slowly fell to their knees in the shallow water. Locked together, and as indistinguishable as a pair of clams, the waves caressed them as they moved as one. 'Viddy, I'm in love with you,' whispered Jonathan, and Viddy's heart leapt with hope and love.

Later, they drove home in silent wonder at the turn their relationship had taken. Everything took on a warm glow as they basked in the joy of new love. Just before they reached the lane leading to Viddy's lodgings, Viddy reached out for Jonathan's hand.

'You never told me your idea,' said Viddy, 'about France.' Jonathan stopped the car, and then turned to look earnestly into Viddy's face.

'I want to come with you,' he said. 'We're going to do this together, Viddy.'

'If only that were possible,' said Viddy sadly. 'You don't know my mother. I can't live a lie, Jonny. No,' he said slowly, 'I can never go back, not if I want to remain true to myself.' Jonathan sighed and turned into the lane.

'Never say never,' he said. 'Have faith my friend.' He leaned over to kiss Viddy, and then drove away.

'Viddy, is that you?' called Sarah as he let himself in through the kitchen door.

'It is,' he called back. 'How was your day?' Sarah walked into the kitchen with a serious look on her face.

'My day has been eventful,' she said, looking meaningfully at Viddy.

'Oh?' he said. 'In what way?'

'I received an unexpected visit this morning. It was a French lady, the Vicomtesse Christine de Courcy.' Viddy turned as white as a sheet.

'Oh, mon Dieu,' he said, covering his face with his hands, in an uncharacteristic display of emotion. He stifled a sob and then turned and ran out of the door, into the fading light.

'Viddy, come back!' shouted Sarah after him. She pushed her feet into a pair of shoes and rushed outside. She could just make out Viddy running up the side of the hill and around the golf course, towards the cliffs. 'Viddy!' she shouted again, but her voice was carried away on a gust of wind, as the weather began to change.

Low clouds obliterated the sinking sun and fine drops of rain began to fall. Sarah hurried back inside to grab a coat. So the woman had been speaking the truth, she was Viddy's mother. Why else would he have reacted this way?

Sarah's astonishment at finding the elegant Frenchwoman on her doorstep was surpassed only by the news that her lodger was almost certainly the Vicomte Daveed de Courcy, heir to a Château in the Loire Valley in France. There was no time to lose. Sarah grabbed her raincoat, pulled it around her and slammed the door shut. She dashed towards the golf course, following the path along the side of it, to the cliffs beyond. By the time she reached the top of the cliff path, her breath was ragged and she was soaked. The rain was driving down and it was getting dark.

'Viddy!' she shouted, 'Viddy, where are you?' She stopped for a moment to catch her breath, straining to hear him. Then, as the wind and rain stilled, she heard the faint sound of sobbing coming from among the rough, long grass near the cliff edge. 'Viddy!' she called rushing towards the sound. Then she saw him hunched over in the long wet grass. 'Oh, Viddy,' she ran to him and knelt down, wrapping her arms around him. 'Listen to me, you may not be able to see it now, but everything will be alright. Please come home. Let's talk about this. Your mother loves you, that is very clear.'

'You don't understand!' he shouted, over the wind and the rain. 'Nobody does! I'm gay, I'm queer! Can't you see, there's no place for me in this world?' He turned his face into the grass again and his shoulders heaved, as he sobbed his heart out into the wet earth.

THE DE COURCYS

Back at the Grand Hotel, Christine reflected on her conversation with Sarah. Her hopes were initially dashed, when Sarah said she didn't know anyone named Daveed. It was only when she'd called him Viddy, his childhood nickname, that Sarah realised she knew him. 'Actually, I do have a lodger, called Viddy,' she said. 'He's been with us since early April.'

'Thank God,' she said to Sarah, almost passing out with relief. That was when Sarah invited her in for a cup of tea. 'He's out today,' she explained. 'He usually helps us in the garden.' She paused, and then said, 'He is the most considerate person, so gentle and kind. Does that sound like your son?'

'It sounds exactly like him,' said Christine. 'You have no idea how much I've missed him. Can you tell me more, Sarah? How is he? What has happened to him?'

'Unfortunately, I must respect his privacy,' said Sarah. 'I know you are his mother, but he is an adult. Any decision to talk about this must come from him.'

Christine tried desperately to hide her disappointment. 'Of course.'

'What I can tell you is that I have been keeping an unofficial eye on Viddy since he was discharged from hospital a few months ago. I am really pleased with his progress. I am a nurse, you see,' said Sarah. 'He's still quite vulnerable, emotionally, but he's made a friend, and his health is improving every day. He seems happy and settled, but he's been reluctant to talk about himself, or his future.'

'You really have been kind to him, thank you so much,' said Christine. There was a silence, while they both reflected on their new understanding of the situation. 'Do you know when Daveed will be back?'

'I'm afraid I don't,' said Sarah, 'but I'll be glad to give him a message for you. This is going to come as quite a shock to him, after all this time. He must have had his reasons for keeping his background so quiet. It is almost as if he didn't want to be found.'

Christine stood abruptly then, 'I have taken up enough of your time, Sarah. When Daveed is ready, please ask him to call me. I will be staying at the Grand Hotel, on the seafront, for as long as it takes. My son means everything to me.' Then she added, 'Thank you, for everything you have done for him.'

A few days later, Sarah called Christine, to say Daveed was ready to meet her. Following her instructions, the concierge brought him directly upstairs, knocked, and then let him into the suite.

Daveed stepped through the ornate doors, and there was his mother, standing in the middle of a small, elegant drawing room overlooking the sea. Over the preceding days, Viddy had become used to the idea of seeing her again. 'I'm relieved, if I'm honest,' he'd said to Sarah. 'I can't go on hiding who I really am from myself or from the world any longer. You see, I'm in love,' he admitted. 'It changes everything.' The thought of continuing to live a lie was unbearable – it was time to tell his mother the truth.

'Mon Cheri,' exclaimed Christine, moving towards her son, arms outstretched. 'I have been so worried about you! Merci à Dieu you are safe.'

'Maman,' said Daveed, walking to her and hugging her petite frame to him for a very long time. 'So much has happened; there is so much I need to tell you.' He smiled lovingly into her face, appraising her. She had lost too much weight and she had aged. Her normally taught skin had settled into soft wrinkles of sadness around her eyes and mouth. He felt a painful pang of guilt. 'I'm so happy to see you, and so sorry for what I've put you through.'

'If only you could have left me a note, talked to me,' she said sadly, pulling away and looking into his face. 'You know I would have supported you, no matter what.'

'Maman, you say that, but there is so much you don't know about me.'

'My darling, I have known you since your tiny body emerged from mine. I know you through and through. You are my son.'

Daveed could see the love shining from his mother's face. He looked at her for a long moment, then said, 'Maman, I've been living a lie. I just can't do it anymore. The strain of trying to be who everybody wants me to be is more than I can bear.'

'What can you mean, Daveed? In what way have you been living a lie? Come, let's sit down and talk. Tell me, please. You know you can tell me anything, however dreadful you think it is.' Daveed sighed.

'Actually Maman, I'm starving,' he said, wanting to deflect her. 'I haven't eaten anything this morning.' He needed some time to think. Whilst telling his mother the truth was his plan, he realised he was going to struggle to find the right words.

'Well, that's easy,' said Christine, 'I'll order you a nice breakfast and you can enjoy it at your leisure, with a view of the sea.' Christine picked up the telephone, 'Hello, is that room service? This is the Sea View Suite. Yes. Could you please bring up a full English breakfast for one and tea for two? Thank you.'

Daveed looked at her and smiled gratefully, then said, 'Since you have fluffy robes and a huge bathroom, do you mind if I shower before breakfast? I've been in the sea.'

'Go ahead darling, make yourself comfortable. We have all the time in the world.'

Daveed shut the bathroom door behind him, and then let his clothes fall to the marble floor. He stepped into the huge shower, pushing the lever fully over to switch it on. Hot darts of steaming water hit his skin and then gushed, as the jets quickly reached their full capacity. The tension he had been holding in his body slowly melted away, as the hot water caressed his limbs and shoulders. He lifted his face into the jets, letting the water cascade through his salty hair. Tears of relief began to run down the sides of his face. Finally seeing his mother again and the imminent prospect of telling her the truth, overwhelmed him; but he was determined to do it.

By the time he emerged from the bathroom, fresh, dried and reclothed, his breakfast was set out on a small table near the open balcony doors. His mother was at a small desk writing a letter. 'Darling, enjoy your breakfast,' she said over her shoulder. 'I have a few things to catch up on. We needn't talk until you are ready. We can even make it another day if you like.' Daveed's body language and poorly hidden anxiety before his shower, made Christine realise the importance of what he had to say to her. She wanted to give him time.

Later, they strolled along the promenade, enjoying the sight of children running into the waves and families setting up deckchairs and picnics.

'How lovely it is to be on the British coast!' said Christine. 'It's so very different to Deauville and Houlgate, isn't it?' Daveed nodded.

'I used to love our summer holidays there,' he said, turning to smile at his mother. In the old days, the Château kept horses and they would be stabled at one of the many Haras near the coast during the holidays, so that the family could gallop them along the wide flat beaches. 'Do you remember the time you and Philippe raced the horses along the full length of the beach, to win some prize or other your Papa had offered? They were such happy days,' said Christine wistfully.

Daveed, sensing his moment said, 'I loved him you know Maman, Philippe I mean.' Christine looked at her son and reached for his hand. 'I think I did know, darling. You mean you loved him like a brother, or was it something more than that?' This last question gave him hope that his mother might, after all, be able to understand.

'It was a long time before it became something more,' he said. He took a deep breath and plunged in, 'I suppose you could say Philippe was my first love, the one who finally made me see who I really am. I was heartbroken when the family left.'

'Darling, it is natural for friendships to become very intense, especially when there is nobody else. You and Philippe were inseparable growing up; the way you felt at the time is understandable.' Daveed said nothing and she continued, 'The world is full of lovely girls, I am sure the right person will come along for you. You just haven't met her yet. There is no pressure to marry my darling, I only want you to come home and take your rightful place as head of the family. Don't forget, we are all still grieving over the death of your brother.' Daveed's heart sank, his revelation had fallen flat. Perhaps his mother didn't want to understand.

'I'm sorry Maman, I have to go,' he said suddenly. 'There is so much more I need to say to you, but I can't do it now.' Christine was surprised at the change in Daveed's tone, and stopped to look at him as he continued, 'Why don't we meet for a drink this evening? I'll come up to the suite later.'

'Alright darling, if that's what you want. I'm going to walk for a bit longer. I'll see you later.'

LOUIS

When Daveed arrived at the hotel later, he had a plan. After a large gin and tonic with his mother, he said, 'Maman, I have a surprise for you.'

'A surprise?' she said. 'How lovely, what kind of surprise?'

'I'm taking you to see a fashion show tomorrow,' he said. 'A close friend of mine is at the end of his fashion design course; this is his final show. Afterwards, the three of us are going out for dinner.'

'This is a surprise!' said Christine. 'Who is this friend of yours? I didn't realise men did fashion design courses.'

'Of course they do!' said Daveed. 'You only have to think of all the greats; Christian Dior, Yves St Laurent, Hardy Amies – all men. It's the same with chefs. I have always wondered why cooking and fashion are perceived as the preserves of women. It doesn't make any sense.'

'Yes, I suppose that's true,' said Christine. 'I don't think I've ever thought about it like that.'

Daveed paused for a moment, then said, 'His name is Jonathan, Maman. I don't think you realise what a bad way I was in when I came to England. Jonathan has helped me to recover.'

'In that case, I look forward to meeting him,' said Christine. Then she paused, before saying more quietly. 'Daveed, you still haven't told me why you disappeared the way you did. You said just now that you were in a bad way. I can't bear to think of it. Was it my fault that you left?' Christine rummaged in her small handbag and brought out a handkerchief, dabbing the corners of her eyes.

Daveed knelt on the floor beside her, and pulled her to him, 'Of course it wasn't your fault Maman. I love you, you know that.'

'Then why?' she asked him.

Daveed sighed, moving back to his chair. He looked into her face and said, 'I know that Louis was the hero of the family. He was brave, he was intrepid, and he faced dangers most people would run away from.'

'The dangers he faced were of his own choosing, Daveed, you know that. I hated the way he put himself at risk, constantly. If he wasn't racing yachts, it was cars. He was addicted to danger, like a drug. I honestly believe he thought he was invincible. Believe me, if I could have stopped him, I would have.'

'He watched you struggling to manage the Château, after Papa died, and he didn't lift a finger. Not once did he cancel a race or a party to help you. That task fell to me. I didn't have Louis' strength or stamina, and without Philippe to help me, I felt useless.' Daveed looked up at his mother as he continued, 'How do you think it felt, to do as much as I could to help you, but to know that it would never be enough? Face it Maman, Louis was just a playboy.'

'Daveed!' said Christine, shocked, 'I won't let you speak of your brother like that,' but Daveed carried on as if she hadn't spoken.

'There is so much you don't know about Louis! He was always your golden boy, wasn't he? Did you know he used to bully me?'

'Bully you?' said Christine.

'Yes, bully me,' said Daveed. 'He used to hurt me in so many ways, and then tell me that this was what he had to endure at boarding school. "Why should you get off scot free you little Mummy's boy," he'd say, as he twisted my arm behind my back. One day he even pressed a lighted cigarette butt into my back.'

'Mon Dieu,' said Christine under her breath, as Daveed's voice trailed off and he quickly wiped away a tear. Then he looked up, 'Look at me!' he shouted suddenly. 'I'm pathetic, I'm nothing!' Now it was Christine's turn to go to her son. She got up and stood behind his chair, putting her hands on his shoulders and leaning her face down next to his, so that their cheeks were touching.

'Oh Daveed, why didn't you tell me?'

'I couldn't tell you,' he sobbed. 'Louis threatened me. He said he'd tell you about me and Philippe.'

'What about you and Philippe?' said Christine. 'What was there to tell?'

'He knew me for what I was. Relationships between boys were commonplace at his school – they were all doing it apparently.'

'At his school?' said Christine, as if watching a film, she couldn't quite comprehend. She stood up and moved back to her chair, trying to process this new picture of the world, being laid before her.

'Maman, look at me. I left home because I hated myself, and I hated Louis for being everything I could never be. You see, he was my hero too, until the bullying started. The depth of disillusionment and grief I felt at his betrayal of my love was worse than losing him when he died. I always looked up to him, but in the end I hated him. When he died, I felt nothing but relief.' Christine took a sharp intake of breath, as Daveed finished, 'There, I've said it. The guilt has been eating me up, and now I feel as if I have betrayed you too. I know how much you loved him. I'm so sorry Maman.'

When Viddy called Jonathan later that evening, he was despairing. 'I just can't make her understand that I am not the person she wants me to be. In spite of everything I have said it's as if she hasn't heard me. I couldn't have spelt it out any more clearly, but she just glosses over it. She thinks everything will be alright when I marry, but it won't Jonny. I won't do it. What am I going to do?'

Jonathan sighed, he'd been mulling over a plan, perhaps now was the moment. He said, 'Don't worry, I'm going to help you. Have you arranged for us to have dinner with your mother tomorrow?'

'Yes,' said Viddy quietly, 'but right now, I'm not sure I can face it.'

'You'll feel better tomorrow,' said Jonathan. 'The most important thing is that we see her alone, with no distractions. We're going to win her over,' he said, confidently.

THE FASHION SHOW

Lydia had waited in vain for a call from Jonathan. Berry must be back home by now, so she supposed he no longer needed her to walk the dog. She'd tried to ring several times, but hadn't left a message. What would she say? 'Jonathan, I fancy you, do you want to get together?' He'd probably laugh in her face. 'Lydia, why do you tell yourself things like that,' went her internal monologue. 'Jonathan's a nice guy, why would he laugh at you?' The little voice laughed back, 'Because he doesn't fancy you, of course. Look at yourself!'

Lydia sighed, why did she always have such a downer on herself? She'd tried to conquer the little voice in her head, she really had, but it just kept creeping back to taunt her. It waited behind every bit of dubious courage she mustered. She thought back to the evening with Anya, at the yurt. Things were so much better for a few days after that – everything took on a new perspective. She somehow managed to rise above the little voice, laughed at it even, but now it was back in charge.

As she walked towards the kitchen, Lydia caught sight of herself in the mirror. She was surprised to see an attractive girl with dark eyes and a new pixie haircut looking back at her. The person she saw before her was everything she believed she was not – poised, attractive, alluring even. She sighed, perhaps she would buy herself a new dress, and then she would walk round to Jonathan's house and surprise him.

It was the middle of the afternoon, when Lydia walked up the path to Jonathan's front door and rang the bell. She wore an emerald green, jersey dress that clung to her slim figure. The base of the skirt flared at her ankles, and swung jauntily over chunky flat sandals. She hoped she didn't look as if she'd gone to too much trouble. As she waited at the door, she began to lose her nerve. She was on the verge of turning back, when the door opened.

'Berry!' said Lydia. 'Hi, is Jonathan in?'

'No,' she said. 'He's got his end-of-year fashion show this afternoon. I was just getting ready to go and watch it. Why don't you come with me? I'll be ready in a few minutes, come in.'

'OK,' said Lydia, 'Do you think he'd mind?'

'Of course not,' she said. 'The more the merrier.'

'Did you have a nice holiday?' asked Lydia.

'Amazing!' she said, pulling up her sleeve. 'Look at my tan! You look nice by the way.'

'Thanks,' said Lydia. Berry always looked good, lucky thing; blonde hair, blue eyes and an English rose complexion. Some people have all the luck, she thought ruefully.

'Jonathan's got a dinner afterwards,' said Berry, 'so I doubt we'll see much of him. Apparently he's meeting a friend's mother, and he wants her to like him, for some reason.'

As they walked into the public hall half an hour later, it was thronging with people. There was a sense of excitement, as demob-happy students and their visitors, waited for the show to begin. Rows of chairs faced a low stage, from which a catwalk extended into the middle of the room. Many of the students, already seated, were outrageously and magnificently dressed. One girl had long feather plumes set into piled up hair, and another wore a floor skimming velvet coat, over ripped jeans. Next to them, a boy wore a red chiffon top stretched across his chest, with huge pleated puff sleeves. His face was made up in the style of Boy George, with eyeliner and lipstick. Lydia blinked in surprise, but Berry took it in her stride. 'Hey Marcus,' she said, slapping palms with him. 'This is Lydia,' she added. Marcus waggled his fingers at her.

'Hi,' said Lydia awkwardly. 'Oh look, there's Viddy.' She spotted him on the end of one of the rows in front of her, so she got up and walked over.

'Viddy,' she said, touching him on the shoulder. 'I thought it was you. How are you?'

'Lydia,' he said. 'What a surprise. What are you doing here?' Didn't it occur to him that Jonathan might have invited her? Obviously not.

'Berry invited me.'

Then, Viddy turned to the elegant woman seated beside him, and said,

'Maman, this is Lydia. Lydia, my mother.'

'Enchantée,' said Christine, smiling at Lydia, as if they had never spoken.

'What a surprise,' said Lydia. 'Very nice to meet you Mrs . . .' she hesitated.

'Vicomtesse de Courcy,' said Christine, 'but please, call me Christine.'

Of course, thought Lydia, suddenly making the connection. This was the woman who had called her for Viddy's address. At that moment, the lights over the catwalk came on, and Lydia moved back to her seat ready for the show.

'Good evening, ladies and gentlemen,' said a diminutive woman from the stage. She wore a Cleopatra style bob, with a thick straight fringe and heavy turquoise glasses. Her loose linen suit was terracotta coloured, with tribal style turquoise and green motifs at the sleeve and trouser edges. 'Welcome to our end-of-year fashion show. You are about to see the culmination of many months of work, by our talented design students. We invite you to sit back, relax and enjoy the show.'

As the lights went down, Madonna's 'Papa don't Preach' began to pump, at full volume, from the speakers. The spotlights lit the catwalk and the show began.

A tall model strode out in a red, triangular coat. The scarlet satin was offset by her white blonde hair and thick fringe, over heavily kohl-lined eyes and red lipstick. The padded shoulder lines of the coat extended well beyond her own, and the sides tapered dramatically to a point, just above her knees. Red tasselled cones in homage to Madonna, protruded from the breast pockets and thigh-length, red satin boots completed the look. She stopped several times, turning and swinging her hips to the beat.

As she walked back through the curtain, the music faded to be replaced by the loud opening propeller whirls of 'Silver Machine'. A model with a chiselled face and short spiky hair, walked boldly onto the cat walk. He wore a silver body suit, slashed to the waist, and sprayed silver Doc Marten boots. A billowing, red crinoline skirt cascaded from his waist to the floor, in sparkling ruffles. The skirt opened at the front as he walked, to reveal silver clad legs. Four models followed behind him. Two were dressed in city style, silver suits with red bowler hats. They wore big red glasses, in the style of Elton John. The other two, wore silver sprayed jeans and T-shirts, bearing red 'Ban the Bomb' logos. The parade continued, showing a series of spectacular outfits, each pushing the boundaries of fashion a little further.

The finale was a long turquoise dress, with a spiral of silver circles falling from the model's shoulders. These surrounded her body, forming a silver vortex, in which she walked. A matching headdress of turquoise silk, formed enormous roses on top of her head. Their circular, silver stems swirled round her head and face, to create an open helmet.

When the show came to an end, there was huge applause. Christine looked at Daveed; he had tears in his eyes and was beaming and clapping for all he was worth. 'What a triumph!' he said. 'What did you think, Maman?'

'I really enjoyed it,' she said. 'It was unlike any fashion show I have ever seen,' she said truthfully. Her fashion experience was limited to the Parisian couture houses of Dior and Chanel, so Daveed was not surprised.

As the clapping died down, Christine turned to her son, 'By the way darling,' said Christine, innocently, 'Who was that girl? The one in the green dress, earlier.'

'That was Lydia,' he said. 'She's a friend. I've done some work in her garden.'

'What a beauty,' said Christine. 'She would be perfect for you, Daveed. Why don't we include her for dinner this evening?'

'I don't think so Maman, she almost certainly has plans.' They wanted his mother to themselves this evening; Jonathan was sure they could win her over, but it was unlikely to succeed with the distraction of other people at the table.

'Well, at least we should ask,' persisted Christine. 'Let's go and find her and ask her what she thought of the show.' Christine looked towards the back of the room and spotted Lydia, and a pretty blonde girl, chatting to one of the young men from the show. 'There they are,' she said, picking up her handbag and moving briskly towards the group. Daveed hurried behind her, wondering how he could avert disaster.

'Vicomtesse de Courcy,' said Lydia, as they approached. 'Wasn't it a marvellous show? Isn't he clever?' Her cheeks flushed as she turned to gaze adoringly at Jonathan. Viddy stepped forward to introduce his mother.

'Maman, may I present my friend Jonathan, and his sister Berenice. Lydia, you met earlier.'

'How lovely to meet you all,' said Christine. They each acknowledged her with a handshake and a smile. 'Jonathan, I believe you are to be our dinner companion this evening.'

'I am,' he replied meeting her gaze with a disarming smile, 'I'm looking forward to it.'

Christine looked round at the group, 'Why don't you all join us?' she asked. 'We can celebrate the success of the show together.' Jonathan caught his sister's eye, panic written all over his face, while wide-eyed, he imperceptibly shook his head.

Lydia, oblivious to Jonathan's aside, thought it must be her lucky day. She was about to accept, but Berry was too quick for her, 'That is so kind of you Madame de Courcy but Lydia and I already have plans this evening, don't we Lydia?'

'We do?' said Lydia, mystified.

'What are you like, Lydia,' said Berry. 'You remember, I mentioned it earlier.' She dug her elbow into Lydia's ribs.

'Oh yes, that's right. We do have plans,' said Lydia, without much enthusiasm.

'Oh, what a shame,' said Christine. Viddy caught Jonathan's eye, his face flooded with relief. 'Perhaps another time. Come on boys, shall we go?'

THE DINNER

In the end, Christine insisted on hosting the dinner, not least because she wanted to be comfortably installed in her hotel, at the end of the evening. Viddy was under the impression there would be a big reveal about their relationship this evening, and he was anxious. Jonathan knew they would have to be much more circumspect. 'Trust me, Viddy. I'll do my best to make this work, but remember Rome wasn't built in a day. We need to take this one step at a time.'

The Mirabelle restaurant had a table reserved in a quiet corner, at Christine's request. She wanted privacy. Her objective this evening was to persuade Daveed to come home with her. It was a little awkward that he wanted to bring a friend, but she would make the best of it. He seemed pleasant enough, and the fashion show would give them plenty to talk about.

'This way, Vicomtesse,' said the waiter, as he led them to a round table at the side of the restaurant. He handed them each a menu and gave the wine list to Jonathan.

'It is so kind of you to include me this evening, Vicomtesse,' said Jonathan. 'Would you like me to choose some wine?'

'Yes Jonathan, thank you; and please, call me Christine.'

'Would you prefer white or red wine?'

'White please.'

'Yes, for me too,' said Viddy. Jonathan – quite accustomed to good restaurants and wines thanks to his parents – chose a Burgundy.

'We'll have a bottle of Saint-Véran and some water please,' he said to the hovering waiter.

'Je voudrais une coupe de champagne,' said Christine, impulsively, as she examined the menu.

'Bien sûr Madame,' returned the waiter.

'Why don't we all have a glass of champagne?' said Viddy. 'It's so good to see you again Maman.' Christine reached out and took her son's hand.

'You too, mon Cheri. Alright, we'll start with a bottle of Laurent-Perrier.'

'Oui, Madame.'

'Maman, I'm so glad you are meeting Jonathan. He has helped me so much with my recovery. We have become close.' He swallowed, wanting to say more, but Jonathan nudged him gently, with his foot.

'I am very happy to meet you, Jonathan. We find our best friends in the most unexpected places. I am blessed that Daveed met you, when he so badly needed a friend. I thank you from the bottom of my heart, for everything you have done for my son.' She raised her champagne glass towards the boys, and as their glasses touched, a tiny ring of fine crystal sang into the room. 'To friendship,' said Christine.

'To friendship,' repeated Viddy and Jonny, glancing at one another.

Once they had ordered their food, Christine said, 'Now Jonathan, tell me more about your course. Your fashion show was unlike anything I have ever seen. Believe me; I have been to many in my time.'

'I'll take that as a compliment,' he said, smiling. 'Thank you. Well, the course was primarily a course in fashion design and creation; there were modules in interior design and the history of textiles. In addition to that, we covered marketing and event planning. The course has given me a fantastic grounding, in the concepts of getting a creative business up and running. There was an accounting module as well, but that was the part I enjoyed least,' he said honestly.

'It sounds interesting. Your parents are obviously very forward thinking,' she said.

'I think they always recognised where our strengths lay, and supported us in finding the right path. My sister, Berenice, is attending art college. Eventually, she wants to become a portrait painter.'

'What are your plans, now the course is finished?' asked Christine.

'In an ideal world, I would like to be an events planner,' said

Jonathan. 'That's where the money is. There is a big gap in the market at the moment, for creative people to organise ventures in our stately homes. They are all finding that they need to bring in some income, to help them stay afloat. Many old families in this country are struggling to make ends meet. Often they have no idea how to bring their beautiful homes into the modern world.'

'Perhaps they have no wish to be part of a modern world,' said Christine. 'After all it is the old way of life and our beautiful buildings that most of us want to preserve.' Jonathan was pleased that Christine was already thinking of his words in the context of the Château de Courcy.

'This is where my idea takes wing,' said Jonathan. 'Using my historical study of interiors, my intention is to improve the interiors of these lovely old buildings, whilst remaining true to the original. Enhancing the character if you like, rather than in any way changing it. Once those improvements are made, they make the most marvellous backdrops for weddings. Country houses and castles are hugely popular now, it's an up-and-coming trend. Imagine the fashion show I have just put on, with the backdrop of a stately home for example. It would be spectacular.'

Christine tried to visualise Dior or St Laurent shows taking place in such a setting, and she was surprised at how right it felt. The boy had a good eye. 'How interesting,' she said thoughtfully. Viddy was beginning to see the way this was heading, and he smiled tentatively at Jonny.

Just then, the waiter appeared with their starters, 'I have your escargot in garlic butter Vicomtesse et Monsieur, and for you Monsieur,' he said to Jonathan, 'Gravadlax.' He served small baskets of crusty bread for each of them, and poured their wine. 'Bon apetit,' he said with a flourish.

'Oh Maman, what a treat this is,' said Viddy. He was so happy to have the two people he cared about most in the world, at the table together. 'You are not returning to France too soon are you, I couldn't bear it.' Christine's face became serious and she turned to her son.

'Daveed, I won't be going anywhere without you. I am sorry to say, it has all become too much for me in France.' She looked up at them both. 'I had hoped for us to have this conversation in private, but as Jonathan is such a good friend to you, perhaps it is better that he hears it too.' She paused. 'I'm sorry Jonathan if this is awkward for you, but I must speak frankly to my son.'

'Of course,' said Jonathan diplomatically. As Christine turned back to her son, Jonathan concentrated on his food.

'I am finding the responsibility of our heritage quite overwhelming,' she said to Daveed. 'I need you to come back to France with me, to take up your rightful place at the Château de Courcy. Now your brother is gone, it is you who must lead us into the future.' She paused to allow the considerable weight of her words to find their mark, as she carefully extracted an escargot from its shell. Viddy looked in despair at Jonathan, but they continued to eat in silence.

After thoughtfully chewing the snail, and following it with a piece of crusty bread dipped into the garlic butter, Christine dabbed the edges of her mouth with her napkin. Then she said, 'The Château roof needs some repairs and there is something more major; a water course has appeared near the building. Unfortunately, our funds are not unlimited, so these things are a concern. I need you by my side to help with some of the decisions, Daveed, not to mention the heavier garden jobs. You always loved and nurtured the gardens so beautifully darling, they need you – we all do. After all, Chateau de Courcy is your home.'

'If it would help, Christine, I could come to France with you both,' said Jonathan. 'You could think of me as an extra pair of hands for the summer. I would be company for Daveed, and perhaps I could come up with some ideas for the Château for you, to help generate some extra income. The English country houses can wait,' he said, warming to his theme. 'I'm sure between the three of us, we could make short work of the gardens, and get things organised.'

'What a generous offer,' said Christine. Viddy held his breath. 'I wouldn't be able to pay you, I'm afraid.'

'Of course not,' said Jonathan, 'and I wouldn't expect it. In fact, it would be just the change I need now that my course is finished.'

'Would you like it if Jonathan came back with us, Daveed? Would it change the way you feel about coming home?'

'More than you can ever know, Maman,' he said simply.

'Well then Jonathan, it looks as though we have a plan. What will your parents think about the idea?'

'I think they will be supportive. They arrive home next week, thankfully. They would not have wanted Berry to be left alone, so the timing works well. When were you thinking of returning?' he asked her.

'The sooner the better,' she said, smiling at them both and reaching out across the table, to take one each of their hands in hers.

LYDIA

Anya was walking among her indoor plants in a comfortable, long kaftan. It was early morning, her favourite time of day. The sky was peachy pink and getting brighter as the sun began to slope into the kitchen. She was about to water her plants, when the telephone rang. She glanced at the clock, wondering who could be calling her at this hour. 'Hello,' she said.

'Anya, it's me, Lydia. I'm sorry to call you so early, but I'm going crazy. I've been awake all night. I didn't know who else to turn to. Can I come and see you?'

'Lydia, what's the matter? Are you alright?' asked Anya, concerned. Lydia left the sewing group so suddenly last time, and Anya had been meaning to call her.

'Not really,' she said. 'I'm in a complete state. I don't think I can even go to work this morning.' Anya was worried now.

'Slow down, Lydia. Come straight over, I'll put the kettle on and we can talk. Don't worry about work; we'll call them when you get here.'

When Lydia arrived soon afterwards, her face was red and puffy and she fell against Anya with relief, and began to cry. Anya enveloped her in a big hug, 'Lydia, my dear, whatever is the matter?' she said quietly. 'Has something happened?' but Lydia couldn't speak, she just wept quietly against Anya's shoulder. 'Come on, let's sit down. I'll make you a cup of tea.' Lydia took the tissue Anya held out to her, then wiped her eyes and blew her nose.

'I'm sorry, I didn't mean to be like this. It was just the relief of being here. I'm exhausted, I haven't slept.'

'Don't worry about anything, we're going to sit down together and have a nice talk over a cup of tea. You can tell me everything, but first we need to call your work. It's the library, isn't it? Would you like me to call them for you?'

'Yes please, just tell them I'm ill or something. I definitely can't go in today. I feel as if I'm falling apart.'

Once the call was made, Anya poured them each a cup of tea and made Lydia some hot buttered toast. She didn't press her, knowing she would speak when she was ready.

After a few quiet minutes at the pine table, sitting in the morning sunshine, Lydia bit into the last of her toast and wiped her mouth. Then she looked at Anya, 'I don't know where to begin.'

'There's no rush,' said Anya, 'take your time. I've got all day.' Then she carried on sipping her tea.

After a few minutes, Lydia said, 'I met Mum last week, out of the blue, on the seafront. I haven't seen her for almost two years, it's a long story, but things have been difficult between us. I'm much closer to my grandma, even though she lives in Florida. We write to each other regularly and she's always interested in my life. Grandmère Clémence has felt more like a mother to me than my own, over the last few years.'

At this she stopped, hung her head down and took a deep breath, before continuing, 'It was thanks to Clémence that I was able to leave home and have some independence. I think she could see that Mum was stifling me. Not that I'm blaming Mum, she's had a lot to cope with in her life. The trouble is, it was me she kept turning to, as if I was her counsellor or something, but I was still a child. I still don't understand why she couldn't see that. When I eventually found the courage to break free from her and make a life for myself, it was a relief, but I've struggled.'

'I know you have,' said Anya, then she paused. 'Unfortunately, life is rarely straightforward. It is full of highs and lows, challenges and heartache. We just have to deal with it as best we can. You've been doing so well though, cutting back on your drinking, sea swimming, making new friends.'

'That's the thing, I've been drinking again. I feel horrible about myself.'

'Oh Lydia, what's brought this on? You were doing so well.'

'It started after the last sewing class, and now I can't seem to stop.'

'Do you mean the drinking? Does this have something to do with the reason you left so suddenly last time?' asked Anya.

'Actually, it does' she said.

'Do you want to talk about it?' asked Anya. There was a long silence and then Lydia's words came out in a rush.

'When I first moved down here, something happened, at my flat.' Lydia said it without emotion. Anya waited for her to say more. 'It happened because I was drunk.'

'What happened, Lydia?'

'That's the thing – I don't know what to call it. I had sex with a horrible old man, a complete stranger. He rang my doorbell and because I thought he was a neighbour, I let him in. He'd been spying on me through my window after dark, but I didn't know that at the time.' Anya took a sharp intake of breath.

'Do you mean he forced himself on you?'

'Not exactly,' she said. 'I was lonely and desperate for some company. When I fell against him, struggling to keep my balance, he assumed I was willing to have sex with him. Once it started, I felt powerless to stop him. I'd had too much wine. I was half out of it. I experienced the whole thing as if it was happening to someone else.'

'Have you reported this?' said Anya.

'No, I haven't told anyone,' said Lydia. 'It was my own fault, I should never have let him in, but it haunts me. I feel disgusting and worthless, as if I deserve bad things to happen to me.'

Anya was horrified, but before she could speak, Lydia continued.

'Then I saw him again, on the front of the newspaper,' said Lydia.

'Which newspaper?' asked Anya.

'The one you got out at the end of the last sewing class, to look up the craft fair. His face was on the front page.' Anya looked at Lydia.

'Lydia, you can't mean the local man who has been arrested on charges of rape?'

Once again, it was as if Anya hadn't spoken.

'He came to my door late one evening and I was drunk, so I let him in. He said his name was Norman. I was lonely and I was drunk,' she said again, for emphasis. 'It was as simple as that. I just wanted some company. I didn't think he was going to do what he did, it all happened so quickly.' She hung her head again and began to cry.

'I just can't get it out of my head. I thought I was putting it behind me, but seeing Mum again has brought it all back. It was something Mum said to me, something that happened when she was a child. I felt angry on her behalf, angry that she didn't stand up for herself. Then, as I was blaming her, I realised with sudden clarity that I too had let this bad thing happen to me, yet I'd done nothing. I didn't stand up for myself either. So why was I angry with Mum, why was I blaming her? She was only a child at the time and I was an adult. I should have fought him, but I couldn't. I was too bloody drunk.'

She cried again, deep wrenching sobs, as Anya looked on. 'In the end I gave myself up to it. I blanked out reality. Then, when I opened my eyes and saw his disgusting, leering face . . .' Lydia couldn't go on. Then she said more quietly, 'I just can't get over the shame I feel. How could I have let it happen?'

It took a lot to shock Anya, but she was lost for words.

'Lydia, we should call the police. You need to report this.'

'I can't,' she said. 'They'll say it's my fault, I know they will. I can't face the humiliation of it. I feel so ashamed.' Anya realised that this situation was far more serious than she could have imagined and beyond her experience. Lydia needed professional help.

'Lydia, is there anybody else you feel you could talk to, apart from me, I mean?' said Anya.

'The only other person, but I haven't seen her for ages, might be my therapist, Jane. I'm not sure there's any point, she'll just take me round in circles and I'll have to keep reliving it. What I want to do is forget it ever happened, but my mind won't let me.'

'Lydia, why don't we call Jane, to see if she can see you? I think it would help. I also think you should consider going to the police. Don't you see that your statement, alongside those of his other victims, will help to ensure he goes to prison for what he has done.'

Lydia carried on as if Anya hadn't spoken. 'I've been a wreck since I saw his face in the paper. The relief that he's been caught has allowed me to let my guard down. The problem is that now I have, the feelings are bubbling up and threatening to overwhelm me.'

'Do you have Jane's number?' asked Anya.

'Not on me, but I do at home. I'll phone her later and I promise I'll think about what you've said, about the police I mean.' Lydia seemed to have recovered herself, perhaps because she didn't want to be pressured into contacting the police.

'Lydia, if you do decide to go to the police, I'd be happy to come with you to offer moral support. You have only to let me know.'

'Thank you so much Anya, you have been so kind. I'm sorry to burden you with this, but I had nowhere else to turn.'

'Come on, I'll drive you home. I'm so sorry you've been through this. At least you felt able to come to me, and I'm glad of that. I'm always here, come over anytime if you need to talk.'

When Lydia was back home she took a deep breath, she would write an account of that night in every detail, as she remembered it. Jane always advised writing things down, saying it could be cathartic. Now the man was locked up, she would find the courage to face this, even her own miserable and flawed part in it. It would be a bit like making a confession, she decided, and help her come to terms with what had happened.

Lydia felt sullied, knowing she was in some way to blame. She also knew that if she was telling Jane about it, they would eventually make a circuit back to the fact that her problem with alcohol was an illness. Jane would say that her judgement was not sound when it happened. She would ask Lydia what she would say to a friend, in the same situation.

This always made Lydia see herself in a kinder, more forgiving way. Didn't she, of all people, deserve her own compassion?

Lydia pulled out a piece of paper and a pen, and sat down at the dining room table to write down the terrible truth of it. She would leave nothing out.

CLÉMENCE

The next morning, Lydia was still unsure whether to call Jane. Unburdening herself to Anya had helped, and writing it down brought her some closure. She was taking another day off work, thanks to Anya telling them she wouldn't be in until after the weekend. She was glad – it would give her time to recover.

Just then, the letter box opened and several envelopes dropped onto the mat. She picked up a long, neatly typed airmail envelope, with an unfamiliar address in the top left corner. It appeared to be from a law firm in Florida. Lydia's heart stood still for a moment, as she tore it open.

Charles Retford Associates
Attorneys at Law
Captiva Island
Florida

Dear Miss d'Apidae
  It is with the deepest regret that I must inform you of the death of your grandmother, Clémence d'Apidae. She passed away peacefully at home on 30th September 1986. Please accept our sincere condolences.
  As you are the executor to Mrs d'Apidae's estate, I would appreciate it if you would call my office upon receipt of this letter.
  Yours very sincerely
  Charles B Retford, Attorney at Law

Lydia was stunned, and began to sway on her feet. She moved to sit down in one of the armchairs. How could her beloved Grandmère be dead? She had only written to her a few days ago. Numb and in a state of shock, Lydia had cried so many tears in the last twenty-four hours that she had nothing left.

As she sat in the armchair, she came to a decision. She picked up the phone and first, she called the library. Mr Hanratty answered after two rings, and said in a sonorous voice, 'Seahaven Library, how can I help you?'

'Hello Mr Hanratty, this is Lydia.'

'Lydia, I heard you are unwell. I am sorry. How are you now?'

'Mr Hanratty, I'm afraid I have some bad news. I have been unwell and now, just this morning, I have received news that my grandmother has died.'

'Oh my dear girl, I am sorry. My deepest condolences.'

'The thing is Mr Hanratty; I have to go to Florida, immediately. I'm not sure how long I will be away, so I think it best I hand in my notice. I'm so sorry to let you down like this, without warning.'

There was silence at the other end of the phone as Mr Hanratty took in the news. Then he recovered himself and said, 'It sounds as if you have no choice, Lydia. You will be missed, especially on Friday afternoons.'

'Thank you, sir. Please could you ask Angela to box up my few personal items, and keep them for when I return?'

'Yes, of course. If you could send a letter before you leave, so that we have your notice officially, we can start to search for your replacement. It will not be an easy task. Thank you so much for everything you have done to improve our library, Lydia. We all wish you the best of luck for the future.'

'Thank you, Mr Hanratty. Goodbye.' Lydia cut the call off and then dialled the travel agent.

'Hello, is that Star Travel? I need to fly out to Florida first thing in the morning, could you please book a flight for me? Ideally, I would like to fly into Fort Myers International, but Miami will do, if that's all you can get.' Lydia gave them her details, along with a credit card and then rang off. She was in a high functioning state of shock. She moved automatically around the flat, pulling down her suitcase, packing summer clothes, and putting away winter ones. She wrote lists of people to write to, and things she needed to do before she left. She had no idea when she would be back.

When her packing was finished, she pulled some writing paper and envelopes out of the drawer, and wrote to her mother first.

Dear Mum
    I'm glad we met the other day and I'm sorry I was in a bit of a state. I've had a lot on my mind.
    On top of all that, I'm writing with some bad news. I received a letter from Florida yesterday. It was from Grandmère's lawyers telling me that she has passed away. It is a terrible shock. I am so distraught that I can hardly think straight. I was close to her; and although I know she was quite old, I wasn't expecting her to die.
    I need to get away for a number of reasons, but in particular, the lawyers have asked me to come over as soon as possible. Apparently Grandmère has chosen me as her executor. I'm not sure what that means, but they are going to explain everything when I arrive.
    I am flying to Florida tomorrow morning. By the time you receive this letter, I will be on the plane. I'm sure you know the address and phone number of Windsong, but I'm enclosing Grandmère's card, in case you want to get in touch.
    With love
    Lydia

Lydia wrote a similar letter to her father, keeping it more formal. He may also have received a letter from the lawyers, but she wanted to be sure he knew. Next, she wrote to update Viddy on her plans, just in case he was thinking of coming over to help in the garden, although she thought it unlikely. She hadn't seen him since the fashion show.

She wrote to Berry after that, enclosing a card and asking her to let Jonathan know she would be away. She had almost given up hope that he might want to get in touch, but you never knew. Finally, she wrote to Anya, thanking her for all her support and telling her she had written a statement and would post it off to the police station. That would please her. Lydia carefully sealed and stamped the envelopes, before walking up the road to drop them into the post box.

When she returned, she cleaned and tidied her flat, packed the last of her belongings and pulled out her diary. Turning to a blank page, she wrote in large letters: *'Today is the first day of the rest of my life.'* She put down her pen, leaned back in her chair and allowed herself a hopeful smile. Maybe things could be better from now on. She shut the diary, opened the desk drawer and pushed it to the back. Time to move on.

The next morning, finally on the plane, Lydia pushed her bag into the overhead locker and sank gratefully into her seat. She stretched her legs out in front of her, clicked her safety belt, and let out a sigh of relief.

Everything had happened at once, over the last few days. After months of tormenting herself, Lydia felt better since speaking to Anya about her ordeal. The statement to the police was enabling her, finally, to put it behind her. As for her mother re-entering her life out of the blue, Lydia just wasn't ready to handle that as well. Clémence's death was the final blow. She needed time to take stock and gather her thoughts. She wanted to start afresh.

When the flight landed, a driver met Lydia at the airport, to take her to Captiva Island. By the time the car turned off the narrow lane towards Windsong, it was mid-afternoon. The driveway was flanked by banana trees and swaying pink and white oleanders. When the pale pink house, set against a blue sky came into view, childhood memories came flooding back. Magnolia trees stood on either side of the wooden steps to the front door, their blooms fluttering in the warm air. Parrots trilled in the trees, mysterious in the semi darkness of their deep foliage.

The driver opened the car door for Lydia, and carried her cases up to the front door. 'Do you need help with anything else, Mam?'

'No, nothing else thank you.' As the car drove away, Lydia pulled the key from its hiding place over the porch. She pushed it into the lock, turning it easily, and the door swung open into a vast room, full of light.

Azure blue sofas faced floor to ceiling windows, with a view to a wide, white deck, facing the beach and the ocean beyond. Steamer chairs with blue and white upholstered cushions, were arranged at one end, and at the other, a round rattan dining table was encircled by four comfortable chairs and matching cushions.

Lydia walked over to unlatch the glass doors and slid them open all the way so that the wall of glass was open to the sea, and the sound of the waves. She let her jacket slide to the floor, and kicked off her shoes and socks – she would have no need for them here. Then she sat down on the sofa facing the window, and put her bare feet up on the large, low ottoman. She gazed at the view, unable to believe the beauty of it. She lost herself in the palest blues, turquoises and soft navy lines that made up the ocean. It brought to mind a line from Yeats's poem, 'The blue and the dim and the dark cloths of night and light and the half-light . . .'

Lydia awoke with a start some time later, the light had changed, and the air was cooler. She felt disorientated for a moment, and ran her fingers through her hair, yawning and rubbing her eyes. She pulled herself up off the sofa, where she had slumped against the cushions in sleep, and walked through to the kitchen. Although the kitchen was separate from the living space, a marble topped breakfast bar linked the two rooms with comfortably upholstered bar chairs arranged invitingly along it.

In the kitchen, Lydia pulled open the refrigerator and poured herself a glass of water from the bottle. She picked up her glass and wandered barefoot out onto the deck, still warm from a day of sunshine. Small creatures were making rhythmic ringing sounds in the hedges around the balcony. Tiny lights encircled the palms near the deck, softly illuminating the beach as the light began to fade. It was beautiful. Lydia smiled, breathing deeply of the salty air; content and relieved to have finally arrived.

She pulled her cases through to a large bedroom and let her clothes fall to the floor. The first thing she would do was have a shower and put on some fresh clothes. Clémence's lawyer was to call by shortly, to take her out for an early dinner. She hoped her snooze would keep the jet lag at bay for long enough to get through the evening, which was primarily to discuss the key details of Clémence's estate.

The restaurant was elegant with twinkling lights and a small jetty reaching into the water. Yachts were moored along its length, their occupants slowly making their way ashore. Once they had ordered a light supper, Charles Retford got down to business.

'Well young lady, first may I express, once more, my deepest condolences. I know you and your grandmother were close. It seems that you are the main beneficiary of her significant estate. She chose you as executor, rather than your father, for personal reasons.' Lydia was surprised; she expected Clémence's estate to go to her father.

'What exactly does an executor have to do?' she asked, uncertain she would be up to the task.

'Generally, the executor is the person with the most to gain from the estate, thus giving that person some incentive to manage some of the more arduous tasks involved. However, in your case, Mme d'Apidae has asked me to deal with all that for you, unless you prefer to do it yourself.

'I can also tell you that the bulk of their business interests passed to your father, Étienne d'Apidae, upon his father's death. This would have formed the largest tranche of their significant joint assets. Simeon didn't want your grandmother to be burdened by the responsibility of all that.'

'Thank goodness,' said Lydia, relieved that she wouldn't have to deal with her father over any of this.

'I am going to leave you with a copy of Mrs d'Apidae's will to peruse at your leisure. The main things you need to know are that she has left her property, Windsong, to you in its entirety. She also bequeaths to you her substantial annual income, mostly derived from stocks and shares in Paris, as well as an annuity left to her by her father. This will allow you to live very comfortably indeed Miss d'Apidae, so you need have no financial concerns at all.'

'What about my brother?' asked Lydia. 'Does Grandmère mention Roger, at all?'

'No she does not. I asked her about that, when the will was drawn up. She said your brother had already been substantially provided for with another legacy. I believe the name she mentioned was Alice Gardener.'

'Yes, of course, that's true,' said Lydia. 'I didn't expect this. Perhaps Grandmère wanted to give me the gift of independence and a fresh start.'

'Indeed,' said Mr. Retford. 'Your grandmother adored Windsong, and from what I can gather, she adored you too. It would make her very happy to think of you living there. She did not put any restriction on you selling the property, if you so wish, but I know it was her hope that you would not.' Lydia said nothing, there was so much to take in and she was beginning to feel tired.

The waiter appeared to offer them desserts and coffee, but Lydia shook her head.

'Just the bill please,' said Charles. Then turning to Lydia he said, 'You must be exhausted, Miss d'Apidae. I'll settle the bill and then drive you home.'

'Thank you,' said Lydia.

Later, as the car drew up outside Windsong, he said, 'There is just one other thing I should mention, the funeral home will be in touch with you, probably tomorrow. They are in the process of making all the arrangements for your grandmother. I believe she had everything planned with them long before her death. They will only want to meet you to advise you of the details.' He paused, 'Good luck with everything, Miss d'Apidae. Please ask me if you need any assistance.'

'Thank you, Mr Retford,' said Lydia. 'No doubt we will be in touch.'

.

WINDSONG

The next morning, Lydia awoke from a deep sleep, uncertain where she was. The dappled shadows of palm leaves swayed over the pale walls of her room, and the gentle ring of birdsong floated through the open window. In the background, the rhythmic ssschhhhh of the tide rising and falling on the shore was a tonic to her weary soul. Of course, she was at Windsong, her new home.

She stretched luxuriantly in the deep, comfortable bed, refreshed and energised. She pulled on a short robe, stepped over her suitcases and made her way into the bathroom. Then she padded out of her bedroom into the vast, vaulted living space. She was just lifting her arms above her head for another luxuriant stretch, when she heard a voice behind her.

'Good mornin' Mizz d'Apidae, can I get you anythin'?' Lydia swung round, astonished. Alberta seeing the look on her face was quick to introduce herself. 'Jeez, I'm sorry to startle you, Mizz Lydia. I'm Alberta, you remember? I've worked here for your grandma since you was all kids.'

'Alberta, of course,' said Lydia, recovering from the shock. 'I'm so sorry, I just wasn't expecting to see you.' Lydia smiled, remembering that it was Alberta who made pancakes for them when they visited Windsong as children. 'Now you come to mention it Alberta, I am starving. I would love some of your pancakes!'

'Comin right up, Mizz Lydia. There's coffee in the kitchen, shall I pour you a cup?'

'Thank you, yes. I'm going to sit outside.' She slid back the glass door and stepped out onto the sunny deck, taking a great lungful of the fresh sea air. Lydia sank down into a large wicker chair with a comfortable blue and white cushion, as Alberta placed a steaming mug of coffee on the low table beside her. 'Thank you, Alberta. It is so lovely to be back here. I just wish I had seen Grandmère before she died.'

'Don't you go worryin' your head with all that, Mizz Lydia.

She had a real good life. She missed Mr Simeon after he gone, and I think she was ready. She knew you had a busy life, but she sure loved receivin' your letters.' Alberta paused, and they both gazed out to sea reflecting on Clémence for a moment. 'Alright, I'm goin' inside to fix your pancakes, they won't be long.'

'Thank you, Alberta, you're making it feel like home.' Lydia was glad to have Alberta here, the connection to her childhood, bringing to mind happier times. She'd been lonely for too long. Perhaps things would be different now.

The pancakes were plentiful, served with bacon, sausages and maple syrup, along with more coffee. Lydia enjoyed every mouthful and then leaned back in her chair, replete. The warmth of the sun and the wide horizon of the sea were working their magic on her. There was no hurry; today, she would take her time. When she carried the tray inside much later, she said, 'Alberta, thank you. That was delicious, just what I needed.'

'You're welcome, Mizz Lydia.' She paused. 'I hope I'm not speaking out of turn when I tell you, I've taken the liberty of preparing the master bedroom suite for you. Windsong is your home now, and I know your grandma would want you to have it.'

'Oh,' said Lydia. She hadn't considered this. In fact, she barely remembered the room; it was so long since she'd seen it. 'Yes, I suppose that would be the best thing,' said Lydia. 'Thank you, Alberta. I haven't unpacked anything yet, so why not?' Between them they carried Lydia's cases up the white staircase, tucked away at the far end of the room. The stairs were camouflaged by a wall of white shelves, full of books and sea sculptures.

When they reached the top, nothing could have prepared Lydia for the beauty of the vast bedroom. It was mostly white, with vibrant blue bedlinen. The bed was centrally positioned, facing the sea. Its padded headboard seemed to sway with white and turquoise sea fans and plants, embroidered across its width. At the end of the bed, a white ottoman was covered in cushions in every possible shade of turquoise and blue, and in front of that, a rug covered the white boarded floor.

Double glass doors opened onto a balcony, overlooking the sea. At the far end of the room, a door opened into a generous bathroom. There was a large shower and a bathtub on one side and on the other, double washbasins with white cupboards beneath. The white walls were decorated with paintings of sea life, in shades of blue and green. The other end of the room opened into a vast, walk-in wardrobe. The rails were still filled with Clémence's beautiful clothes from Paris.

'This is lovely Alberta, thank you so much for getting it ready for me.' Alberta turned to leave the room, and Lydia said, 'I am expecting a call from the funeral home today Alberta, so could you please take a message for me, if I'm not down? Just say I'll call them back this afternoon.'

'I sure will, Mizz Lydia.' Once Alberta left, closing the door behind her, Lydia breathed a sigh of relief. Now she could unpack some of her things, run herself a nice long bath and get ready for the day.

After soaking in the delicious bubbles and hot water for far too long, Lydia was preparing to dress. She opened her suitcase and realised, quite suddenly, that she wanted to shed her British skin. Spurning the dreary clothes in the case, she decided to look through the things Clémence had left in her wardrobe. She slid the elegant outfits along the rails, pulling out a beautifully cut cream muslin coat dress with matching palazzo pants, and a colourful silk sash. Small buttons covered in matching silk, ran all the way down the front of the coat dress, with one at each sleeve and two more at the fitted waist of the trousers. The outfit was completed with a silk vest top to match the sash. It perfectly channelled Florida cruise wear, meets Parisian chic, Lydia decided.

She was delighted with the effect. Why shouldn't she reinvent herself in this new world, start afresh? After all, nobody here knew anything about her. She tied the sash around her short hair and added a dash of lipstick. Quite a transformation, she thought, as she looked approvingly at herself in the full length mirror.

As Lydia descended the stairs, the doorbell rang. By the time she reached the hallway, Alberta had opened it and was talking to a lady on the porch. 'I'm not sure whether she is available, Mz Greenwood, I'll go and find out.'

Lydia called out then, 'I'm here Alberta, please show Mrs Greenwood in.' Mrs Greenwood stepped forward to shake Lydia's hand.

'Hello Lydia, I'm so pleased to meet you. I'm your neighbour Cassie Greenwood.'

'How nice to meet you,' said Lydia.

'Your grandma and I were great friends, I'm so very sorry for your loss,' she paused. 'Clémence talked about you often, you are very like her.'

'Thank you,' said Lydia, pleased she had made an effort. 'Please come in, can I offer you a cup of coffee?'

'That is so kind,' she said, 'but I'm sure you have a busy day, having just arrived. Why don't you come and join me for lunch tomorrow? We can have a salad out on the deck.'

'I'd love to,' said Lydia.

'Shall we say 12.30?' said Cassie.

'Thank you; I look forward to it.'

'Good,' she said. 'Me too. Turn left out of the drive and first left. See you tomorrow.'

Palm Cove was just as lovely as Windsong. At the end of a palm lined driveway, the pale yellow house was elegant and colonial. White wooden shutters stood either side of its many windows and the porch had white pillars with steps up to the front door. Two pots of red hibiscus bloomed on either side of it, as Lydia stepped up to ring the bell.

She wondered for a moment whether these people realised how privileged they were. She too had taken the d'Apidae lifestyle for granted; it was all she had ever known. Her time in her little flat on the south coast, along with her job at the library, changed all that. She had finally grown up, and the journey had not been an easy one.

'Lydia!' called Cassie, opening the front door. 'Come on in, I'm so pleased to see you.'

'Thank you,' said Lydia, smiling. 'It was kind of you to invite me.'

They walked into a square hallway with a pale pink tiled floor. A wide staircase rose up from the centre of it, becoming a galleried landing at the top. Large stained-glass windows in shades of pink and green spanned the width of the wall, filtering warm, colourful light down the stairs and over the tiles at their feet. 'How beautiful,' said Lydia. 'I don't think I have ever seen anything like those windows.'

'I know, I love them,' said Cassie. 'We were in the South of France for a holiday a few years ago, and we visited the chapel Matisse designed in Saint-Paul-de-Vence. It made such a profound impression on me. The building was all white, lit by these beautiful stained-glass windows. They were designed so distinctively, in his own style, and yet like nothing else he had done before.

'It wasn't just the light; it was the feeling inside. I couldn't get it out of my mind. When we got home, I showed my photographs to a talented glassmaker I know, here on the island. This was the result. The design is different of course, but the colours are almost the same.'

'I love it,' said Lydia, gazing up in wonder. She followed Cassie through a door to the left of the staircase into a large, bright room. Several palms in colourful pots were lit with slices of sunlight, creating a tropical atmosphere. A comfortable suite of pale pink furniture faced the ocean, and this was scattered with small lilac and pink cushions. To the right, double doors opened into a large dining room. A white table and chairs, with matching sideboard, were offset by more of the pale pink floor tiles. Lydia could make out colourful sculptures of heads along the sideboard, and a large vase of roses and stocks bloomed lavishly, in the centre of the table.

She followed Cassie outside onto the deck, where a round table was set with a jug of cordial, a salad and a selection of appetizers. 'Let me pour you a nice cool drink,' said Cassie. She put a long glass of cordial with ice and lime into Lydia's hand and then poured her own. Lydia walked to the edge of the deck, where a low white wall separated it from the beach and the sea beyond.

'Clémence loved it here,' said Lydia. 'She often wrote to me, describing her walks on the beach. She enjoyed the birds and the intricacies of the shells she found. I believe it made her truly happy.'

'It did,' said Cassie. 'I can't imagine her life in Paris, but she told me it was very different to this one.'

'It was,' said Lydia. 'It could not have been more different, but I think this life represented who she really was. She told me once that I should try to discover my own truth, no matter what it cost me, and to live it with all my heart. I know now that it takes many years of experience to understand what that truth is, and I am still finding my way.'

'You and the rest of us,' said Cassie. 'One of the philosophers, I think it was Goethe, said, "As soon as you trust yourself, you will know how to live." I love that one. The challenge is finding the courage to put that trust in yourself. It's the challenges life throws at us and our responses to them that make us who we are. I think if we experience difficulties early on in our lives, wisdom comes sooner. I'm ashamed to say, I have led a very sheltered life so far. It's had its ups and downs of course, but nothing serious. Nevertheless, I like to think of myself as a well-adjusted, happy person.'

'What's all this philosophising I can hear?' said a voice from inside the house. A young man in jeans stepped out to join them. He wore an old shirt with the sleeves rolled up, and splashes of what appeared to be white powder and paint up his arms.

'James, what a surprise!' said Cassie, stepping forward to hug him. 'Lydia, this is my son.' James reached out to shake Lydia's hand. 'James, this is Clémence's granddaughter, Lydia.'

'I'm glad to meet you,' he said, his eyes crinkling as he smiled. Then more seriously, he said, 'I'm so sorry for your loss. My mother told me.'

'Thank you,' said Lydia.

They were all quiet for a moment before Cassie said, 'James, would you like to join us for lunch, now you're here?'

'I thought you'd never ask,' he said, laughing. 'I'm just going inside to wash, I won't be a minute.' When he returned, Cassie poured him a glass of cordial and they sat down at the table.

'James is a sculptor,' said Cassie. 'His studio is on Sanibel Island, just over the bridge.'

'Is that some of your work I noticed inside, as we walked through?' Lydia asked him.

'The heads you mean?'

'I think they were heads, yes. I only saw them fleetingly.'

'Yes those are mine,' he said. 'I went on a trip to Sicily last year and they were everywhere. When I came home, I was inspired to create one to represent each member of our family. I'll show them to you properly, later,' he said.

The main course of salad and warm, savoury pastries was

followed by a pecan pie with whipped cream and coffee. Over lunch, James talked about his career as an artist. 'It isn't always easy,' he said. 'Many people, especially among my parents' friends, feel that I'm just drifting. They see the good education I've had and they feel I'm wasting it. They wonder why I'm not a doctor or a lawyer. It is hard for them to understand that I have this overwhelming passion for my art.' He paused.

'When I'm creating something, I feel at one with myself and with everything around me. It's a kind of flow of creativity, and maybe something else.'

He paused, searching for the right word, but Lydia found it for him, 'Truth,' she said.

'Yes, that's it,' said James. 'Truth.' He looked at Lydia and smiled, as if seeing her properly for the first time.

'We've come full circle,' said Cassie. 'That was the conversation we were having just before you arrived James. Lydia was telling me that Clémence was a great advocate of living one's truth, mostly because it took her so long to discover hers. She said it came to her late in life, as it does with most of us. If it comes to you early, it's a gift.'

'It is,' said James, smiling at her. 'On that note, let me show you my sculptures Lydia, and then I need to get back to the studio. Thank you for a delicious lunch Mom, and great company.' At this he smiled once more at Lydia. 'If you're free one day next week, I could show you around the islands if you like. We could go to the Ding Darling Nature Reserve.'

'Ding Darling?' said Lydia. 'Is that really its name?'

'I know, crazy isn't it. It's named after its founder, Jay Norwood Darling. He was a cartoonist by trade, he knew Walt Disney apparently. Anyway, he had a passion for birds and conservation. He managed to block the land from being sold to developers and convinced President Truman to sign a conservation order. That was twenty years ago. It's an idyllic place, so tranquil and expansive.'

'I'd love to,' she said.

MEMORIES

For all the semblance of normality among new friends, and the novelty of her new lifestyle, Lydia was struggling to come to terms with the loss of Clémence. She found memories of her in every box of trinkets, in every drawer and among her many books, photographs and papers. When the Reverend Swift visited to finalise arrangements for the funeral, Lydia took the opportunity to tell him how she was feeling.

'The thing about death is that the clock has stopped. You think it is going to go on ticking forever, until you are ready to say goodbye, but it doesn't work like that. All the things you knew you would say one day, when the time was right, will never now be said.' The Reverend looked at Lydia, with a gentle and sympathetic expression on his face. His quiet presence encouraged her to go on.

'I've found small things, perhaps in a drawer or a box, carefully wrapped things I'll never know the story of. There are photos of people I don't recognise, happy groups of people with my Grandmère among them. Should I keep them, even though I might never now know who those people are, or what part they played in her life?'

Lydia sighed, and looked at Reverend Swift. 'These are interesting questions my dear, and they tell us much about life. It can be so fleeting, and yet we think we have all the time in the world. It is only when we can no longer have those conversations that we realise how much we have lost. It is one of the great mysteries of the human condition, that we only appreciate things when they are gone. If we could learn to appreciate what we have, in every moment, our lives would be so much richer.'

'The thing that makes me sad,' said Lydia, 'is that we accumulate so many little things over a lifetime, things that have special meaning to us. Yet one day, those things will be given away by others who have no idea of their significance, or of the special memories they held. Our precious homes will be cleared of our memories and we will leave this world without a trace.'

'No my dear, we never leave without a trace. Each and every person leaves their mark on this world. Kindness and compassion in particular, are never forgotten.'

'I regret that I didn't speak to Grandmère about things that really mattered. We wrote to one another regularly, and yet I never asked her about her life or her memories. I was too busy telling her about the trivia of my own, and in doing so, I glossed over so much that really mattered.'

'Perhaps that is something your grandmother can leave you with,' said Reverend Swift. 'The knowledge that the time is always now. Clémence was such an understanding person and much loved by so many people. She learned some profound lessons in her life, as you will, no doubt, in your own.'

'Thank you Reverend, that has really helped.'

They sat quietly together for a few minutes, and then he said, 'Mrs d'Apidae's funeral will take place at the Chapel by the Sea, here on Captiva. Your grandmother worshipped there for many years. She always donated generously and she did so much to help us. She was marvellous at organising the carol service, traditionally held there on Christmas Eve. Have you been to see the chapel yet?'

'Not yet, but I will,' said Lydia. 'The funeral home has organised all the flowers. They tell me Clémence had everything planned, down to the last detail.'

'That sounds like your grandmother,' said the Reverend, smiling. 'Do you have any particular hymns in mind for the service, or do you think she may also have chosen those?'

'I'll give the funeral home a call and ask them,' said Lydia. 'I would like to do a reading, if possible,' said Lydia.

'Yes, of course. Will there be any other family present?' asked Reverend Swift.

'My father, Étienne d'Apidae, is coming, but other than that, it will just be local friends. We will be holding a memorial service at a later date in Paris.'

'Your father might want to say a few words too, but if not, I am happy to speak on your behalf. I was privileged to know Mrs d'Apidae rather well. We had a lot of conversations, of a spiritual nature, towards the end of her life. It was as if she was preparing herself, as we all must, eventually,' he said.

When Alberta came in to work the next morning, Lydia asked her to tell her about the day she found Clémence. 'I know you're trying to protect me Alberta, but I need to know. I can't stop thinking about it. I wish I had come to Windsong sooner.'

'Everythin' was just as it always was when I left,' she said. 'I brought Mz d'Apidae her tisane with some special cookies. She asked me to post a letter for her on my way home, which I did. Before I left, I reminded her that I wouldn't be here the following day and we said goodbye.' Alberta paused, pulling a handkerchief from inside her sleeve to dab her eyes. 'That was the last time I saw her alive. Oh Mizz Lydia, if only I had come in as usual the next mornin', she wouldn't have been alone for so long.'

'So what happened when you did come in, the next day?' asked Lydia.

'I can hardly bear to tell it,' she said, dabbing her eyes again. 'I came in through the kitchen door at the side, as usual, and I prepared some tea for Mz d'Apidae. She always liked to take it on her balcony upstairs. I came out of the kitchen with the tray, and that's when I saw her. She was sittin' in an armchair, with her head laid back, just as if she was sleepin'.'

'Strange thing was she wasn't in her usual chair. She was sitting over there, as if she was looking at that painting.' She pointed to the girl in the red dress. 'Her tea and biscuits were untouched beside her, that's when I knew. I put the tray down and ran over to her, and then I took a hold of her hand. It was as cold as ice. Oh Mizz Lydia, that was a bad day.'

'I'm so sorry you had to go through that, Alberta.'

'Course I called Dr Redman, just as soon as I could get myself to the telephone. He came straight over. He said she died peacefully, most likely of old age.'

'I think the painting may be Clémence as a child,' said Lydia. 'I wish I had asked her about it, I would love to have heard the story, but now I'll never know.'

'Now I come to think of it,' said Alberta, 'When I found her, she was holding an old piece of paper in her hand, as if she had been reading it.'

'Do you still have it?' asked Lydia.

'I put it over here, on her desk,' said Alberta, walking over to look for it. 'It looks like it's written in another language to me, 'cos I sure can't read it,' she said, handing it to Lydia.

Lydia looked at the note. The paper was yellowed at the edges and folded into four, with an old piece of sellotape stuck to the back. Lydia unfolded it and began to read. It was written in French, her second language, having been brought up with both a French father and grandmother.

> *My darling Clemeen,*
>
> *I treasure this painting. Henri has not only seen, but managed to reveal the true essence of you. I think of you now as my Clemeen, and it gladdens my heart. It brings to mind the formidable spirit of you, my dear daughter.*
>
> *I know not why courage fails me in matters of love, but I struggle to show my heart.*
>
> *Stern rigour, as my own father showed to me, is all I know.*
>
> *Forgive me Clemeen, for what I am. Please know that you are so very much loved.*
>
> *Your loving Papa,*
> *Julien d'Apidae.*

'It's from her father,' said Lydia, amazed. 'It looks as if it may have been taped to the back of the painting.' She looked up at Alberta who was standing there, curious.

'I reckon she must a been reading that letter when she passed on,' said Alberta.

'I always felt the painting was of Grandmère as a child, and now I know for sure. I can't think why I never asked her about it. I was so wrapped up in myself and my own problems.'

'Don't you beat yourself up, Mizz Lydia. She wouldn't a wanted that. You loved her and she knew it. Hearin' about your life was always a great comfort to her.' Lydia smiled sadly.

'Thank you, Alberta. I've found so many photographs of her looking happy, on a beach, or laughing at a party with people I don't know. There were stories behind all those pictures, and now I'll never hear them. I find myself scrutinising words, hastily scribbled on the back of a photograph, or trying to understand the significance of a letter like this. They become filled with meaning and the lost opportunities for connection. The things left behind become the only information we are left with, to decode a whole life.'

Alberta didn't have an answer to this, so she sighed, hands on her hips, as Lydia said, half to herself, 'Suddenly you see how little, in the end, any of it matters. I suppose what matters is how she felt when she was with those people, and the stories she might have told as a result of knowing them.'

'Shall I bring you some tea, Mizz Lydia? It always used to make your grandma feel better.'

'Yes please, Alberta, thank you.' Soon after Alberta left the room, the telephone rang. 'Don't worry Alberta, I'll get it,' called Lydia.

'Lydia, it's me,' said Juniper. 'Darling, I've only just received your letter. I'm so sorry.'

'Hello Mum,' said Lydia. 'I can't believe it has only just arrived, I posted it two weeks ago, before I left.'

'Well it has been here for quite a while by the looks of it, but I've been on the coast with Jed. We only got back today.' Lydia noticed her mother's use of 'we' and wondered whether there was more to the relationship than she had admitted. 'Darling, I had no idea Clémence had passed away. What an awful shock. How did you hear about it before anybody else?'

'I'm her executor, Mum. The lawyers wrote to tell me. The letter arrived a couple of days after our lunch together. I decided to quit my job and come straight to Florida.'

'Does your father know?' she asked.

'Yes, I wrote to him when I wrote to you. He's arriving later today.'

'Do you think I should come over?' asked Juniper, 'For the funeral I mean.'

'No, Mum. Clémence wanted a small affair on the island, something to represent who she was when she was here, at her happiest. It will just be Dad and I from the family. Dad is planning to arrange a memorial service for her in Paris in the spring. Perhaps you and Roger could attend that.'

Juniper sighed. 'Clémence was my mother-in-law for most of my adult life, Lydia. I would like to have paid my respects.'

'Yes, I know Mum, but this is how she wants it to be. Everything has been arranged by the funeral directors, and Clémence gave them very clear instructions. She arranged it all, down to the last detail, apparently.'

'I see,' said Juniper. 'Well, there is nothing more to say then. I will send some flowers. At least you will have your father with you for the funeral. I'm thankful for that at least.'

'Thank you, Mum. I'm so sorry.'

'It's alright,' said Juniper. 'I'm sorry too. Goodbye, Lydia.' Juniper put the phone down and Lydia's heart sank. She had been waiting for a call from her mother for days, hoping for some soothing words, but as usual, they were not forthcoming.

THE FUNERAL

The funeral took place on a bright, sunny day. The blue sky framed the little white chapel, which was lavishly decorated with white roses and blue stocks for the occasion. Lydia arrived early, accompanied by her father. She was dressed in a black linen bolero jacket with a high collar. The sleeves and bodice were embellished with fine black cord, twisted and moulded to make swirls and floral shapes. Her skirt, also in black linen was flared and calf length. Two strips of fabric had been cut from the lower part of the skirt and replaced with fine black organza, giving fleeting glimpses of her slim legs both above and below her knees, as she walked. She wore a white camisole top beneath the jacket, a small black hat and large pearl earrings.

Étienne, still jet lagged, was white-faced. He was immaculately dressed in a black suit, as he accompanied Lydia to sit at the front of the chapel, beside his mother's coffin. Lydia noted dispassionately, that some of his boyish charm had left him. He looked older. Perhaps life as a divorced man was not suiting him after all.

The coffin was lavishly covered in blue, pink and pale yellow flowers, reminiscent of Clémence's best times beside the ocean, the funeral home explained to Lydia when they went through the details.

By the time the service began, the church was full to bursting with the many friends and acquaintances whose lives had been touched, in some way, by Clémence. The organ rang out with the first bars of 'Morning has Broken,' and then the church filled to the roof, with the sound of their singing. A song known to almost everyone, and a favourite of Clémence's, the congregation sang out their joy in celebration of her life.

As the hymn faded, Reverend Swift stood and motioned for them all to sit.

'We are here today to celebrate the life of a remarkable woman. Clémence d'Apidae was a most generous patron of our chapel and a kind and thoughtful friend to so many, in our small community. In the years she has lived among us, she has touched many lives. Our sincere condolences go to her son, Étienne, and her granddaughter, Lydia. May I now invite you, Lydia, to share the reading you have chosen to honour your Grandmother today?'

Lydia stood and walked slowly to the lectern. She looked nervous, thought James, wondering why she had avoided his calls since the lunch at his mother's. She was beautiful in her grief, and he couldn't take his eyes off her. 'I chose this reading for Grandmère, from a book she read to me many times as a child. It is still one of my favourites. This is from 'The Little Prince', by Antoine de Saint-Exupery.' Lydia read very slowly,

"For some, who are travellers, the stars are guides.
For others they are no more than
little lights in the sky.
You –You alone will have stars
as no one else has them.
In one of the stars I shall be living.
In one of them I shall be laughing.
And so it will be as if all the stars
will be laughing when you look at the sky at night.
You, only you, will have stars that can laugh!
And when your sorrow is comforted
(time soothes all sorrows)
you will be content that you have known me . . .
You will always be my friend.
You will want to laugh with me.
And you will sometimes open your window, so, for that pleasure . . .
It will be as if, in place of the stars,
I had given you a great number of little bells that knew how to laugh."

At the end, the congregation was spellbound as Lydia returned to her seat. 'She is so like her grandmother,' whispered Cassie to her husband. When the next hymn began, the congregation stood to join the choir's gentle and soaring rendering of, 'Be Still for the Presence of the Lord'.

When it was Étienne's turn to stand and read, all eyes were

upon him.

'It is a great honour that so many of you have come here today to celebrate my mother's life.' His slight French accent sounded exotic among the mostly American congregation, and there were discreet looks and murmurs of appreciation, as he spoke.

'My mother has always managed to be a leading light in so many areas of her life. She was multi-talented and always worked extremely hard for the good of others. When I was a child she led by example, even though as a result, I did not see as much of her as I might have wished. When she bowed out of her tireless charity work in Paris, and moved to Captiva to be with my father, it was a very happy day for them both.

'Sadly, by then, it was me who was leading a busy life. It is a source of great regret to me that we spent so little time together over the years. However, it is a comfort to know that my mother found a home among your generous hearts, and I thank you for your tributes today. May you rest in peace, Maman.'

Sympathetic murmurs accompanied Étienne's return to his seat, but Lydia's heart was cold. He had never had time for anyone but himself. He had certainly been no father to her, as far as she could remember. Clémence wrote often, how much she missed him.

After the service, a few words were spoken as Clémence's coffin was lowered into the ground, and that was when it all became too much for Lydia. She could barely contain her sorrow. She excused herself as soon as she could, to return to Windsong with Alberta. An elegant buffet was set out in the great room for the wake. Chairs and tables were arranged out on the deck, dressed with white cloths and small bowls of flowers. 'Them caterers sure done a nice job, Mizz Lydia,' said Alberta. This was praise indeed.

Lydia went upstairs to remove her hat and jacket, and swapped her heels for a pair of flat, black sandals. What a relief. For the first time since arriving here, she felt the need for a glass of wine to calm her nerves. Instead, she drank a large glass of water, deciding that although she would have some wine, it would be much later. This was a party for Clémence, and Lydia did not want to let her down.

Downstairs, Alberta was showing the first guests in. Lydia

stood at the door to greet each one of them, as she knew Clémence would have done. 'Thank you so much for coming to the service,' she said, again and again. Each new arrival introduced themselves and offered their condolences. 'We loved your reading, marvellous choice,' said some. Others commented on how very alike she and Clémence were, praising Lydia's fortitude in this difficult situation. When James, Cassie and her husband walked in, Lydia sighed with relief to see people she recognised. 'Thank goodness,' she said smiling, ' familiar faces.'

'This is my husband, Edward,' said Cassie, introducing them. 'It was a lovely service, thank you.'

'My sincere condolences, Lydia, we are sorry to have lost a true lady as our neighbour. Your grandmother was a wonderful friend to Cassie, and a great support when she needed it most,' said Edward.

'Thank you,' said Lydia. Just then, Étienne appeared at the door and Lydia made introductions, before allowing her father to lead them inside to find them a drink. Then there was a lull.

Most people had arrived, and were outside in the shade of the palm trees, a drink in their hand. Lydia was walking towards the kitchen to find Alberta, when she heard someone calling her name. She turned to see James coming towards her, arms outstretched. It looked as if he was moving in for a hug and she was momentarily unsure, but he took both her hands in his and said, 'Lydia, you are managing this really well. It can't be easy.'

Dropping the idea of anything other than complete honesty, she replied, 'I'm doing what I know Grandmère would have wanted. I'm putting my best foot forward and doing the best I can.'

'Atta girl,' he said.

'You don't have a drink,' said Lydia. 'What would you like?'

'There was a time when I would have killed for a chilled bottle of wine, but alas, I don't drink anymore.'

'Oh?' said Lydia, interested now.

'Between you and me, I'm a recovering alcoholic. My life was close to going down the tubes. It was the pressure of Uni, the party life of New York City and if I'm honest, too much money to spend. My parents had no idea; they thought they were paying for me to live in a decent apartment. I don't mean luxurious, just reasonably nice. You probably know how expensive it is to live in New York,' he said. 'In fact, I was bunking up with friends and spending all the money on booze. I was trying to fit in, and the alcohol gave me the courage to rise to the challenge, but it was never really me. When I look back, I think they would have liked me more if I'd just been myself.'

Lydia said nothing. This was very close to home, and it was as if a door had opened and shone a light onto her path. As they stood there, she wondered whether this was what Edward meant about Clémence supporting Cassie, 'when she needed it most'. If only she'd had more faith in her Grandmère. It never crossed her mind to confide in her. She knew now, too late, that she would have supported her, no matter what. 'I'm sorry I didn't take your calls,' said Lydia. 'I've been so busy with all the arrangements.' She knew it wasn't a good enough reason. How long would it have taken to have a brief conversation with him? It wasn't just a conversation though, was it? He wanted to take her out, to show her the island. She'd made such a mess of her life so far, she didn't trust herself not to mess this up as well. James was too nice for her. Then she remembered Cassie's words from Goethe, *'As soon as you trust yourself, you will know how to live,'* and she made a decision.

'Sorry James, you deserve the truth. If I'm honest, I've been scared of getting involved. I've made a bit of a mess of my life up to now.'

'You and me both,' he said. 'So, come on, how about it? I'll take you out to the nature reserve. We can take some pictures there and maybe do some sketching. Do you draw?'

'Actually I do, a bit,' she said. 'I have a small set of watercolours I could bring.'

'Me too,' he said. 'We'll take our paints, a couple of deckchairs and a picnic.' He looked at her and said quietly, 'I think we may have more in common than you realise.' If only he knew just how much, thought Lydia.

'Why not,' she said in the end. 'Come on, I'll get us both some sparkling elderflower.' He looked at her then, comprehension dawning.

'Thank you,' he said.

DING DARLING

Lydia awoke early as usual, and opened the doors to her balcony. It was going to be a beautiful sunrise. The turquoise sky was already streaked with pink and apricot, announcing the sun's imminent appearance on the horizon. This was a quiet and contemplative time of day. Lydia enjoyed the gentle silence, punctuated with the occasional bird call and the slow rhythmic ssschhhhh of the sea on the pale sand. She visualised Clémence walking on the beach, looking out for shells, enjoying the breeze in her hair. 'Oh Grandmère,' she whispered to herself. 'I wish I had told you how important you were to me. I hope that in your heart, you knew.'

Lydia took a deep breath, and settled into her morning meditation. The serenity she found in the yurt with Anya had shown her the way to find peace in her heart, whenever she needed it. Meditation was now an integral part of her day.

James was taking her to the nature reserve today. She didn't feel any anxiety about spending the day with him. She wondered whether he might even be a kindred spirit. There was going to be no more pretence in her life. She was as she was, flawed, well-meaning and with a tendency to be prickly at times, especially around her mother. So be it. From now on, people would have to accept her as she was.

There was no more alcohol to prop her up – she was going to manage without it. She'd so nearly succumbed to a glass of wine at the wake, but James had unwittingly saved her. When he spoke with such honesty about his own addiction, it made her realise that she wasn't alone in her struggle. It made everything easier; knowing somebody else had been through it too. Perhaps one day, she might confide in him.

James arrived to pick Lydia up in a well-used, VW camper van. She smiled as she saw it turn into the driveway and make its way slowly towards the house.

'He's here, Alberta,' called Lydia, as she opened the front door, just in time to see the cheery yellow van pulling up outside. She raised her hand in greeting. 'Hi,' she said, smiling, as he climbed out of the van.

'Are you all set?' he asked.

'All ready,' she said. 'Alberta has packed us a picnic.'

'Ooh, nice,' he said. 'I've brought deckchairs and an icebox full of drinks to share.'

'I've got my camera, some paints and a sketch pad, just in case I feel inspired.'

'Oh, you will,' he said, smiling.

Once everything was in the car, they turned onto the narrow main road, the only one that ran the length of the island. As they drove along, there was a feeling of being a long way from anywhere, almost in the wild, with occasional tell-tale signs of life. There were discreet entrances to long driveways, marked by jaunty letter boxes here and there, several of them pelican shaped and carved from wood. 'I love the pelicans,' said Lydia. 'We don't have them in England.'

'Have you seen them diving for fish yet?' asked James.

'I have,' she said. 'I often sit on the deck, looking out to sea. The strangest part is seeing the underneath of their beaks stretching like baskets to accommodate the fish, and then they look up to the sky and swallow their catch.'

'I know,' he said. 'It amazes me that they can dive vertically out of the sky and somehow catch a fish.'

'It's ever changing isn't it? The sea, I mean. Different colours reflecting a changing sky.'

'I agree,' he said. 'My studio looks out over the sea. There is something about the lack of a visual boundary, the sense of looking out towards the edge of the world. It gives me the sense of freedom I need, to be creative.'

'The sea is important to me too, but in a different way,' said Lydia. 'When I was at my lowest ebb, I started sea swimming. Somehow it turned things around for me. The water can be really cold in England – it's not like taking a dip here. It was the cold that made the experience so transformative for me. It was the complete shock of it. It took me right out of my head and into my body. It had a profound effect on me. From that moment on, I began to see things differently.' She stopped, she'd already said more than she intended.

James listened closely, reflecting on her words for a moment, and then he said, 'You know, if you want to talk about any of it, any time, I'm happy to lend an ear. I've been through quite a lot myself over the last few years, so I'm an understanding listener.'

'Thank you,' she said.

'Look ahead,' he said. 'There is the bridge, over to Sanibel Island.'

'It's very small,' said Lydia.

'Well, the islands are actually quite close together,' he said. 'Closer than you think. The only way off the island, other than this bridge, is by boat.'

'My grandpa had a yacht. I've only just remembered that. I wonder if it's still in the boathouse. It was called 'Little Song', after the house.'

'Do you sail?' asked James.

'I wouldn't say I sail exactly,' she said. 'But I know how. Grandpa used to take us out as children; he treated us just as a captain might treat his crew. As a result, we all know how to trim the sails, drop anchor and navigate. It's been a long time since I was afloat though,' she said. 'Do you sail?'

'My parents have a small yacht, so yes, I was brought up around sailing. Like you, it's been a while since I went out.'

Once they were on Sanibel Island, it took only a few minutes to see the first signs for the nature reserve. Soon after that, they turned off the main road and into Ding Darling. The rangers at the entrance gave them a small map, and they drove slowly in. At first there was nothing to see, just wild grasses and trees either side of the road, and then the landscape opened up into a wide expanse of shallow water and marshland.

'Look!' said Lydia. 'Flamingos.' She pointed across the wetland towards a row of long-legged pink birds, intermittently dipping their large curved beaks and long necks into the water. James pulled the van into a lay-by, and they got out to have a better look.

'Look how beautiful they are,' said Lydia.

She gazed out over the hazy marshland, which was made up of wide stripes of colour. Lines of sea reflected the pinks of the sky, offset by deep navy blues. These were interspersed with pale sandbars and a multitude of birds. The scene shimmered in the heat, and seemed to go on as far as the eye could see.

'Wow,' said Lydia. 'I'm going to get my camera out. Do you mind if I set up the tripod?' she asked. 'I want to zoom in close, without the camera shaking and spoiling the shot.'

'Be my guest,' he said, smiling, pleased she was enjoying it.

As Lydia gazed through the viewfinder, she closed in on the flamingos. Their bright pink plumage glowed against a shimmering haze of blue and beige. She clicked the shutter. 'Nice one,' she said.

She pulled the focus back then and tried to capture the wide horizon before her, in all its glory. 'It's very hard to capture this, isn't it?' she said. 'You have to be here, be part of it, to truly appreciate its beauty.'

'I know what you mean,' he said. 'There is an incredibly immersive atmosphere about the place.'

They drove slowly through the four-mile reserve, stopping often to get out and take pictures. The vantage points across the water were from wide wooden bridges, placed at regular intervals through the park. From one they saw a family of alligators swimming through the water, and from another, Lydia saw some more pink birds. 'Those look a bit like pelicans,' she said, pointing at them.

'I think they are from the pelican family,' said James. 'They are Roseate Spoonbills. See the way their beaks are spoon shaped at the end?' Lydia was about to get her camera from the car, when there was a flurry of splashing, and the group of birds took flight. Their large, pink wings filled the sky, momentarily blocking the sun as Lydia watched in awe. James watched her, watching the birds and smiled. It was a privilege to see her relaxed, with her guard down.

Later, they found a shady spot among some palms, with wooden picnic tables set out beneath the trees. Lydia opened the hamper Alberta had packed for them. There were plates, glasses and cutlery strapped inside the lid. The hamper contained several sealed boxes of soft lunch rolls. Some were filled with egg mayonnaise and cucumber, others with crab in a pale pink sauce. Another box contained sticks of cucumber and carrots with two smaller boxes of creamy blue cheese dip.

'We have a feast!' said James when he saw the food. 'What would you like to drink?' he asked her. 'I have pink lemonade, ginger beer and diet coke. There is also water.'

'Ooh, pink lemonade please,' she said, smiling at him. She handed him a plate and a pot of the cheese dip, then she arranged the open containers in the middle of the table. 'Help yourself.'

'Here's to Alberta,' he said, raising his can of ginger beer.

'To Alberta,' said Lydia. They enjoyed a lingering lunch, leaving nothing untasted. As well as the filled rolls and dips, there were cold sausages, some salad and two pots of Alberta's lemon syllabub. Lydia was just taking the last spoonful of her lemon dessert, when she heard loud rustling in the undergrowth. She looked out beyond the palms, and to her horror saw an alligator making its way out of the bushes. Thankfully it was moving away from them, towards the water's edge. She looked at James, who was sitting stock still, watching it too. He lifted his finger to his lips to indicate they shouldn't make a sound, then, just as quickly as it had appeared, the alligator slid into the water and swam away.

'Oh my gosh,' whispered Lydia. 'I have never seen an alligator as close as that before.'

'Nor me,' he said quietly. 'I think we should pack away the rest of the food and get back into the car. It may have been the smell of the food that attracted it.' So much for sitting in the open air to do some painting, thought James. He didn't think he'd be able to relax after that. Just then, a Ranger's vehicle pulled into the car park and James walked over to have a word with him.

'Good afternoon,' said James. 'We just had a bit of a scare out here.'

'What happened?' asked the Ranger.

'We were eating our lunch in this picnic area and an alligator came out of the bushes. Were we in any danger, do you think?'

'I doubt it,' he said. 'Did you see where he went?'

'He walked over there and moved into shallow water. Then he swam away. Thankfully he didn't see us.'

'It's only in shallow water, that a 'gator might mistake you for food,' he said. 'Their little legs mean they can only move slowly on land. It is in the water that they become swift and powerful. They use their huge tails to propel themselves, at lightning speed, towards unsuspecting prey. Anything they think may be food, could potentially be dragged under. How big was the one you saw?'

'Maybe five feet long,' said James.

'That's a small one,' said the ranger. 'I doubt it would take on an adult human. Nevertheless, it's best you stay well away from the water's edge. This isn't the first time 'gators have been seen here. I'll see to it that some more signs are put up. Unfortunately, some people throw food for them, which is not only a big mistake, it's against the safety rules of the park. Thank you for letting me know. You folks have a good day now.' He tipped his fingers towards his hat, before getting back into his truck and driving off.

'That was the last thing I expected,' said Lydia, as she packed the picnic things into the car. 'Did you have enough to eat?'

'I did, thank you,' he said. 'It was a delicious lunch. Have you seen enough here for today? What do you say to a drive and then some ice cream? We could go to the far end of the island to see the old Sanibel Lighthouse, then on the way back, I know a wonderful ice cream shop. They have every flavour you can imagine. Sanibel Crunch is my personal favourite,' he said, grinning.

'Sounds like the perfect end to a really nice day,' said Lydia.

CHÂTEAU DE COURCY

The preparations to leave for France were completed in a couple of days. Jonathan's parents agreed that Berry could manage alone for a few days, before they arrived home. Viddy had barely any possessions to pack up at Sarah's, and she was truly sorry to see him go.

Christine joined Juniper and Jed for dinner at the marina before she left. 'Thank you both, for everything,' she said. 'I don't think I could have done this without you.'

'We were happy to help,' said Jed. As they said their goodbyes, Christine couldn't help noticing how close they seemed, and it pleased her. She would soon be reunited with Alain. She had missed him more than she thought she would.

The journey across the channel and the subsequent drive to the Château took them the best part of the day. Eventually, when they left the main road, they began to pass through small villages. Narrow roads meandered past houses of the palest stone, and flowers rambled over pretty walls, illuminated by afternoon sunshine. Christine sighed and visibly relaxed, 'We are nearly home,' she said.

She turned off to the right and they approached a small railway crossing on the narrow road ahead of them. The car bumped over it and almost immediately they turned into a long, tree lined avenue. Christine slowed the car, 'Here we are,' she said. 'These are our trees; I never tire of their beauty. If you look carefully, their leaves are shaped like tulips.' The boys craned their necks to get a better view. 'I still remember the day your father brought me here for the first time Daveed, after our wedding. It was June, and the tulip trees were covered in their white waxy flowers. It felt as if the blooms had been hung out to welcome us home, as man and wife.' Viddy hadn't heard his mother mention her wedding for a very long time. Christine continued, almost as if they weren't there.

'Isn't it strange the way we have to be away from something

before we can see it with fresh eyes? I sometimes feel as if the best parts of my life are behind me, but when I come back here, everything falls into place.'

As they reached the end of the long avenue of trees, two sphinx-like stone statues sat on pillars, on either side of the entrance. Between them, the Château rose into view against a clear blue sky. Jonny gasped, as he took in the pale white turrets of a castle to rival anything he had seen in a fairy tale. Sweeping, green lawns were laid out on either side of the approach. Beyond those, formal gardens stretched out on each side as far as the eye could see. 'That is the Medici garden,' said Christine, gesturing to the right. 'On the left is the garden of Diane de Poitiers. They were both powerful women who left their mark on this Château, long before we were born.'

'I am absolutely blown away by this,' said Jonathan. 'Viddy, why didn't you say your home was so, so . . .' he searched for the right word before settling on 'spectacular!' Viddy blushed with pleasure at Jonny's reaction, then looked at him and grinned.

'I suppose to me, it's always been home. No more, no less. Coming back again though, when I thought I never would, makes me realise how much I've missed it.'

'Darling, what can you mean?' interjected Christine. 'There was never any question of you not coming back, was there?'

'It doesn't matter Maman, I'm here now.' He glanced sideways at Jonny; it was such a relief to have a friend who knew his heart. No secrets. Jonny understood how he felt about everything, especially how difficult it was for him at the Château before he left.

As Christine pulled up outside, a man rushed out to greet them, smiles all over his face. 'Bienvenue, Vicomtesse.' Then he turned to the boys, his face becoming serious as he bowed briefly to Viddy. 'Monsieur Le Vicomte, nous sommes très contents de vous voire.' Viddy coloured slightly, as the reality of his life in France came face to face with the very different one he had been living in England. To deflect the awkwardness, he gestured towards Jonny and said, 'Jean, je vous présente mon ami, Jonathan.' Jonny smiled and stepped forward to shake the Butler's hand, then they all smiled and Jean relaxed. 'Jean has been with us forever,' he said to Jonny. 'His wife, Guillemete, helps in the kitchen, she was a nanny to us too, when we were small, wasn't she Maman?' But Christine hadn't heard him and was already walking over the wide, stone bridge towards the front doors.

'What's this?' asked Jonathan, pointing to a large round tower with a turret beside the bridge?

'Oh, that was my father's den,' he said. 'It was part of the original castle and mill in the sixteenth century. Much of it was knocked down so that the Château could be re-designed and built out over the river. It was long before our time. The old keep was the only bit they kept.

'Traditionally, it has always belonged to the Vicomte.' He looked at Jonny, 'So I guess it will be mine.' Their eyes met for a moment before they walked over the bridge and through the ornate doors, into a pale, marble hall.

Christine led the way into a large, comfortable salon to the right. Warm red on the walls made the pale white and gold of the Renaissance fireplace light up like the sun. A group of comfortable velvet sofas and chairs in soft greens and reds were grouped around a large beige rug. The rug was edged with small animals, echoing those carved in gold above the fireplace. Heavy white drapes, trimmed with braid hung either side of the windows, framing the view out across the river. 'This is our family salon,' said Christine. 'Opposite,' she said, leading the way out into the hall again, 'is the dining room.' They stepped into a large square room hung with tapestries in shades of beige, blue and red. An ornately carved sideboard matched the enormous dining table, which was spread with a blue and green striped table cloth. A small vase of flowers was the centrepiece, and the many carved wood chairs had their seats upholstered in pastel shades of linen. The overall effect was a welcoming, informal dining room.

'What a lovely home you have,' said Jonathan.

'Thank you,' she said. 'Despite living in a castle, I have always tried to make it feel like home. I'm afraid I don't have much time for formality.' She paused, glancing around her, seeing it through Jonathan's eyes. 'We eat most of our meals in here,' she said. 'My suite leads off this room, and Daveed's is directly above it.' Christine registered the look of surprise on her son's face, and added, 'Yes, darling, we have moved you into that one, now you are the Vicomte.' Daveed knew that both suites comprised a spacious bedroom with a private bathroom, dressing room and study, all enjoying plenty of light and views over the water.

'Thank you, Maman.' Then he walked towards the carved wooden doors behind her, 'Ah, the chapel,' he said, pushing the doors open.

'I know you always loved it,' she said to Daveed. 'There were times when he was a child, that he would disappear,' she said to Jonathan. 'We would eventually find him sitting peacefully here, in the family chapel.' Jonny followed Viddy into the fairly small, almost circular room. It had a soaring ceiling, culminating in a white dome of curved vaults. Tall, narrow stained-glass windows illuminated the mostly white space, at the centre of which, was an ornate altar of white and gold. Simple family pews lined both sides of the room. On the wall to the left, there was an oil painting of the Virgin Mary and to the right, Viddy gazed at another, depicting St Anthony of Padua, kneeling before a young Christ.

'This is where Henri II's widow, Catherine de Medici, came to worship after her husband's death,' said Christine. 'She governed the country from the study in my suite. She had to remove her husband's mistress from the Château first. Diane de Poitiers was a woman of beauty and intelligence. Henri gave her the Château in recognition of her as his favourite lady. It was her vision that led to it being extended out across the water. Some say, it became the most beautiful bridge in France.'

'How fascinating,' said Jonathan.

'There is so much history here,' said Christine. 'We are very lucky.' She paused, 'Anyway, let me show you up to your room, Jonathan, so that you can get settled in.'

She led the way back out into the hall and up a beautiful, white stone staircase. Its steps were smoothly curved, where hundreds of feet had trodden before them. The staircase was narrow and curving with high, white ceilings. A series of curved vaults overhead, culminated in small sculptures of fruit and flowers.

At the top of the stairs, they found themselves in a light hallway, lined with tapestries in shades of beige, grey and green. The polished, terracotta tiled floor was illuminated by double glass doors at one end, leading to a balcony. Christine turned to the right and led Jonathan into a large, light bedroom with the same terracotta tiled floor and ornate gold ceiling joists. An enormous four poster bed with drapes of scarlet and gold stood to the right of an equally ornate fireplace, with two red leather chairs in front of it.

'This is spectacular,' said Jonathan. He couldn't believe his eyes.

'If you think it is grand,' said Christine, 'you are right. This bedroom once belonged to César, Duke of Vendôme and son of King Henri IV. The decor has been preserved and refreshed in keeping with the original design. It is an important part of the history of the Château. I hope you will be comfortable.'

'Christine, I honestly don't know what to say, except thank you.'

Christine smiled and said, 'I'll leave you both to get settled. Guillemete has planned dinner for 7 p.m. See you later.' She moved off down the stairs and Viddy grinned at his friend.

'Like it?' he said. Jonny walked over and put his arms around him.

'Thank you for bringing me here,' he said simply, looking into Viddy's face. Viddy smiled back, but instead of leaning in more closely, he stepped back.

'Better get unpacked before dinner,' he said. 'See you down there.'

'What do I wear?' asked Jonathan.

'Oh, it's casual,' he said. 'We only dress for dinner when we have guests, or for special occasions.'

'Great,' said Jonny. 'See you at dinner.'

BELONGING

A few days later, Christine was relaxing with Alain at Le Manoir, happy to be back on familiar ground. Although she would not have said it, she was very glad indeed to be with him again.

'So, you have brought back the Vicomte,' he said. 'I am happy for you, ma Cherie. That is what you wanted, no?'

'It is what I wanted, yes.' She paused. 'Unfortunately, there is so much more to it than that. I really struggled to persuade Daveed to come home. I honestly believe that in his own mind, he was never going to return.' Christine put her hands over her face and bowed her head. 'The whole thing has been exhausting,' she said.

'Why would he not return?' said Alain. 'This is his home, his destiny.'

'It has always been his home, but his destiny? That is something new for him. His becoming the Vicomte, rides on the back of grief at the loss of his brother, confusion about how he wants to live his life, and the sheer weight of responsibility now resting on his shoulders. Louis was always going to be the one to take on the Château, and he would have taken it in his stride. For Daveed, it is more difficult. He is a sensitive soul, he loves his plants and the garden, but beyond that . . .' Christine's voice trailed off, then she said, 'Alain, I feel as if Daveed has had some sort of mental breakdown. Apparently he was in a very bad way in England. People were very kind to him and he made some new friends. Without them, I'm not certain he would have survived.'

'Was it really that bad?' asked Alain.

'I believe it was. I still don't know the full extent of it, Daveed won't tell me. Sarah, the person who kindly took him in, hinted that he was attacked while sleeping rough, in Brighton.' Alain looked incredulous.

'Are you sure?' he asked.

'That's what she said,' confirmed Christine.

'It has been worse than I thought,' said Alain. 'Ma pauvre,

come to me.' He beckoned her over to the sofa and she sat down beside him and laid her head against his broad chest. He smelt of lemons, horse leather and home. Imperceptibly, Alain had become the person she felt most at ease with. She closed her eyes and sighed.

Since the death of her husband three years ago, Alain had provided Christine with comfort, practical advice and steady friendship. She enjoyed evenings like this with him at the Haras du Manoir and was increasingly reassured by his presence. She wouldn't want to say that she had come to rely on him, but she valued his counsel. It was easier to make important decisions with the input and sounding board of a trusted friend.

Alain's business was racehorses. He'd been around them all his life, both breeding them and racing them. The British Royal Family had visited the Haras du Manoir on more than one occasion, to purchase horses from among his pure bred Normandy stock, but this was something he kept to himself. He knew his horses were the best, and it followed that the most discerning of people would want to buy them.

'Where would I be without you, Alain?' said Christine quietly, comforted by the steady beat of his heart as she rested against his chest.

'It is so good to have you back,' he said into her hair, before kissing the top of her head and pulling her closer.

'Come to the Château for lunch tomorrow?' she said impulsively. 'Daveed has brought a friend with him from England. I'd like you to meet him.'

The next day, Viddy was finding his rhythm again and revelling in the feeling of being outside among his plants. The idea that it was his Château and his land was growing daily and he was beginning to feel a pride in it.

In the kitchen downstairs, Guillemete was preparing fresh soup using the celery Viddy had just brought in from the garden. He watched as Guillemete washed and cut up the tender stalks, dropping them into hot olive oil, along with plenty of garlic and a few potatoes.

'Smells good,' said Viddy, picking up the wooden spoon and stirring the pot. Guillemete leaned across and dropped a big handful of chopped celery leaves in, then added some stock.

'All ze flavour is in ze leaves,' she said, grinning at him. One of her lower teeth was missing, but she was familiar, and she was home. 'Where is zat lazy friend of yours? 'E spends 'alf 'is time in bed,' she said.

'No idea,' said Viddy.

"E's missing a beautiful day,' she said.

'Do you need anything else from the garden for lunch?' asked Viddy.

'Non, c'est bon,' she said.

Viddy headed back outside, he didn't mind when Jonny reappeared. What mattered, was that he'd found his rightful place again. Being back in the Château garden, among his plants, was like a return to the lifeblood that had sustained him for as long as he could remember.

Everything felt different. He was different. Viddy had been so fearful of being found out by Christine, of being discovered leading the kind of life she would never have believed possible. It had been all consuming. It wasn't just the love affair with Jonny, but sleeping rough, living on the streets among the lowest of the low. At least that is how he'd seen himself in the early days. He knew now how easily it could happen to anyone, given enough bad luck or bad judgement, and sometimes both. People could be brought low, but it did not make them bad people, any more than he was a bad person. He was ashamed of his prejudice now and resolved to use his privilege, in future, to make things better for people who were down on their luck.

His decision to leave home cost him months of unhappiness. His deception over many years, eventually cast a long shadow over his once open, and loving demeanour. He wasn't sure now, what it had all been for. Everything changed for him after he was honest with his mother. If only he could have been honest with her sooner. It didn't matter that she chose to misunderstand him. He had spoken his truth and the pressure he was carrying, the burden of it, had gone. He felt free to be who he had always been, a loving son with nothing to hide. No more guilt, no more lies.

What he'd had with Philippe was a deep connection, born of many years shared experience, and a mutual love of nature. In every other way, they were worlds apart, he thought ruefully. He smiled, remembering the day Philippe gave him a tiny teddy bear and told him he loved him. The bear was long gone, but the ribbon from around its neck was something Viddy carried with him always. At least he had, until he was taken to hospital in England. He hadn't seen it since. It didn't seem to matter anymore. Not since he'd met Jonny.

When he thought about Jonny, he could imagine him being comfortable in any setting. With Philippe, he always pictured him in the natural world, where everyone and everything were equal.

Wasn't that how it should be, in God's eyes, he asked himself. Why was it that the trappings of wealth and privilege created frameworks, within which people either fitted, or they didn't? It didn't seem right that a building or a set of conventions, should determine the outcome of a relationship, or of anything for that matter. Viddy sighed.

The experience of loving Jonny, and his joy at rediscovering his happiness at home, opened his heart wide. He found himself smiling in sheer appreciation of the world. Love could be so pure, when guilt and shame were not a part of it. The more open-hearted he became, the closer he felt to God. He knelt down to pick some late summer strawberries, just as the sun emerged from behind a cloud and covered him with light.

Jonny looked out of his bedroom window at that moment, and stared at Viddy. It was as if he was looking at someone he didn't recognise. In England he was Viddy's protector and strength, but here in France, he was seeing a new side to his friend. From the moment they arrived at the Château, Viddy's demeanour changed. He held himself with confidence and bearing, like the Viscount that he was. He belonged here. Jonathan sighed; they hadn't been alone for any length of time, since arriving a week ago. It was almost as if Viddy was avoiding him, but why would he?

JONATHAN

Jonathan immediately liked Alain when they met over dinner. Conversation flowed easily and he found himself speaking with enthusiasm about his end-of-year fashion show, and some of his plans for the future.

'I want to start my own business, eventually, once I have some experience,' said Jonny. 'I've seen a lot of people make a success of event management. I think it's something I would enjoy.'

'So, what brings you to France?' asked Alain.

'I met Daveed through a friend in England,' said Jonathan. 'When I heard he was returning to France, I offered to come over and help.'

'Speaking of events,' said Alain, turning to Christine, 'Have you heard that there has been a fire at one of the hotels in Tours?'

'Yes, I did read about it. What a tragedy. They suspect an electrical fault, don't they?'

'It is unconfirmed at the moment, but the hotel is closed for the foreseeable future. Unfortunately, Marie-Claire de Villemont was due to have her wedding reception there in a few weeks. Do you remember the family?'

'Yes, I do, although it's a few years since I've seen them, but Daveed knows Marie-Claire, don't you darling?' said Christine.

'I haven't seen her for a while,' he said. 'We were at École Primaire together, back in the day.'

'I wonder what they will do, about the reception I mean?' said Christine.

'The mother and daughter are distraught, apparently. Sebastian de Villemont mentioned it the other day. Everywhere they've tried is fully booked, at such short notice. It's such a shame.' Alain let his words hang into the silence. Viddy and Christine carried on eating but Jonathan looked up and caught his eye, and Alain winked at him.

For all Jonathan's plans to be an extra pair of hands at the

Château, things had not worked out as he imagined they would. The family, including Viddy, slipped into their traditional roles almost as soon as they arrived and Jonathan was left to his own devices. He was beginning to see that he had been outmanoeuvred by Christine, and in the nicest possible way, used as a vehicle to persuade Viddy to return to France.

He'd done quite a lot of sketching, in particular of some of the tapestries in the drawing room. Other than that, if he was honest, he was finding it rather lonely in the countryside. He needed a purpose.

The silence continued as they ate, while Christine remained oblivious, or so they thought. But it turned out that the wink had not been lost on her.

'What are you two cooking up?' she said, looking first at Alain and then at Jonny.

They both grinned at her, and then Alain said, 'I suppose I'm wondering, with all the space in the ballroom, whether it might not be an opportunity to let this young man cut his teeth, and organise an event here at the Château? Sebastian tells me that the caterers are booked and paid for. They would provide everything required.'

'Alain, you can't be serious?' said Christine.

'Maman, it is such a good idea,' said Viddy. 'Imagine how Marie-Claire must feel about all this. You could save her day.' Christine said nothing, her face inscrutable, as she thought about it. Perhaps she could help. She imagined having music and dancing at the Château again, and found she liked the idea.

'What about Marie-Claire?' she asked. 'Do you think this is something she would want?'

'We won't know until we ask her, Maman,' said Viddy.

'Jonathan, how do you feel about all this? Do you think you would be up to the task of organising it?'

'I would love to,' he said confidently. 'I would need to brush up on my French, but otherwise, I would enjoy doing it. I haven't helped here as much as I expected to. A project would make me feel useful.'

'Jonny, your French is good,' said Viddy. 'Don't forget that quite a lot of people speak English too. Marie-Claire definitely does.' Then he turned to Christine. 'What do you think Maman, shall I call Marie-Claire?'

'Just a minute, Daveed. Let's not get ahead of ourselves,' said Christine. 'I would like to think it over, but I would also like to help if I can.' Alain reached for her hand under the table and gave it a squeeze.

'Of course, Maman.' Viddy was quite used to deferring to her.

Then Christine said, 'Daveed, darling, I know this should ultimately be your decision. I just need time to get used to the idea of handing over the reins. I hope you understand.'

The next day Jonathan made an effort to get up early, as soon as he saw Viddy outside. Since arriving, he'd ditched his silver trousers and flamboyant jacket in favour of jeans covered in multi coloured patchwork and a pink t-shirt, his concession to the countryside. He pulled on a pair of short garden wellies from a selection by the garden door, and went outside. 'Hey friend,' he called, as he strode across the garden towards him. The grass was increasingly dewy in the morning and evening, as the weather became more autumnal.

Viddy looked up, surprised, Jonny wasn't part of his early morning communion with the garden, but he put a smile on his face and walked over to meet him.

'You're up early,' he said. 'Did you sleep OK?'

'Yes, yes, I did, but can we drop the formality? I hardly recognise you since we've been here,' said Jonathan, playfully slapping him on the shoulder.

'Well, this is who I really am,' said Viddy. 'I was a lost soul in England and you saved me with your kindness, Jonny. I can't thank you enough for that.' He looked into Jonathan's face, and stepped forward to hug him. Jonny wrapped his arms around him and pulled him close, but just as quickly, Viddy stepped away. There was an awkward pause, and then Viddy said, 'I hope Maman agrees for Marie-Claire to hold her wedding reception here. I think you'll like her.'

Jonny looked at Viddy, trying to fathom the change in his friend. Then he said, 'I'm sure I will.' Jonny waited for Viddy to say something else, but he didn't. Then he said, 'I'll leave you to get on,' and turned to walk back to the Château. Viddy watched him walking away, his heart heavy. Then he knelt down to pray. He found enormous solace in these quiet moments with God. Lately, it felt as if He was calling him.

When Jonny walked into the dining room for breakfast, Christine was sitting reading the paper. 'Bonjour, Jonathan,' she said, smiling. 'Did you sleep well?'

'Good morning, Christine. Yes, very well, thank you.'

'That's good. Please, help yourself to some breakfast. Guillemete has laid everything out on the sideboard. I'll ring for some coffee, or would you prefer tea?'

'Coffee is fine, thank you,' he said. Christine thought he seemed quieter than usual. He looked sad too this morning, which was very unlike him.

'Bonjour, Monsieur Jonathan,' said Guillemete, bustling in with a pot of hot coffee and another of hot milk for him. 'Would you like me to make you some eggs for your breakfast?'

'That is very kind of you Guillemete, but I'll have some croissants from the sideboard. Thank you.'

He and Christine sat in silence for a while as he ate, and she continued to read the paper. After a while, she folded it and put it down beside her.

'I have been thinking about Marie-Claire's wedding,' she said. 'Do you think you would like to organise it here for her?' Jonathan's face lit up.

'Yes,' he said. 'I really would.'

'In that case,' she said, 'I will call the family this morning and make our offer. I will suggest that they visit this week to see whether Château de Courcy would suit their needs.'

'How could it not,' he said, excited now. 'I can't think of anywhere more beautiful to have a wedding reception.' Ideas were rushing through Jonathan's mind now. He pictured guests rowing elegantly on the river, in the long blue rowing boats the family kept tied up on the water. He imagined photographs of the bride outside the Château, set against a blue sky. The gardens too, in autumn, would lend themselves beautifully to a spectacular wedding album.

Christine smiled as she watched him, his breakfast forgotten, lost in the world of his imagination.

'Christine, do you mind if I familiarise myself with the other rooms in the Château, especially the ballroom, in readiness for their visit?'

'Not at all,' she said. 'Be my guest.' Jonathan spent the rest of the morning exploring, making himself thoroughly familiar with the house and gardens, with the event in mind. He looked over some of his notes about event planning and made a list of everything he could think of, that would need to be discussed when the de Villemonts came over. He was determined to make a success of this.

If the family had been let down at the last minute, it was likely that all the other services for the wedding were booked, and ready to go. It would just be a matter of bringing his creative flair to bear, and pulling everything together.

He was just on his way out of his bedroom, to get some fresh air, when he heard the telephone ringing. He knew that Christine had gone shopping and Viddy was likely to be in the garden, so he picked it up. 'Hello, Château de Courcy.'

'Jonny, is that you? It's me, Berry.'

'Berry,' he said surprised. 'Are you alright?'

'Yes, I'm fine,' she said. 'How are things in France?'

'Very grand, as it happens.'

'Lucky you,' she said, pausing for a moment. Then she said, 'Jonny, do you remember my friend Lydia?'

'Do you mean the skinny girl with glasses? Of course I do,' he said. 'It was me who brought her home to meet you.'

'Well, I've had a letter from her. She's moved to Florida.'

'Florida?' he said. 'That was sudden. What's she doing there?'

'Apparently her grandma died and left everything to her. She's living in a huge house on the beach, on some exotic island!'

'It's alright for some,' he said, thinking he could do with some sunshine and warmth himself.

'She really liked you, you know Jonny.'

'Did she? I never knew that. She looked as if she wouldn't say boo to a goose!'

'You must have seen the way she looked at you.'

'To be honest, I didn't. You know me, I like to keep my options open.'

'You mean you're gay,' she said. 'Do you think I'm stupid?'

'I'm not gay Berry, I just like to keep an open mind.'

'Well, whatever,' she said. 'Anyway, Lydia asked me to tell you where she is. She's invited me over for Thanksgiving on 27th November.'

'Invited you over?' he said, incredulous.

'Yes, invited me over,' said Berry. 'She's holding a big get together at her beach mansion, with roast turkey and all the trimmings. I'm going to ask Mum and Dad if I can go.'

Jonathan was taken aback to hear his sister's news, was he jealous? Probably, but in light of the way things were turning out with Viddy, he wondered whether he should put himself forward as Berry's chaperone.

'Do you think they'll say yes?' he asked her.

'Who knows,' she said. 'They'd probably prefer it if you came too. My term ends mid-November, and Thanksgiving is soon after.'

'Am I invited?' he found himself asking.

'Not specifically, but as I said, she likes you and she asked me to tell you where she is.'

'OK let me know what Mum and Dad say about your trip. I might come with you. It just depends on things here.'

'What things?' she asked.

'It's all happening here,' he said. 'Get this. Your bro' has been asked to plan a wedding at the Château!' he said, sounding delighted. 'This may be the start of my career as an events planner.'

'That's amazing!' she said. 'Go Jonny!'

THE DE VILLEMONTS

As soon as she saw the de Villemont car approaching along the tree lined avenue, Christine stepped outside to greet them. When the car pulled up, Sebastian and his wife got out, followed by two lovely young women. 'Quelle plaisir de vous voire,' said Christine, stepping forward to greet Adèle, air kissing her on both cheeks. 'You too Sebastian, it has been a long time.'

'This is our daughter, Marie-Claire,' said Adèle. Marie Claire stepped forward,

'Enchantée, Vicomtesse de Courcy,' she said. Then turning to her right she said, 'This is my sister, Francine.'

Francine stepped forward to shake Christine's hand, 'Enchantée,' she said.

'Please, come inside,' said Christine. As they moved over the bridge towards the Château entrance, they marvelled at the vista of the river and the extensive gardens on either side.

'This is magnificent,' said Sebastian.

'Wow,' mouthed Adèle silently to her husband. Marie-Claire exchanged excited glances with her sister, as they stepped into the pale marble hallway. Its ceiling was decorated with sweeping curved vaults, embellished with rosettes of cherubs and roses. The walls and floor were of matching pale stone, the whole illuminated by a vibrant display of purple and blue flowers.

Christine led them into a large, elegant room hung with vast tapestries. Jonathan, dressed in smart navy trousers with a white shirt, stepped forward as they entered. 'Je vous présente Jonathan, un ami de la famille,' said Christine. Jonathan stepped forward to shake hands, as Christine introduced them one by one. 'Jonathan is just beginning his career as a wedding and events planner, so this would be a marvellous opportunity for him.' There were smiles and murmurs of greeting, as Christine continued, 'This is the room we are proposing for the reception of your wedding guests. Jonathan will tell you more.'

'Thank you,' he said, stepping forward. 'As the Vicomtesse said, this beautiful salon would serve to welcome your guests, perhaps with a glass of champagne. It may be that during this time, as people arrive, the bride and groom will use the opportunity for photographs in the gardens.'

'Indeed,' said Sebastian. 'We have our photographer already booked, don't we ma Cherie?' he said to Adèle.

'Good. Let me make a note of the date the wedding will take place,' said Jonathan, pulling out his notebook.

'It will be October 25th, two weeks from now.'

'Alright,' said Jonathan, taken aback that it would be so soon. 'I'm sure we can manage that. The autumn colours in the gardens will be glorious, then.' He paused as the family admired the room.

'What beautiful tapestries,' said Adèle.

'They are,' said Jonathan. 'They were embroidered in Flanders around 1500. The subjects of ladies, animals and flowers were ground-breaking, at a time when scenes of bloodshed, and battles were more fashionable.'

'The colours are still so vibrant,' said Adèle.

'The colours have been carefully protected. The tapestries are actually museum pieces,' he said. 'The French government bought them from the Château in 1882 and restored them.[2] Part of the agreement was that every five years, they would be returned to the Château, to be displayed in their original place for two years. The rest of the time they are on display at the Musée de Cluny in Paris, so that other people can enjoy them.'

'I wonder what inspired them,' said Adèle.

'They were made for a nobleman in Paris. He commissioned the artist to paint battle scenes initially, to be made into tapestries. During his time at the nobleman's house, rumour has it that the artist fell in love with one of his daughters and then, with his wife. The nobleman was persuaded that tapestries of ladies and animals would be more pleasant to look upon, than scenes of bloody battle. So, the commission was changed. I don't think the nobleman ever knew that it was his wife and daughter who inspired the finished works. Perhaps love is, after all, the greatest inspiration.'

'How fascinating,' said Sebastian.

2   Please see notes at the end of the book

'Perfect for a wedding too,' added Adèle. Jonathan glanced at Christine, who had taken some trouble to explain all this to him, a few days before the visit. She smiled at him, pleased.

'Shall we go through to the ballroom now?' said Jonathan. 'This is where we are proposing that the wedding breakfast be held.' They walked back into the marble hall and Jonathan led them through an almost hidden doorway, such was its pale colour.

There were gasps of amazement as they stepped into an enormous ballroom with windows along both sides, overlooking the River Cher.

'This room must be sixty metres long,' said Adèle, 'and maybe six metres wide? It is absolutely beautiful!'

The floor was made up of squares of slate and white stone, placed to form monochrome diamond shapes, over the full width and length of the room. The many ceiling joists were stained with lime wash, and the walls were painted white. Eighteen windows, of the palest of pastel stained glass, were set into a series of archways. These ran the length of the vast room, on both sides, their glass warming the light that flooded the space.

'As you see,' said Jonathan, 'this room is a blank canvas for any theme or colour scheme you may wish to use for the wedding. The fir trees in the alcoves,' he pointed along the sides of the room, 'will be illuminated with white lights, so that as evening falls, they will provide a soft glow. The chandeliers too can be lit, as darkness falls.'

Adèle turned to Christine and said, 'I had no idea how beautiful this would be. I cannot thank you enough for the opportunity – you really will be saving the day for us.'

Sebastian added, 'Naturally we are willing to pay for the space. The hotel has refunded us and still feels in our debt after letting us down as they have. It is one of the best hotels in the area, but of course, they are blameless in all this.'

'Yes, of course they are,' said Christine. 'It is all very unfortunate. We are only too happy to help, and of course would not dream of accepting any money from you.' Jonathan tried and failed to catch her eye, as Sebastian replied.

'You are very kind Vicomtesse, but I insist,' he said. 'We wouldn't have it any other way, would we Cherie?'

'Certainly not,' said Adèle. 'I would not feel comfortable unless we pay you for it, Christine. Despite the beauty of the hotel facilities, this surpasses anything we could possibly have imagined for the wedding. You really are very kind.' Everyone had forgotten the girls, and now Marie-Claire's parents turned to their daughter.

'What do you think, darling?' said Adèle.

'Oh Maman, Papa, Vicomtesse! Thank you so very much. It is absolutely perfect.' Her cheeks were flushed with excitement, and the sisters flung their arms around each other.

Jonathan smiled and said, 'I am sure you already have an idea of the details, and what you would like for the wedding,' he said.

'We do, of course,' said Adèle. 'Everything was planned down to the last detail. It is only the venue that will be different. Of course if you have any particular ideas Jonathan, we would be interested to hear them.'

They looked expectantly at him and he said, 'I wondered whether a quartet of musicians might play to welcome guests, as drinks are enjoyed in the salon. Later, they could move to the far end of the ballroom, and play during the wedding breakfast. There is plenty of room for a series of round tables at this end, and perhaps some floor space at the far end of the room, could be reserved for dancing later on.'

'That all sounds wonderful,' said Marie-Claire breathlessly.

'I'm sure you will have much to discuss with Jonathan,' said Christine. 'Shall we return to the salon, and I will ring for some coffee?'

'Thank you,' said Adèle.

Jonathan was prepared with a list of all the elements he believed would be required for a successful wedding event, and they went through them together. The wedding service was to take place at the church closest to the de Villemont family home. After that, they would make their way over to Château de Courcy. They discussed flowers and food and the timing of everything, while Jonathan made notes.

'The caterers will be in touch with you directly, Jonathan, to discuss their needs,' said Adèle. 'The menu is already planned, and they will take care of everything, including tables, chairs and so on.'

She looked at Sebastian, and he added, 'The wines and furniture will be delivered to the Château a few days before the wedding.'

Once Jonathan had written everything down and taken all the contact information he needed, he suggested they take a stroll in the grounds. The sun was warm as they stepped outside, and the trees were already dressed in the beginnings of autumn glory. 'There is so much to see in the garden,' said Jonathan. 'If we walk to the right here and onto the bridge, you will have a marvellous vantage point over the Château, with the river on one side, and the gardens on the other.'

'Oh, look at these rowing boats,' said Francine. 'They are like something out of a painting.'

'Aren't they,' said Jonathan. 'I was imagining some photographs of guests rowing on the river, but it may not be the best time of year for that.'

'October can be beautifully sunny,' said Adèle. 'I don't think we should rule it out. If we have photos taken beside the water, the boats and the Château will still be the backdrop, it would be wonderful.'

Marie-Claire's eyes were shining as the event began to take on a dreamlike quality for her. Prior to their visit, she had become very despondent, even wondering whether her wedding would have to be postponed.

'Maman,' she said. 'I am just so relieved we have found such a beautiful place. I can't wait to tell Jacques.'

'You are very welcome to bring your fiancé back here and have a stroll in the grounds,' said Jonathan. 'Perhaps the photographer would like to come too, so that you can identify some nice areas for your wedding pictures,'

'Thank you so much, Jonathan,' said Sebastian, stepping forward to shake his hand. 'We are delighted with the outcome of this morning, and we look forward to working with you to make this a great success.'

'Thank you, Monsieur,' said Jonathan. 'You will not be disappointed.'

As he watched the car drive away, he felt energised. He was good at this, and he would not let them down. He strolled back onto the bridge, to look at the Château through the eyes of the de Villemonts. It was truly magnificent. No wonder they were so pleased. Then he turned to look out across the curving flowerbeds of the Diane de Poitiers Garden, marvelling at their symmetry and the way the curves of the design led the eye further and further into the distance. Then he stopped and stared. Was that Viddy over there by the glasshouses, talking to someone?

Jonathan had hardly seen him over the last few days, and when he joined him in the garden, there was an awkwardness between them. It made his heart ache, but he knew he needed to give Viddy time to readjust to being back home. He was probably chatting to one of the casual gardeners – he certainly wouldn't be able to manage all this alone. He went inside to change his clothes and then strolled out to see how they were getting on, but when he got there, there was no sign of anyone at all.

VIDDY

By the time the ballroom was set up for the wedding, it was a sight to behold. Crisp linen cloths covered round tables, each with a small floral arrangement in the centre. Crystal glasses shone in the sun, as it slanted through the pale glass windows.

The wedding party arrived in white cars, dressed with flowers and ribbon. The emerging guests were chic and elegant in pastel silks and beautiful hats. Their laughter drifted across the lawns, as they posed for photographs with the bride and groom, relieved that the formal part of the day was behind them.

As they eventually made their way inside, Jonathan was there to welcome them and show them into the salon, where glasses of chilled champagne and sparkling elderflower awaited them. As they later entered the ballroom, there were gasps and murmurs of appreciation at the magnificent space, and the views along the river.

Once everyone was seated, with the bridal party at the top table, Jonathan ensured that everything ran smoothly, as the caterers took over. They served elegant plates of food and topped up the wine and water. Jonny went down to the kitchen to make sure that the champagne was chilled, ready to serve with the speeches, and later, with the wedding cake.

There was still no sign of Viddy. For nearly two weeks now, Jonathan had barely seen him except briefly at dinner, when he appeared to be lost in his own world. Once or twice he knocked quietly, before trying Viddy's bedroom door, only to find it locked.

The organisation of his first event had taken up most of Jonathan's time, so there had been little time to think about Viddy. He'd wanted to be sure that nothing was left to chance, and to that end, employed meticulous organisation and attention to detail. It was only now that the day was moving towards a successful conclusion, that Jonny began to give Viddy more thought. Where did he spend all his time? Surely at this time of year, there was less to do in the garden, not more. Today of all days, he really thought his friend might have been here to support him.

With the speeches underway, Jonny knew he wouldn't be missed for a while, so he decided to go outside and get some air. He changed out of his good shoes, tucked his trousers into his socks and pulled on one of the pairs of wellies by the door.

He strode out into the garden, making his way along the curving paths of the Medici garden, then beyond it to the flower gardens. Next, he searched the vegetable gardens, before looping back to look in the glass houses. Both were empty. After that, he walked along the perimeter of the de Courcy estate with growing determination to find his friend. Enough was enough.

He had almost given up, when he noticed a pale stone church some distance away, beyond the estate. He remembered Christine's words about Viddy, and the times they found him sitting quietly in the family chapel. So he walked through the gate at the exit to the de Courcy land, and then across the lane towards the church.

When he eventually walked unobtrusively through the door, and into the dimly lit church, he could just make out his friend kneeling in one of the front pews. Jonny walked over to him and said quietly, 'Viddy, what are you doing here? Come up to the Château with me and join the wedding celebrations.' When Viddy turned his face to Jonny, tears were running down his cheeks.

'Viddy, what is it?' said Jonny, kneeling down beside him.

'Leave me Jonny, I'm not worthy of your love or the faith you have put in me,' he whispered, half choked with tears. Jonny helped him up.

'Come on,' he said, 'Let's talk outside.' He took his jacket off and wrapped it round Viddy's shivering shoulders. When they stepped out into the autumn sunshine, Jonny could see that his friend had been crying, for a very long time. His eyes were red rimmed and his face pale. 'Let's walk back towards the Château. We'll find a warm place to sit and talk. I've missed you, buddy,' said Jonny.

As they walked through the gate, and back onto de Courcy land, Jonny saw that the glasshouses were bathed in afternoon sunshine. 'How about the glasshouse?' he asked. 'Shall we go and sit in there? At least it will be warm inside.'

Once inside, Jonny closed the door behind them and made his way to the far end. He pushed through some ferns, beyond which he could see a couple of upturned wooden boxes that would serve as seats. Once they were sitting facing one another, Jonny leaned forward and put his hands gently on Viddy's shoulders.

'I can't bear to see you like this, Viddy. What has happened to you?' he asked gently.

There was a long silence, and then Viddy said, 'I'm just so confused about everything. When I was away from Château de Courcy, everything seemed easy. Now I'm back here, all that has changed. This land, this place, they are in my blood and in the beating of my heart. Château de Courcy is part of who I am, but everything I have suffered here is a part of that too. I wish I could separate myself from it, but I can't.' Jonny waited quietly, considering what he should say. Viddy continued.

'God is calling me, Jonny. It is only with Him that I feel at peace, even as I struggle to shake off the confusion in my heart.' Jonny looked at him, sympathy in his eyes, trying to understand.

Then they both heard footsteps entering the glasshouse and a voice called out, 'Daveed, tu es là?' They looked at each other and Viddy put his finger to his lips. He knew his world was about to come crashing down, and he screwed his face up in silent pain. In an effort to stay quiet, Jonny accidentally knocked a plant pot with his elbow, and it fell to the floor and smashed, making them both jump. A moment later, a pair of slim legs clad in faded jeans appeared from among the ferns, and Jonny stood up.

He came face to face with a dark haired man of about his own age. He had the suggestion of a beard, pale green eyes and smooth olive skin. The man looked mystified, and then surprised, when he saw Viddy was there too.

Viddy stood up quickly and said, 'Jonny, je te présente mon ami, Philippe.'

'Philippe?' said Jonny. 'Do you mean Philippe, your childhood friend?' Suddenly everything became clear, and he felt a physical pain in his heart.

'Bonjour,' said Philippe, reaching out to shake Jonny's hand.

'Bonjour,' said Jonny, shaking his hand briefly. Then turning to leave, he said, 'I need to get back.'

'Jonny, your jacket,' called Viddy, handing it to him. Instead of letting go of it, he held on so that Jonny was forced to look back at him, then he mouthed, 'I'm so sorry.'

JONATHAN

Viddy did not come down to dinner for the rest of the week. Christine seemed unfazed by his absence, and invited Alain to join them for the first few evenings. They chatted about the success of the wedding, and Jonny's part in it. Alain asked about some of the practical aspects of the day, and whether there had been any learning points to take away for the future.

'I have learned so much just from doing this,' said Jonathan. 'It has been a great experience for me, and I've enjoyed it too.'

'Adèle and Sebastian were delighted with everything,' said Christine. 'They were full of praise for the Château and for you, Jonathan. They said the wedding could not have been more perfect.'

'I'm glad,' he said. Christine noticed how detached Jonathan seemed, and resolved to have a chat with him the following evening, when they would be alone.

Jonathan too made a decision to speak candidly to Christine when he had the chance, it was time. He was tired of pretending and of living in a kind of limbo, in Viddy's absence. Now the wedding was behind them, he needed to make some decisions.

The following evening, it was just the two of them. Once their dinner was served, and they were alone, Christine said, 'Jonathan, there is something I wish to speak to you about.' She paused, and his mind raced with all the possibilities, but she said, 'I thought you would be pleased to hear, that as a result of the success of the de Villemont wedding, I have received three more wedding enquiries. All of them are planning spring weddings.'

'That is wonderful news,' said Jonathan. 'I'm so happy for you.'

'Before I discuss that with you, I want you to know that Monsieur de Villemont insisted on paying me for the privilege of using the Château. I am quite frankly astounded that such large sums could change hands for the use of a room, albeit a rather grand one. I know you worked incredibly hard to make it a success. In fact, without you, it would not have happened. So, I am proposing to give you one third of the money, as a fee for your hard work.'

'That is very generous of you, Christine. I had no such expectation. You have made me welcome in your home, and it has been a real pleasure to spend time with you and your family. Alain has been supportive too, I have appreciated his counsel.'

'It is the least you deserve,' she said. 'If you prefer to have this money in sterling, I can transfer it to you from our bank account in England. Just think it over and then let me know.'

She paused for a moment, as Guillemete came in to collect their plates and bring in some cheese. Then she continued, 'In the meantime, I have an interesting proposition for you.' She paused, and looked at Jonathan, but he already had an idea what was coming.

Christine continued, 'In light of the recent wedding enquiries and the potential for many more to come, I would like to offer you a permanent position here at Château de Courcy, as our events planner. I could pay you a very modest salary, pocket money really, all the year round, but every time there is an event, you will receive a substantial bonus. How does that sound?' There was a long silence and Jonathan sighed; it was now or never.

'A couple of months ago, this would have been everything I could have hoped for, and I would have jumped at your offer,' he said.

'And now?' asked Christine.

'Now, things have changed.'

'In what way have they changed?' she asked.

'Christine, there is no easy way to say this. I know that Daveed has already been honest with you, about himself. You may know that he and I have been . . .' he paused, searching for the right word. 'Involved,' he finished.

'Ah,' she said slowly. 'Yes, I thought as much.'

'Did you know that Daveed's old friend, Philippe, has come back?'

'Yes I did know,' she said. 'There is very little that escapes my notice. I don't suppose Daveed realises it, but I have always known him, almost as well as he knows himself.'

She paused for a moment, as if lost in her own thoughts, and then she said, 'I have felt so desperately sorry for his inner torment, and at the same time, quite helpless in the face of an impossible situation.' She looked calmly at Jonathan, her face serious.

Then Jonathan said, 'Nothing is impossible,' he said. 'If you love your son as I know you do; you will find a way of supporting his choices in life. Sadly, those choices no longer include me.'

Christine said nothing, and the silence lengthened. Then she said, 'May I be brutally honest with you, Jonathan?'

'Of course,' he said, 'If you think it will help.'

'I just want to be sure that we understand one another.' She paused. 'I invited you here because I realised it was the only way I would get Daveed to come home. As it has turned out, I owe you a debt of gratitude for paving the way for a new venture at Château de Courcy. That was something I did not foresee.'

She paused. 'The fact that Philippe is here as well, means that Daveed is unlikely to want to leave again.' Now it was Jonathan's turn to look surprised.

'Christine, I'm not sure that you know, or care to know your son, as well as you believe you do. When I searched and eventually found Daveed, on the afternoon of the wedding, he was kneeling in the village church with tears streaming down his face. He said that the only place he can find peace is with God.

'I had such high hopes of creating a life here with him, hoping that in time you would see what we meant to each other. I hoped you would finally accept your son for who he is.' Jonathan paused. 'I believe you have always understood him, but have remained deliberately blind to what he so desperately needs you to see. How far will you let this go, before you finally acknowledge his truth? This is not going to go away.'

Jonny let his words hang in the air while Christine allowed the silence to lengthen. If she was surprised by his bold statement of the facts, she didn't show it. She was waiting for him to finish, but he was not finished yet. He was not going to hold back. This needed to be said for Viddy's sake. Perhaps, in the end, this would be the only thing he would be able to do for him.

'I care for Viddy so very much, but I can see that this situation is breaking him. He was a different person in England, we had such fun together. He was carefree and happy, but his loyalty to his family and the Château de Courcy come before everything, even his own happiness. I cannot stand by and see him in such pain. If I knew he could be happy with Philippe, painful as that would be for me, I could accept it. The truth is I don't think he knows what he wants. He is both blinded and floored by the truth of who he is, and the terrible conflict he feels, because you will not accept it.'

Christine still did not react. Eventually she drew herself up and said, 'Thank you for your honesty, Jonathan. This cannot have been easy for you.'

'I think it's time I went to bed, if you'll excuse me.' Jonathan got up from the table, then added, 'Thank you for your confidence in me, Christine. I really appreciate your offer of work at the Château. If I may, I would like to think it over. I will let you know of my decision in the coming weeks and certainly before the end of the year.'

'Good,' she said. 'I look forward to it.' As he turned to leave the room, she added, 'And Jonathan, I want you to know that I am going to give some serious thought to what you have said this evening. I know you have Daveed's best interests at heart, as I do.'

'Thank you. Good night, Christine, I'll see you in the morning. Tomorrow, I will make plans to travel home.'

WINTER

WINDSONG

As Jonathan and Berry got ready to leave for the airport, the skies were grey and sleet was falling. Since arriving home from France, Jonny had been out late most nights, clubbing and drinking into the early hours. His face was pale and unshaven when he emerged from his bedroom, after barely an hour of sleep. 'Christ, you stink,' said Berry. 'There's no way I'm sitting next to you for nine hours, looking and smelling like that.' She made him a cup of coffee and pushed him towards the bathroom. 'Pull yourself together Jonny, for God's sake.' He emerged half an hour later a little shaky, but freshly washed and shaved, with his wet hair combed back. He'd packed his case before going out the previous afternoon, so when the taxi pulled up outside, they were soon on their way.

Check-in was straightforward, and with plenty of time before their flight, they treated themselves to a full English breakfast and a large pot of tea. As soon as the plane took off, Jonny fell into a deep sleep, oblivious to the two films that Berry watched back to back. He eventually began to stir as the cabin crew came round offering afternoon tea and sandwiches before they landed.

Jonny stretched out his legs and arms and sighed, refreshed and ready to face the world again. 'Hey sis,' he said. 'We'll soon be in the sun!' He couldn't wait to get into some warmer weather. 'How are we getting to the house?' he asked her.

'Lydia's arranged for someone to meet us,' she said.

As they waited outside the arrivals doors, peeling off layers of clothing to cope with the heat, a yellow VW van pulled up beside them and a man in faded jeans and a t-shirt got out. 'Berry?' he asked. Tanned, muscular arms reached for her suitcase and he flashed her a dazzling smile.

Berry almost swooned as she said, 'Yes, and this is my brother, Jonny.'

'Hey Jonny, I'm James, a friend of Lydia's. My parents are her neighbours on Captiva.' Things were getting better and better, thought Berry.

'Thanks for coming to get us from the airport,' said Jonny.

'No worries,' he said. 'Good flight?'

'Great.'

'What would you know?' said Berry. 'You slept through the whole thing!'

They were soon in the van for the hour long journey. When they eventually pulled up outside Windsong, they were enveloped by tropical beauty. It was like entering another world full of mysterious, trilling birds and deep shadows, cut through with brilliant slices of sunshine. They were just making their way up the steps to the front door, when it opened. Lydia was unrecognisable as the tall, skinny girl with glasses they had last seen in England. Instead, she had blossomed like a beautiful bloom on a slender stalk. Her tanned face was sprinkled with freckles, and an open, silk coat-dress billowed around her slim legs. She wore white frayed shorts and a black vest top, finished off with fine hooped earrings.

'Lydia, you look absolutely amazing!' said Berry, rushing up to hug her.

'You brought your brother!' said Lydia.

'Hope you don't mind,' she said. 'It was a bit last minute.' Then she whispered into Lydia's ear, 'I couldn't leave him, bit of a love crisis.'

'Hi Jonathan,' said Lydia stepping forward. 'It's great to see you! Come on in, all of you.' They stepped through into the beautiful space and when Lydia saw their faces, she remembered how the sight had affected her when she arrived, two months ago.

'Wow!' said Berry. 'This is incredible.' Jonathan was lost for words. He dropped their bags and walked out onto the deck, marvelling at the sight before him. If this didn't have the power to heal him, nothing would.

He turned to Lydia, 'Lydia, I'm so sorry to turn up uninvited like this. Berry kind of insisted and if I'm honest, I was quite jealous when I heard she was on her way to the sun.' They all laughed.

'You are very welcome. There is plenty of room, and it will be great to have some company,' Lydia replied, and then turned to James and said, 'Thanks for picking them up from the airport,

Cheri,' and she leaned forward and kissed him. James flushed with pleasure and the siblings looked at each other and grinned, hiding their respective disappointment.

'Come on,' said Lydia. 'I'll show you up to your rooms, and then you'll probably want a swim.' She led the way up a staircase at the opposite end of the house to her own. At the top, the hallway was all white with a roof-light opening onto a perfect square of blue sky. There were three bedrooms, each with its own bathroom, all predominately white, with sky blue sheets and towels. Large blue rugs covered pale wooden floorboards and each room had a balcony with views across the beach, to the sea.

'I love it,' said Berry. 'How did you get so lucky, Lydia?'

'Ah, that's a long story,' she said. 'My life has changed so much in the last couple of months. There's so much to tell you.'

A few minutes later, suitcases abandoned on the floor, they were racing down the stairs and out over the hot white sand to the sea. Jonathan was the first into the water, followed quickly by Berry and James. 'This is incredible!' said Jonny. 'You have no idea what we left behind in England this morning. It was dark and cold and trying to snow.'

'Welcome to paradise,' said James. It was good for him to see the beauty of Captiva through fresh eyes.

'Lydia, come on in,' called Berry, waving at her, as she watched them from the deck.

'Later,' she called back, 'I'm organising food for us.' Alberta had left marinated chicken, a selection of salads and some of her homemade bread for them. There was also a large key lime pie, one of Alberta's specialities. 'Thank you, Alberta,' said Lydia to herself, as she slid the tray of chicken into the oven.

Lydia planned for them to sit down to an early dinner outside, so that they could enjoy the sunset and the gradual illumination of tiny lights around the palms. She remembered how tired she was when she first arrived.

Refreshed and salty from their swims, they showered and changed before emerging onto the deck in bare feet, relaxed and happy.

'That was perfect,' said Jonny. 'I feel better already.'

When Lydia brought out a jug, clinking with ice and slices of lime, Jonny wasn't sure whether he was relieved or disappointed that it wasn't a bottle of wine. The lime and soda punch with cucumber, mint and plenty of ice was so refreshing, that he gulped it down. He didn't realise quite how thirsty he was, until he was on his third glass of it. 'To think I was hankering after a hair of the dog,' he said. 'This has really hit the spot.'

'Unfortunately, I don't have any wine,' said Lydia. 'I think there may be some low alcohol beer in the fridge. Would you like one, Jonny?'

'You know what,' he said, 'I think I'll just stick to the punch. I've had far too many skinfuls lately, trying to drown my sorrows.'

'Anything you want to talk about, mate?' asked James, helping himself to chicken. 'Feel free to unburden yourself, if you need to.'

'Thanks, maybe I will sometime,' said Jonny.

'Tuck in,' said Lydia. 'Alberta is the best cook ever.'

'Thank you, Alberta,' said Berry, 'whoever you are.'

'You can thank her yourself tomorrow,' said Berry. 'She comes in every day. I inherited her with the house. She's been here as long as I can remember. She used to make us the most incredible pancakes when we came here as children.'

'It must feel strange,' said Berry, 'Having somebody around all the time.'

'Funnily enough, it has been a real comfort to me. Alberta reminds me of happy times and home. I was in such a state when I got here, as if my whole world had caved in. That's a long story too, for another day.' She paused.

'Alberta has been a bit like a guardian angel to me, and a precious link between me and my Grandmère. I'm not sure what I would have done without her these last couple of months.' Then, to lighten the atmosphere, Lydia added, 'Not to mention her delicious food! With any luck, she'll make us a pancake breakfast in the morning.'

THANKSGIVING

The next few days were spent lounging on the deck and swimming, while Alberta, who seemed to be in her element, kept them supplied with timely snacks, meals and refreshing drinks.

'Thank you so much, Alberta,' said the charming Jonny. 'Here, let me help you with that.'

'You're all welcome,' said Alberta. 'This just like the old days, Mizz Lydia. You let me know if there's anythin' else you need, Mr Jonathan.'

Over long relaxing meals, they became more and more at ease in each other's company. Lydia and James were open about their alcohol addictions, it was easier that way, but Lydia had not, so far, managed to tell anyone about the incident at her flat. It was a step too far, and very personal. The statement she sent to the police drew a line under it for her, and she hadn't thought about it since beginning her new life on Captiva.

Her relationship with James was slow to ignite, Lydia was cautious, but he turned out to be a true and understanding friend. James was a steadying and calming influence on her, and a source of strength, following the death of Clémence. He too had lived through many ill-judged, alcohol-fuelled situations, and one day, Lydia found herself telling him the story of Norman and the traumatic incident at her flat.

'The worst thing was,' she said, 'there was a part of me that was grateful for the human contact.' She paused. 'Does that shock you?'

'Shock me? No.' He looked at her for a long moment, gently pushed a few wisps of hair from her face, and kissed her softly on the mouth. Then he said quietly, as he gazed into her dark eyes, 'It makes me want to slowly take your clothes off, kiss your freckled skin and make a sculpture of you, in all your beautiful vulnerability.' A tear began to run down Lydia's cheek then, and she kissed him back, pressing her body against his, as if she never wanted to let him go.

On the eve of Thanksgiving, wonderful aromas came from the kitchen, as Alberta prepared all the traditional dishes for the following day. She would be with her own family for Thanksgiving, of course, but she wanted to leave everything ready for Lydia. All she would have to do was put the dishes into the oven.

Over the last couple of months Alberta watched Lydia blossom from a thin, over-anxious girl, into a lovely, relaxed young woman. She put it down to her meeting those nice neighbours and that handsome son of theirs. Alberta smiled to herself. 'Alright Mizz Lydia, everything is ready and I've written down instructions for tomorrow. I reckon I should get back to my own family now.'

'Of course you should, Alberta. Thank you so much,' said Lydia. 'I hope you have a lovely day off and Happy Thanksgiving.' Alberta hung up her apron, put on her pink straw hat and picked up her basket.

'Happy Thanksgiving Mizz Lydia, I hope you all have a wonderful day.'

'Bye Alberta, Happy Thanksgiving!' They called from outside, as the door closed behind her.

Their Thanksgiving Day was one of the best James could remember, it was the only one Lydia could recall in recent memory, and for the other two, it was their first. They started the celebrations with traditional egg nog, mixed by James the evening before. He'd whipped egg yolks with vanilla sugar, and then whisked these into hot milk and cream. The final touch was plenty of grated orange peel and nutmeg, before chilling it in the fridge. Lydia's contribution was a cranberry and orange spritzer with ice and orange slices. She'd bought a bottle of sparkling wine for Jonny and Berry to share and they clinked their glasses together outside in the sunshine, wishing each other a Happy Thanksgiving.

Lunch was a feast of golden turkey that Jonathan volunteered to carve. There was creamy mashed potato and two dishes that were new to everyone except James; a green bean casserole with garlic and soy sauce and a sweet potato casserole with marshmallows. To complete the meal, Alberta had made a rich gravy, fresh cranberry sauce and home-made turkey stuffing.

When their plates were piled high with the steaming food, Lydia dinged her glass with her knife. 'I just want to say a little prayer, before we eat,' she said. They all became quiet and bowed their heads. 'Dearest Grandmère Clémence, I miss you, we are thinking of you today. Thank you God for this beautiful home, for the gift of Alberta, who has become like family to me, and for our lovely feast today.' She paused for a moment, and then she said. 'We ask you to bless the families and friends of the astronauts killed in the space shuttle 'Challenger', earlier this year. We thank you God for the gift of life and for our friends. Amen.'

There were murmurs of 'Amen' and then Lydia pressed a remote to start the music. The beats of The Pretenders, 'Don't Get Me Wrong' filled the room and everyone quickly slipped into party mood. 'What a feast,' said Jonny, tucking into his food with relish.

'Absolutely delicious,' said James. Jokes were shared, and stories told, along with exclamations of praise for Alberta's cooking and Lydia's generosity in inviting them. By the time they were enjoying a traditional pumpkin pie, or rather, some were, it was not to everyone's taste, 'Love is Forever' by Billy Ocean came on, and Jonathan was on his third glass of wine. His heart began to ache for his friend, and the words of the song tugged hard at his heart strings. 'Memories of love I knew, My heart cried out for only you.' Jonny was the only one thus far, who had not shared the secrets of his heart. It was all he could do to hold himself together when he first arrived.

'Are you OK, Jonny? You're very quiet.' said Lydia, concerned.

He looked up, 'Just thinking about a friend,' he said.

'Who?' asked Berry.

'Someone I've come to love,' he said.

'Jonny, don't tell me you're in love,' said Berry. 'You always said you wanted to play the field!'

'Who is she?' asked James. 'You should have brought her.'

'It's a he,' said Jonny.

'I knew it!' said Berry triumphantly.

'The trouble is,' said Jonny, ignoring her, 'Just as I realised I was in love, I found that I wasn't loved back. There was somebody else.'

'Oh Jonny, that's so sad,' said Lydia. 'Is there nothing you can do about it?'

'Not now, they were friends and lovers long before I came

onto the scene. I even knew about the other man, but I thought it was over. Then, one day I found them together.

'I'd just begun to envision a future for us. Isn't it ironic that seeing them together, was the moment I realised I was truly in love? By then, I was too late.'

'This calls for some sad music,' said Berry. 'Shall I get my violin out?'

'Stop it Berry, don't joke,' said Jonny. Berry's face became serious; she hadn't seen her brother like this before. They all exchanged glances.

'OK,' said Lydia. 'I've had an idea. We need a plan. Something to cheer us all up.'

'What?' said Berry.

'First of all, I want you and Jonny to stay here until the end of the year. If you want to, that is. We could spend Christmas together. After that, I think we should have a big New Year Party, with fireworks on the beach, fabulous music and bring all our friends and family together to celebrate!'

'That sounds amazing,' said Berry. 'What do you think, Jonny? I haven't got to be back at college until mid-January.'

'I've got nothing to go back for either,' said Jonny, despondently. 'When I do go back, I'll need to find a job.'

'I thought you said they'd offered you a job at that Château in France,' said Berry.

'A job at a French Château?' said James. 'That sounds like my idea of heaven.'

'I don't think that's going to work out now,' said Jonny. Berry looked mystified, that wasn't what he'd said on the phone.

A couple of days later, Lydia wrote out the invitations, dropped them into the mailbox and began to plan the party.

CHÂTEAU DE COURCY - LETTERS

At Château de Courcy, Jean brought the post in for Viddy. Among them was a letter from England, and his heart lifted. Could it be from Jonny, he wondered? He ripped it open; trying not to be disappointed when he saw it was from Sarah.

Little Bungalow
Sussex Downs Rd
Seahaven
England

Dear Viddy
I have thought of you often and wonder how you are settling in at home. We both missed you after you left and I have fond memories of how lovely the garden used to look!
I am enclosing a couple of letters that arrived for you last week, and look forward to hearing your news sometime.
We send you our best wishes and hope that you are happy in France.
Lots of love Sarah

Inside was a letter from Lydia, dated 30th September, nearly two months ago.

Flat 3, Sea Rd
Seahaven

Dear Viddy
Sorry I haven't been in touch for a while. I've been in a bit of a state over various things. On top of that, I've just heard that my Grandmère has died.
I have to go to Florida; I'm leaving in the morning. I wanted to let you know in case you decided to come and do

some gardening. I didn't want to leave without telling you where I am.

I'm enclosing a card with my address and phone number over there, in case you want to get in touch. I don't know how long I'll be away.

Lots of love, your friend,

Lydia

Viddy's heart squeezed as he was reminded of Jonny, and the day they met in Lydia's garden. Impulsively, he picked up the phone to call him. The phone was answered after a couple of rings by a man, most likely Jonny's father. 'Hello.'

'Hello, this is Daveed, I'm a friend of Jonathan's. Is he there please?'

'No, I'm afraid he's not. He and his sister went away a couple of weeks ago. They're staying with a friend in Florida.'

'Do you know when they'll be back?' asked Viddy.

'They didn't say, I'm sorry. Would you like to leave a message for him?'

'No, no thank you,' said Viddy, putting the phone down.

So, Jonny and Berry were staying with Lydia in Florida. How did that come about, he wondered? He sat for a moment reflecting on it. His mother was always with Alain these days at Le Manoir, so he'd been alone much of the time, with plenty of time for soul searching. There was so much he had hoped to say to Jonny, but now he thought about it, a letter would probably be better than a phone call.

He went to his bedroom and pulled out some paper from the desk in his small study. The paper had the de Courcy crest printed at the top, its familiar lion standing up on its hind legs. It was the family crest that gave him away, he reflected. Clémence d'Apidae had somehow made the connection, and alerted his mother to his whereabouts.

He knew now that Lydia had played her part too, but he didn't feel angry – he felt quite the opposite. Whatever it cost him in the short term, it led to him being honest with his mother, and he couldn't have gone on without that. It even seemed to him, recently, that she was beginning to acknowledge what she had so far failed to accept.

Viddy picked up his fountain pen and began to write a letter to Jonny. An hour later, he folded the letter into four and tucked it into a Christmas card. He wrote another card for Lydia and another for Berry, and posted them by airmail, the next morning.

Two weeks before Christmas, Alberta came in with some envelopes.

'Mister Jonathan, Mizz Lydia, Mizz Berry, I reckon you all got some Christmas cards.' She handed them round.

'Thanks Alberta,' said Lydia.

'That reminds me, we've normally got our Christmas tree up at home by now,' said Berry.

Jonny recognised Viddy's handwriting immediately. He got up and took his envelope upstairs, then shut his bedroom door behind him. He ripped the envelope open, tossed the Christmas card aside and unfolded the letter.

2ⁿᵈ December
Château de Courcy
France

Dear Jonny

I tried to call you today. Your father told me that you are in Florida with Berry and Lydia. Lucky you. It's getting quite cold here now. Maman is spending a lot of time with Alain, at Le Manoir, so I've been alone a lot. I have had a lot to think about over the last couple of months, and I'm sorry I haven't been in touch before.

The truth is I haven't known what to say to you, Jonny. You saw me that day at my lowest ebb, and then you met Philippe. You made assumptions, Jonny. Wrong assumptions, then left without even asking me about it.

Philippe came back to Château de Courcy two weeks before you met him. He came back to see me and to see the garden once more. You see, he's getting married. He didn't want me to hear about it from someone else.

Jonny put the letter down onto his knee for a minute and sighed.

So, he'd got it wrong. Why hadn't he made more effort to speak to Viddy? He should have had more faith in him. What a mess! He picked up the letter and continued reading.

Hearing of Philippe's plans was a shock, and so disillusioning. You know how much I loved him – I was honest with you about that. It broke my heart when he left with his family, all those years ago.

He told me his love for me was the real thing. He said it took him years to get over leaving Château de Courcy. In the end though, he moved on. He didn't want to disappoint his family, and I can't blame him for that. I know what I've been through myself, and I wouldn't wish it on anyone.

Philippe left the next day to return to the south of France, and you left soon afterwards. I was alone here with Maman and Alain and it was stifling. If only you had tried harder to speak to me, I needed a friend more than anything, but you weren't there for me.

When you found me in the church that day, I was in despair. What you didn't know was that the church had become my regular place of sanctuary. When we first got back to Château de Courcy, all the old feelings of guilt and secrecy came back, and I knew I couldn't go through it again.

At first, I felt relief at having spoken my truth to Maman in England, and I believed it would be enough. All I wanted was for her to see me for who I really am. But as each day passed, I realised nothing had changed.

Anyway Jonny, I have decided to give up on love, at least on love as we have known it. I have been considering going into the church. The love of God transcends any other I have experienced, and it comes without the need to hide one's truth. The truth is the way with God. As long as I accept my truth, I trust that God will accept it too.

These are questions I have spent many hours discussing with the Curé. He has opened my eyes to the many things around me that are full of love. I have learned to see God in every living thing, in every beam of sunlight, in every leaf on every tree. Then at last, I began to feel Him in my heart. I cannot express the joy and solace it has brought me.

They say true love brings you closer to God, but there seem to be insurmountable barriers to ours, Jonny. Unless Maman can give me her blessing, I must live with God's guidance and do the best I can to be the Vicomte everybody hopes I will be.

I wish you every happiness my dear friend and a happy Christmas.

With love Viddy x

Jonathan flung the letter onto his bed and pulled on his swimming shorts. He walked down the stairs, past the girls dozing on their sun beds and launched himself into the sea. He swam and swam for all he was worth, until the house became a tiny square on a distant beach. Then he turned over and floated on his back, hands behind his head as he stared up at the sky. He was such a fool, so focused on himself and his own self-righteous feelings, that he'd failed his friend.

When he eventually swam back, he found the girls about to set off in the yellow van with James.

'We're going to get the Christmas tree,' said Berry. 'Do you want to come?'

'No thanks, I'll see you when you get back.'

'OK, see you later,' said Lydia. Jonny went upstairs to shower and dress. Alberta had left, so he made up his mind he was going to phone Viddy, while he had the house to himself.

He took the phone out onto the deck, and took some deep breaths, before dialling the Château de Courcy. It rang for a long time, before a breathless Guillemete eventually answered, 'Oui allo, Château de Courcy.'

'Bonjour, Guillemete,' said Jonathan. 'Is Daveed there?'

'No Monsieur, 'e is out.'

'Do you know when he will be back?'

'Non, Monsieur.'

'OK, don't worry, I'll call back another day,' he said.

'Very good, Monsieur' she said, and put the phone down.

Jonathan tried to speak to Viddy several times over the next few days, without success.

JUNIPER and JED

Juniper and Jed were kneeling side by side on the grass in Richmond, planting bulbs along the edges of Juniper's flower beds. They were planning a glorious display of crocuses and daffodils in the spring, followed by tulips in the early summer. When the last bulb was pushed firmly into the damp earth, Juniper stood up and took off her gardening gloves. 'Would you like a cup of coffee, Jed?'

'Love one,' he said, as he stood to gather their tools and the kneeling mats. They made their way inside through the hallway door, and Jed stowed the tools and hung up their coats. 'A nice morning's work,' he said, smiling at her.

'Your garden is next,' said Juniper. 'Shall we do it tomorrow?' Jed wondered how much longer he could wait before suggesting that they share both a home and a garden. He was biding his time.

As they sat enjoying coffee with one of Louise's home-made biscuits, Juniper said, 'Have you given any thought to Christmas yet? Do you have plans?'

'Actually, I do,' said Jed. Juniper's heart sank, but she kept her expression neutral. There was a silence as he watched her face. He knew her so well and marvelled at her ability to keep her true feelings hidden. 'As it happens,' he continued, 'I have plans to whisk you away to France. If you are free, that is.'

'To France?' she said; surprised and excited that he was, after all, planning Christmas with her.

'I would love to spend Christmas in France! Do you have somewhere in mind?'

'Yes, I do,' said Jed.

'Well, are you going to tell me where it is?'

'I'm going to take you to a hotel I know, in Honfleur. It is just behind the church of St Catherine. There is a wonderful restaurant there and a spa. It is very near the Vieux Bassin, the old harbour, surrounded by restaurants and boutiques. I think you will love it,' he said.

'Jed, that sounds perfect! I would love to.' She was quiet for a moment and then she said, 'Actually, I have been thinking a lot about Roger lately. It's so long since I've seen him - and Julie, of course. My heart aches sometimes for the rift between us. I sometimes wonder whether it can ever be fully repaired.'

'Everything is repairable, my darling,' he said to Juniper. 'You must never give up hope. You are his mother and he loves you, whatever baggage still lingers from the past. Perhaps it's time you both put it behind you. Where do they live, exactly?'

'They have a small house in Normandy, on my ex-husband's estate. When they are not in Normandy, they live on their narrow boat in Paris. Roger often exhibits his art there, and they use it as a base.'

'When did you last see them?' asked Jed.

'It was at least two years ago; it makes me so sad.'

'Well, we need to change that,' said Jed. 'I've had an idea, leave it with me for a few days, and I'll make a couple of phone calls.'

Then Jed added, 'By the way, how do you feel about taking the yacht over to France? We may be able to moor in the Vieux Bassin?'

'Oh, I don't know, Jed. It's such a long way and it will be winter. Have you sailed the Channel at that time of year before?'

'I have,' he said. 'It is a very long sail, and we may have to wait several days to get the right weather conditions. Perhaps we should travel across in comfort, on the ferry. Let's give it some thought.' Then he got up to put their cups into the dishwasher.

'Leave it Jed, Louise will do that. Come here.' Jed walked over to where she sat on one of the bar chairs. Juniper pulled him close, wrapping her arms around his waist. She laid her cheek against his shoulder, enjoying the feel of cashmere against her skin. 'I love you so much, you know,' she said.

'And I you,' said Jed, pulling her to her feet and kissing her deeply. Her heart lifted with happiness, she was blessed to have this kind and wonderful man in her life. 'I need to get back now,' he said. 'Shall I pick you up tomorrow?'

'No, I'll drive myself over to you, and bring the bulbs with me,' she said.

The next day, Juniper walked along the river in the morning, and stopped for coffee at her usual place. It was chilly, with no sign of the sun, but she sat down anyway, to enjoy her hot drink outside. 'Your friend not with you today?' said the cheery waitress.

'Not today,' said Juniper smiling. As the waitress walked away, she remembered the day she met Jed, and the frosty reception she gave him. If only she had known then, how happy they could be together.

It was early afternoon by the time Juniper swung into the gates of Jed's riverside home, and the sun was pushing through thinning clouds. 'Hello, my darling,' he said, as she stepped out of the car, dressed in her gardening clothes.

'Don't worry,' she said quickly. 'I have brought another outfit with me, but I don't suppose the light will last long. We probably ought to get straight on with the planting.'

'Aye aye, Captain,' said Jed, giving her a mock salute, before taking her in his arms and kissing her. 'Let's get to it.' He led the way down the garden, towards the river. They planned to plant an abundance of daffodils, not only to cheer passing boats, but to frame the river as they looked down on it from the house.

Two hours later, they were back inside and the light was fading. Jed took their coats and boots and went into the kitchen to make some tea. 'I'm really cold,' said Juniper.

'I think it was quite damp by the river,' he said. 'I'll light a fire while we wait for the kettle to boil.'

'While you do that, I'm going to have a hot shower, if you don't mind. I won't be long.' Juniper emerged twenty minutes later in a pair of mustard coloured, flared trousers and a cream high necked jumper. She'd draped an Hermès scarf around her neck and looked the epitome of elegance. A pair of mustard leather loafers completed her outfit, and she kicked these off to curl her legs up under her, on the sofa by the fire.

They sipped their tea in companionable silence and after a while, Jed said, 'I called the hotel in Honfleur yesterday. I have booked a suite for us for a few days, over Christmas.'

'Oh, how lovely! Thank you, Jed.' Juniper looked at him and smiled.

Then he said, 'I have also provisionally reserved a second one, for Roger and Julie. Do you think they would like to join us?'

'Oh Jed, you darling. That sounds perfect! The only hurdle

will be my reaching out to invite them, and them agreeing to come. I wonder whether they could bring their narrow boat along the Seine from Paris?'

'I don't see why not,' said Jed.

'I'll write to Roger tomorrow,' said Juniper.

'Good,' he said. 'Now, about this evening.'

'What about this evening?' asked Juniper.

'I would like to take you out to dinner,' he said. 'There is a little French bistro I know, not far from here. The owners are friends; I think you'll like it.'

The restaurant was enchanting. It was small and intimate, with twinkling candles on the tables and pretty plants trailing from the ceiling in the conservatory. There was a view across the river, where boats and barges were lit with lanterns and strings of lights, over their small decks.

The food was everything good French food should be. The freshest, simplest ingredients, combined with marvellous sauces, good wines and cheese. Juniper and Jed laughed together as they enjoyed their meal, pausing to compliment the chef, as he made his rounds.

Their table was tucked away in a small alcove overlooking the water, and Juniper glanced outside every now and again, enjoying the sight of the boats, imagining people enjoying food together, perhaps listening to soft music as their boats swayed gently on the water.

When Juniper looked back at Jed, he was looking at her lovingly. 'Juniper, my love.' She reached out to take his hand, and he lifted it to his lips, kissing it gently. She watched his dear face, now so familiar to her, and her heart filled with love. Without her noticing, Jed reached into his pocket with his other hand, and pulled out a small velvet box. He opened it and placed it on the table in front of her, revealing a large, oval, yellow diamond. 'My darling Juniper, I have loved you from the moment I first saw you. Will you do me the honour of becoming my wife?'

ROGER and JULIE

Roger was outside, sweeping the remains of the autumn leaves from the terrace, when Julie called to him from inside. 'Roger, there's a letter for you. It looks like your mother's writing.'

'I'll be there in a minute,' he called back. For the last few days he'd been spending long hours in his studio, working on the final canvases for his upcoming exhibition in Paris. Julie wondered whether they may finally be finished.

She was focusing on bringing in cushions, and some of her more fragile garden sculptures, ready for the winter. They would leave for Paris in a few days and spend the next two weeks on the narrow boat. They might even spend Christmas on it, thought Julie. She loved being afloat, it reminded her of happy times looking after Cedric, Astrid's ginger cat. Astrid was the original owner of her narrow boat on the Seine. She'd asked Julie to look after it for her one summer, when ill health unexpectedly forced her to move back to her family in Canada. Soon afterwards, Astrid sent for her cat, and gifted Julie her boat. It was hard to believe it was five years ago. Julie's hand travelled protectively to her belly, and she smiled. There was so much to look forward to.

Roger came in from the garden, cheeks pink from the cold, and took off his boots. They were splattered with paint from the studio, as were his arms and hands. He went over to the sink to scrub up. After drying his hands, he flicked the kettle on for some coffee and slumped down in one of the wicker chairs beside the AGA. 'Here you are,' said Julie, handing him the letter.

Roger took the envelope from her and looked at the date; it was posted a week ago. It was unusual to get a letter from his mother, and he was curious. As he began to read, Julie placed a cup of coffee beside him, and then sat down in the other chair, stretching her legs out in the warmth.

De Montfort House
Richmond
London

Dear Roger

How are you? I hope you are enjoying life and that you and Julie are happy. It seems so long since I saw you both. I had lunch with Lydia recently, which was a rare treat.

I am sure you have heard the sad news that Grandmère Clémence passed away at the end of September. She and Lydia were very close. I found out recently that they wrote to one another regularly. Lydia has certainly had her problems over the years. I am thankful that Clémence was a support to her.

I know that you, Lydia and I, have not seen eye to eye in recent years, Roger. I also know that I am by no means, blameless. Sometimes, I wish I could turn the clock back, and remedy some of my mistakes, but of course, none of us have that luxury. Hindsight is a wonderful thing.

However, there comes a time when we have to accept the past, in all its imperfection, and put it to rest. We have to move forward, learn from our mistakes, and do the best we can.

Anyway, darling, enough of all that. We have had quite an adventure over the last few months and I have many things to tell you. I have made some new friends. A French lady, Christine de Courcy, arrived on my doorstep a couple of months ago, searching for her lost son. Coincidentally, I had also just met a wonderful man, called Jed. Jed has become a close friend and a great supporter.

To cut a long story short, the three of us set out on a quest to find Christine's missing son. Apparently, it was Grandmère Clémence who tipped off Christine in the first place. It turned out that the missing son was to inherit their family Château in France. (I told you, it's a long story.)

Darling, I won't say more now. I would love to properly catch up with you both in person. Now, to the point of my letter. Roger, it would mean the world to me if you and Julie would join Jed and me in Honfleur for Christmas. Jed has taken the liberty of reserving two suites at a lovely hotel, in the

*hope that you will both spend Christmas with us. Perhaps you
could even cruise from Paris, on your narrow boat?*

*Please let me know darling, just as soon as you have
decided. Until then, I will keep my fingers crossed that we can
all be together again to celebrate, in a few weeks' time.*

Your loving mother,

Juniper de Montfort

When Roger finished reading the letter, he passed it to Julie and
said, 'There I was imagining Mum living a quiet life of repentance at
de Montfort House, when in fact, her life sounds more interesting
than ours! Have a read of that.'

Julie took the letter from him, and when she had finished
reading, she said, 'I think it's a lovely letter, Roger. We should
definitely go and meet them in Honfleur. The exhibition finishes
on 19th December, at least your part in it. It will take us a few days
to get there by narrow boat, or we could take the train?'

'Yes, you're right, we should go,' he said. 'It's time to move
on' said Roger. The next morning, Roger dialled his mother at de
Montfort House.

'Hello Mum, it's me, Roger.'

'Darling, what a lovely surprise. How are you both?'

'We are fine, Mum. Thank you for your letter, it was so nice to
hear from you.' Juniper sighed and smiled.

'Is your art going well?' she asked. 'I hear you have an exhibition
coming up.'

'I do, yes. Julie is fine too, she is sculpting now. She loves it.'

'I'm so glad to hear it,' said Juniper. 'Darling, we have so much
catching up to do, and lost time to make up. Do you think you
would like to join us for Christmas?'

'That's why I'm phoning,' he said. 'We'd love to. Jed sounds
nice, I'm glad you've made some friends, Mum.'

'I'm delighted,' said Juniper. 'Jed will be too. He's met Lydia,
and I know he's looking forward to meeting you and Julie too.'

'Likewise,' said Roger.

'It may be that you will also meet Christine de Courcy and
her son. He's about your age. I'm planning to invite them on
Christmas Eve, while we are in Honfleur. Do you think you will

come from Paris on the narrow boat?'

'I'm not sure yet. We're going to give that some thought over the next few days. I am in the run up to my exhibition. That's taking up most of my time at the moment. I'll let you know. If we do bring the boat, we'll probably prefer to stay on it, if that's OK, Mum? It'll be easier.'

'Alright darling, if that's what you prefer. Just let me know once you've decided.'

'I will. Whatever happens, we will be in Honfleur by the end of the day, on 23rd December.'

'That's wonderful darling, I can't wait! Give my love to Julie, and I look forward to seeing you both very soon.'

CHÂTEAU DE COURCY

As Christine left the church after Sunday service, elegant in a cherry red, wool coat with a velvet collar, there was a sprinkling of frost on the ground. She took her soft leather gloves from her handbag, and pulled them on. The sun was breaking through into a clear blue sky, making the holly berries sparkle, reminding her it was almost Christmas. She loved this time of year. The château was so pretty, lit up with white lights, twinkling in the trees. Traditionally, there was always an enormous, decorated tree in the hall, to welcome friends. She wondered whether Daveed would want to continue the tradition next year. After all, by then, it would be up to him.

Alain had tried to make her see that it was unhealthy to try to stay in control at the Château. He even suggested that Christine's reluctance to hand over to Daveed might be stifling him. 'He will make mistakes to start with,' Alain told her, 'but he needs to be allowed to find his own way.' Her reverie was interrupted by the Curé approaching. 'Bonjour Vicomtesse. What a beautiful morning, isn't it?' He reached out and shook her hand, smiling affably.

'It certainly is,' said Christine. 'A lovely service too Curé, thank you.'

'I wonder whether I might impose upon your time later this week, Vicomtesse. There is something I would welcome the opportunity to discuss with you.'

Christine wondered what it could be – perhaps he wanted some help with the Christmas flower arranging. 'Of course Curé, perhaps you would like to come to the Château for a tisane tomorrow afternoon. Shall we say 3 p.m.?'

The Curé arrived promptly, his long cassock billowing in the wind as he came through the door of the Château. 'Please, come in,' said Christine, leading the way into the drawing room. A welcoming fire was burning in the grate, and they sat near it, opposite one another, on comfortable velvet sofas. Christine poured them each a tisane, placing a thin slice of lemon into the wide china cups. She passed one across to the priest.

'So, Curé, how can I help you today?' Christine had already checked her diary, confirming that she would be able to help with the church flowers, if asked.

'This is rather delicate,' said the Curé. 'I hope I am not speaking out of turn, but it concerns the young Vicomte.'

'Oh?' said Christine. She was unaware that the Curé had met Daveed, other than on a few family occasions.

He continued, 'I have been privileged to have a number of private conversations with your son, in recent months, Vicomtesse. He has expressed a wish to join the church.'

'The church?' said Christine, trying to hide her astonishment.

'Yes, I had a feeling this might come as a surprise to you,' he said. For a moment, Christine was lost for words.

Then, drawing on the strength of her family heritage, she replied smoothly, 'It is true that Daveed has always enjoyed spending time in our family chapel. I think it brings him comfort. I understand that he has also, on occasion, spent time in private contemplation in the church, Curé.'

'Yes,' said the priest. 'He has.' He paused. 'You may not be aware, that I happened upon him one day, a few months ago, quite by chance. He was kneeling in one of the church pews. I could hear muffled sounds, and as I approached, I saw that the young man was crying his heart out.' Christine struggled to hide her shock.

'Are you sure?' she asked. 'Could it have been that he had a cold? He does tend to suffer in the winter months.' The priest appeared not to hear this, or if he did, he dismissed it.

'When the Vicomte realised I was there; he was mortified to have been found at such a moment. He dried his eyes, and stood to greet me; but was unable to hide the extent of his distress. That day was the start of many talks he and I have had, over the last few months.'

Christine wondered how she could not have known about this. Her assumption was always, that Daveed was in his garden, happy among his plants. She had seen little of him lately. She had deliberately withdrawn, to some extent. It was her way of convincing herself that she was handing the reins over to her son. In reality, she knew she was still in control of daily life at the chateau. That needed to change, she realised now.

She looked at the priest and said, without emotion, 'Do you think your talks have helped? Have you managed to discover what is troubling my son?'

'It is not so much that I have discovered what is troubling him, at least not specifically. Even if I had, I'm sure you understand that I would not be in a position to divulge any confidence he may have shared.' Christine looked at him, her face expressionless. 'No,' he continued thoughtfully. 'My concern is not so much what is troubling him, but the fact that something clearly is. I believe he feels that whatever it is, is insurmountable.'

Christine's heart began to beat a little faster and she felt a flush creep up her neck. 'What do you advise, Curé?' she asked, to hide her discomfort.

'I wonder whether your son might be persuaded to share with you, what he is unable to share with me,' he said. 'I would like to be able to help him. You see, as I said earlier, he has expressed a wish to join the church.' He paused for a moment, searching for the right words. 'My concern is that he is running away from something. He is looking for a refuge, a sanctuary from whatever is troubling him. These are not the right reasons to seek a life in the church. Of course we, in the church, are here to soothe troubled souls; but we cannot soothe the souls of our flock, if we are deeply troubled ourselves. Do you see, Vicomtesse?'

Christine stood up, 'Thank you Curé, for bringing this to my attention. I intend to make a sizeable donation to the church fund this year, to thank you for your kindness and of course, your discretion.'

'Very kind indeed, Vicomtesse,' he said, rising from the sofa.

The next day, Christine made a point of being in the dining room when Daveed appeared for breakfast. 'Good morning darling, it seems so long since we have sat down together. How are you?'

'I'm well, Maman, thank you.'

'That's good,' she said. As Daveed poured himself a cup of coffee, she continued, 'I had a visit from the Curé yesterday.' Daveed's hand began to shake as he held the coffee pot, his back to his mother. 'He tells me you are considering going into the church.' The colour drained from Daveed's face, and he turned to look at his mother.

'Maman, that is a private matter. It is not something I am ready to discuss with you.'

'Darling,' said Christine, smiling serenely. 'I only want to try to help you see, that running Château de Courcy will be a full time job for you. I'm afraid there won't be time for the church as well.' Daveed said nothing, as he walked towards the table holding his cup. Christine continued, 'Alain has made me see that it is time I got out of your way, darling. How can you possibly step into the shoes of the new Vicomte, if I am always around?'

'Maman, if you insist on talking about this, let's talk; but you won't like what I have to say.' Christine sat back in her chair, and he sat down opposite her, his cup of black coffee in front of him.

'Try me darling, I only have your best interests at heart, you know that.'

Daveed drew a deep breath, and then said, 'Maman, I'm finally going to speak frankly to you. I am tired of tiptoeing around half-truths. I could not have been plainer, in my many attempts to be honest with you, over the past few months. I can see now that I have no choice but to spell it out to you.'

He paused and looked her squarely in the face, 'Maman, I was in love with Jonny. I wanted us to have a life together, here at the Château.' Christine took a sharp intake of breath, but her face remained neutral, and she did not interrupt him. 'With Jonny by my side, I could have taken on the world. Can't you see that my life is not worth living, if it is a lie? That is why I went away.' He paused, then said with emphasis, 'I could not, and still cannot bear, your deliberate blindness to the truth of who I am. I am your son, Maman! Look at me! If I can't be with Jonny, or at the very least, live a truthful life, I will not take on the château. I will not.' Then he said, more quietly, 'That is why I have decided to join the church.'

Christine looked down and contemplated her hands, a flush of shame creeping up her cheeks, in the long silence. Daveed waited, his gaze fixed on her face, hoping she would finally acknowledge him. Eventually, still looking down at her hands, she said, 'Alain has asked me to marry him.'

Daveed looked at her with contempt, then got up from the table and walked out of the room. Christine called after him, 'Daveed, I almost forgot, there is a letter for you. It's in the hall.'

Daveed did not turn round, but picked up the letter as he walked through the hall. Seeing the Florida postmark, he took the stairs up to his bedroom, two at a time, and tore it open. His heart sank; it was from Lydia, inviting him to a party. He threw the invitation down on his desk, pulled on a warm jacket and headed out to the garden.

HONFLEUR

The weather was forecast crisp and cold with some light winds, giving Juniper and Jed near perfect conditions, to sail the Channel. They left the marina early in the morning, having loaded the yacht with plenty of supplies, warm clothes and numerous bags of carefully wrapped Christmas presents.

Juniper's Christmas wardrobe was stowed in a large suitcase, in one of the two smaller cabins that extended beneath the cockpit. She was apprehensive about the trip, but Jed's enthusiasm was infectious. It would be so exciting to arrive in Honfleur, aboard the yacht; even better, Roger and Julie would be there. With Jed by her side, Juniper felt she could face almost anything.

After a few hours on the water, with the wind behind them, they began to cross the busy part of the Channel. Jed was on full alert; he explained that it could be like crossing a busy motorway, such was the volume of traffic coming through the shipping lanes.

At Jed's insistence, before the trip, Juniper attended a basic, competent crew course. She needed to understand how to help him, in the event of an emergency, he explained; as well as be conversant with sailing terms and language.

They sailed often along the coast to Chichester, and Juniper became increasingly familiar with the navigation equipment, and the things she could do to be helpful on board. It was all a bit of an adventure for her. It hadn't crossed her mind, until now, that her competence could mean the difference between life and death. Juniper shuddered, as they continued to navigate the busy shipping lanes. 'The Dover Straight is the busiest,' Jed told her, raising his voice over the wind and chop of the water. 'That's the narrowest crossing point. It's much wider here, but we need to be vigilant for ships straying from their lanes. There is a lane in each direction, so there will be a quieter area as we move between the two.'

Once they were well clear of the shipping lanes, Jed's relief was palpable. Juniper too, breathed a sigh of relief, as the Channel became quiet and darkness began to fall. Jed set the yacht to auto-helm, on a course for Le Havre, and Juniper brought up two mugs of tea and some biscuits. They sat companionably on the rear deck, sipping their drinks as Jed explained the plan. 'There is a marina just inside the mouth of the Seine, at Le Havre. We will anchor there overnight, then find somewhere for dinner. Tomorrow, we'll sail along the Seine to Honfleur.'

By the time they had finished their tea, it was dark. 'Come on,' said Jed, 'there's something I want to show you.' Clipped safely to the yacht, and bundled up in warm clothes and safety jackets, Jed led Juniper along the narrow deck, until the bow was wide enough for them to lie down together, side by side. Once they were comfortably resting on their backs, Jed reached out for Juniper's hand and they gazed up into the night sky.

'Have you ever seen anything more beautiful?' he said. The myriad of stars over their heads were like yellow diamonds, piercing a velvet sky; shining brightly through unadulterated, deep, midnight blue.

Juniper was reminded, quite suddenly, of a night in Normandy, and a moment that changed her life. The stars studded a vast, velvet sky then, too. She sighed – it was time to let it go.

'I'm so thankful that I met you, Jed; and yes, this is probably one of the most beautiful moments of my life,' she said, turning her face towards him. He pushed up onto his elbow then and leaned over to kiss her cool, soft lips.

The next day, as Jed waited on the yacht, behind towering lock gates at the entrance to the port of Honfleur, Juniper was on the pontoon beside it. She had looped ropes from the yacht, around the base of the cleats, and then thrown the ends back to Jed. This enabled him to hold the yacht in position, as the water level and the pontoon rose. Another yacht bobbed on the other side of the lock, and Jed gave them a brief nod and a raise of his hand, in acknowledgement, as the water level brought them slowly up. Once they were alongside the harbour wall, Juniper stepped back on board, and the lock gates opened, allowing them into the port.

As they sailed into Honfleur, small flags were flying, and the old port thronged with little boats. Around the bassin, colourful awnings fluttered over people enjoying seafood in the winter sunshine. Tall, narrow buildings were squeezed together to form a four storey wall of colourful, colombage architecture on every side. Little boutiques jostled for position along the quayside. It was a feast for the senses.

As Jed manoeuvred the yacht alongside a narrow pontoon, someone stood ready to grab the line, loop it around the bollard and pass it back to him to secure to the yacht. 'Merci beaucoup,' he called, with a raise of his hand. 'That's it, we're in!' he said to Juniper, cutting the engine.

The hotel was just a short walk from the bassin. When the narrow, cobblestone lane opened out onto a pretty square, Jed pointed to their hotel, 'There it is,' he said. Juniper took in the pretty, flint-finished building nestled among soft, evergreen climbers and fairy lights. Grey awnings extended towards slate planters of box hedges, creating an intimate terrace where guests were enjoying tea and coffee, with a view across the square.

'This is lovely, Jed,' she said. 'Such a beautiful church, too.'

'That's the Église St Catherine,' said Jed. 'It is many centuries old, and said to be the largest wooden church in France. I'll take you over there before we leave; the inside is quite beautiful and unique. I believe there may be a Christmas Eve service.'

'If there is, I'd love to go,' she said.

The hotel welcomed them like old friends, with informality, relaxation and charm. They were shown to a large suite, with a view across the square and rooftops, to the sea beyond. It was comfortable and stylish. Juniper breathed a sigh of relief, happy to have her creature comforts restored to her. After nearly forty-eight hours on board the yacht, she was tired and longing for a soak in a deep bath.

She admired the pretty sofa and armchairs, and the fruits and flowers set out on a low table, before walking through to the bedroom. The bed had a sumptuously padded, floral headboard and generous feather pillows. 'I won't be long,' called Jed. 'I'm just going downstairs to make sure our dinner reservations are in place for tomorrow. Enjoy your bath, darling.'

When Jed reached the reception area, a young man in beige chinos, deck shoes and a white t-shirt, was at the desk. He was broad shouldered, with thick dark hair. 'Hello,' he said to the receptionist. 'I'm Roger d'Apidae. Has my mother checked in yet?'

Jed stepped forward, his hand outstretched, 'Roger, welcome. I'm Jed; your mother's friend.'

'Jed, how nice to meet you,' said Roger. 'We've just arrived. We're on the boat, but I wanted to let you know, we're here.'

'Did you have a good journey?'

'Pretty good, yes, thank you. So, what's the plan?'

'We only arrived ourselves, half an hour ago. We came across the Channel on my yacht; it was quite an adventure. Juniper is exhausted. I believe, as we speak, she is soaking in a hot bath.'

'I don't blame her,' he said. 'I look forward to hearing more about your trip later.'

'Why don't you come and meet us for a drink at the hotel, around seven?' said Jed. 'Afterwards we can stroll around the harbour. I've booked a little restaurant, overlooking the water, for 8 p.m.'

'Sounds perfect,' said Roger. He shook Jed's hand, then turned and left.

Later, Juniper and Jed made their way down the elegant staircase in good time, to greet Roger and Julie in the cocktail bar. Juniper wore a red, silk-jersey dress with an elegant cowl neckline. The dress curved in soft folds from her shoulders and skimmed her trim body, before flaring around her calves. Her shoes were red flats, each embellished with a neat, gold oval.

Jed couldn't take his eyes off her. She moved with such grace, he reflected, as he watched her make her way to their table in the bar. Her dark hair was held off her face with a velvet hairband and she wore gold twists in her ears and at her throat. When she sat down and smiled up at him, Jed's heart filled with love and gratitude. 'Would you like a glass of champagne, my darling?' he asked her.

'Mmmm, I'd love one, thank you.' Jed ordered their drinks, then sat down beside Juniper and took her hand.

'Are you ready?' he asked. She smiled serenely at him.

'I'm as ready as I'll ever be,' she said. A moment later, Roger and Julie walked into the bar. Roger wore beige trousers, a white shirt and a navy, tweed sports jacket, and Julie, a pale pink dress with a matching wrap. 'Come and join us,' said Jed, stepping forward to greet them, smiling. 'You must be Julie.' Julie smiled, and as she reached out to shake Jed's hand, he lifted it to his lips, and placed a gallant kiss on her knuckles. 'Delighted to meet you, Julie,' he said.

'Jed, you are a charmer,' said Juniper, smiling, as she moved towards Roger. 'Hello darling,' she said, reaching out to take both Roger's hands in hers.

'You look lovely, Mum,' he said, pulling her to him in a big bear hug. She was relieved.

'I'm so happy to see you,' she said. 'You too Julie, you look absolutely radiant.'

'Juniper is having champagne, and I'm having a scotch,' said Jed. 'What can I get you both?'

As they sipped their drinks, Roger talked about his exhibition in Paris. 'It went really well,' he said. 'I've received a few commissions. It felt good to show my face in Paris again, after so many months in the country, preparing for the show.'

As they strolled out to the restaurant, lights twinkled around awnings, and little boutiques spilled their colourful wares onto the quayside. People with rosy cheeks and shining eyes, watched the carousel, as its horses rose and fell, to the music of the accordion. The atmosphere was vibrant and festive, and a sense of excitement, lit Juniper's face.

The bistro specialised in seafood, so they ordered langoustines in a creamy lemon sauce, as well as artichokes to pull and dip. After that, they chose freshly caught sea bass, grilled, with butter and herbs. Their table had a view of the yachts bobbing on the water; each was flying flags on its mast, the tips of which shone with a small white light. 'There's ours,' said Juniper, pointing out one of the yachts nearby, swaying on its moorings.

'Wow,' said Julie. 'How was the trip across the Channel?'

'I loved it,' said Juniper. 'I didn't expect to, but as it was, I don't think I will ever forget it.' Her eyes became dreamy and wistful, and then she looked up and smiled at Jed. 'Actually darling,' she said to Roger, 'we have something to share with you both, don't we Jed.' At that moment, Roger caught sight of the oval, yellow diamond flashing on his mother's finger, and his face broke into a smile.

'Mum, don't tell me the two of you are engaged?' he said, delighted.

'We are,' said Jed. 'I feel like the luckiest man on earth.'

'Congratulations,' said Julie and Roger together.

'I'm so happy for you Mum,' said Roger. They gently touched their glasses together, to toast the news. 'Have you set a date for the wedding?'

'Not yet, but perhaps next summer,' said Juniper. She smiled – delighted that Roger had taken the news so well.

'Why wouldn't he?' Jed said later. 'Roger has his own busy life to lead, and seems happy with Julie. They're much too busy to worry about what their parents are doing,' he said, wisely. 'All they really want, I think, is to know that their parents are happy, so that they don't have to worry about them.' They'd laughed then.

'You always manage to put things into perspective for me Jed, thank you.'

CHRISTMAS EVE

Without Alain's intervention, Daveed would probably not have joined them for Christmas Eve, in Honfleur.

When Christine told Alain the whole, sorry story, she included her conversation with Jonathan, which up to now, she had kept to herself. 'When I heard some of the same things from the Curé,' she said, 'I felt so ashamed. I have let my son down so badly, Alain. I have denied his feelings, refused to listen to him.' She sighed. 'It was a different world when I was growing up. Duty came before everything else. It was always, "do this for the family, do that for the family, don't let the family down", and so on. It is all I have ever known. How could I have been so lacking in compassion?' She paused. 'I have lost my way Alain, and I don't know what to do.'

Alain held Christine close, stroking her hair. 'Don't you worry, ma Cherie. It is late now but we're going to have a long conversation about this in the morning. Everything is going to be alright, I promise you.'

'Daveed, have you got a minute to show me the vegetable gardens?' said Alain, a few days before Christmas. 'Guillemete wants me to bring in some broccoli.'

'Sure,' he said. 'I'll get my coat. I can go, if you like.'

'No, come on,' said Alain, 'Let's get some air.' As they strolled over the frosty ground, coats buttoned up, hands in pockets, their breath rose in clouds around them. 'I love this time of year,' said Alain. 'The frost seems to create a special kind of silence, insulated somehow, muffled. A bit like when it snows.'

'I know what you mean,' said Daveed, surprised. He hadn't put Alain down as a man, sensitive to the rhythms of nature. As if reading his mind, Alain said, 'I've looked after horses most of my life; I often came out at dawn to take care of them. I've always loved the changing sights and sounds of the seasons – mostly the stillness of it.' They walked on in companionable silence.

'How's Maman?' asked Daveed. 'I haven't seen much of her lately. We had a bit of a fall out, actually. I may have spoken more harshly than I intended. I hate to think I might have hurt her.'

'She's alright,' said Alain. 'Like many of us, she struggles to keep up with an ever changing world. It isn't always easy for us dinosaurs, you know?' Daveed laughed, he liked Alain. He was a kind man, and easy to talk to.

'Did Maman tell you, I'm thinking of joining the church?'

'She did,' he said. 'I was surprised.'

'Were you?'

'Well, yes, I was. I thought your future was here, at the Château. What makes you want to cut yourself off like that?'

'I don't want to cut myself off, exactly. The problem is I'm in love with someone. If I can't be with that person, then my life has no meaning.'

'Ah, I see,' he said. 'Yes, that does tend to be the nature of love. What is stopping you from being with the person you love?'

'Maman refuses to give me her blessing; it doesn't fit in with her vision of my future.'

'Ah, I see,' said Alain. He paused, 'Does this have something to do with the young man who spent the summer here? Jonathan?' Daveed went quiet; his mother must have told Alain. 'Yes, your mother told me,' Alain continued. 'Do you want to know what I said?'

'Yes,' said Daveed, surprised. 'What did you say?'

'I told her, I wanted her to start thinking about us; about her and me. You see, I've loved her for a very long time, Daveed. Perhaps with my own selfish motives in mind, I asked her to give it all up. I said that you, like every other person, must choose the life you want. You should not be held back by what others think of your choices.'

'It's easy for you to say that, but Maman's blessing means everything to me. I cannot live freely and happily, if I am under the cloud of her disapproval. I care for her too much for that.'

'Give her time, Daveed. She knows she has treated you badly; she said as much to me the other day. I want you to give her a chance to make this right.'

There was a silence while Daveed reflected on this, then he

said, 'Are you asking me to come to Honfleur with you both, for Réveillon?'

'Yes, of course I am. We have all been invited; it will be an opportunity for you to build bridges with your mother. Apart from that, there will be a young couple of your own age there. I believe they'll be coming from Paris on their narrow boat.' Daveed was interested now.

'That sounds cool,' he said. 'Alright, I'll come.'

The de Courcys arrived at the hotel with Alain, in the early afternoon on Christmas Eve. Alain had managed to reserve their last two rooms, so that everyone could relax over a leisurely evening.

'I wonder why the French call Christmas Eve, Réveillon,' said Julie, as she applied her make up, using a tiny, inadequate mirror over the galley sink.

'It's basically a night when people don't sleep, they stay awake to watch out for Father Christmas,' said Roger. 'The word comes from réveiller, to wake up.'

'Ah, I see,' she said. 'Did you finish wrapping the gifts?' she asked him, examining her lipstick.

'Ju, I don't think I've seen you in make up for the longest time,' said Roger. 'Come over here,' he pulled her onto his knee, and buried his face in her soft curls, as he kissed her neck. 'You look beautiful.' He smiled at her, 'There's just one thing missing.' He took out a small, gift-wrapped box, and handed it to her. 'Happy Christmas, Ju.'

She opened the box to reveal a dazzling, dark green pendant, set into fine, hammered gold. 'I want you to wear this tonight,' he said.

'Oh Roger, it's beautiful,' she said. She carefully took the necklace out of the box, and held it up to the light.

'It's a green diamond,' said Roger. 'They are rare, like you my love. I hope you like it,' he said smiling.

'I love it,' said Julie, taking his face between her hands and kissing him gently on the lips. 'It will be perfect with my dress.'

They stepped off the narrow boat, looking for all the world, like a couple of film stars. Roger wore a black bow tie and smart dinner suit, while Julie was graceful in a deep green, satin dress. It fitted neatly across her narrow shoulders, which were framed with ruched satin sleeves. The dress fell to her knees in a wide A-line, its hem gathered to form a fashionable puff-ball skirt. Her shoes were low court shoes, in matching green.

When they arrived at the hotel, they were directed up to Jed and Juniper's suite. Jed answered the door, wearing a smart, black dinner suit, 'Come on in,' he said, smiling. 'Don't you both look nice.' As they stepped into the suite, Juniper emerged from the bedroom in a pleated column of sage-green silk, falling to her ankles. The dress had wide organza sleeves, finished with long, silk cuffs.

'Juniper,' said Julie, stepping forward to greet her. 'You look gorgeous.'

'You too,' said Juniper. 'What a lovely colour on you. We're the girls in green,' she added, conspiratorially.

Just then, there was another knock at the door. Christine, dressed in a midnight blue, velvet gown, walked in on Alain's arm, followed by Daveed. Both men were immaculately dressed in black dinner suits.

'Come in, come in,' said Jed, arms held wide. 'How lovely to see you again, Christine. You must be Alain,' he said, turning to him and shaking his hand.

'Enchanté,' said Alain. 'This is Daveed, Christine's son,' he said.

'Viddy,' he clarified, stepping forward to shake Jed's hand, and to kiss Juniper lightly on both cheeks.

'Viddy,' said Juniper, 'this is my son, Roger, and his partner, Julie.' As the young people chatted, Juniper and Christine lit up at the sight of one another. They had shared so much over the last few months. They were a little like kindred spirits; cut from the same cloth, thought Juniper, as she stepped forward to kiss Christine on both cheeks.

'How lovely to see you again, Christine,' said Juniper, delighted.

'Juniper, it feels like such a long time. How are you?'

'Very well indeed, as it happens,' she said winking at Christine. 'I'll tell you more, later,' she whispered.

'Great to meet you, Viddy,' said Roger.

'You too,' said Viddy. 'Is it true that you came to Honfleur on a narrow boat?' he asked.

'It is,' said Roger. 'We came from Paris – I had an exhibition of my work there.'

'That sounds interesting,' said Viddy. 'I'd love to see the boat.'

'Come on board after dinner, if you like,' said Roger. 'We can have a nightcap.'

'Now, what can I get everyone to drink?' said Jed. 'We have chilled champagne, gin and tonic, lime cordial and almost everything in between.' There was a selection of delectable canapés arranged on the table, and a wide bar had been provided for them on the sideboard.

An hour later, the group emerged from the suite, laughing and chatting, as they headed downstairs for dinner. The restaurant was lit with twinkling lights, and a large Christmas tree decorated with red bows. Jed led the way to their round table, set with crystal glasses and red linen napkins. In the centre, a wreath of holly and yew, encircled with tiny white lights, cast a warm glow around the table.

The Christmas meal was an elegant feast, starting with two neat squares of foie gras, served on white oblong plates. A deep china spoon, placed beside it, held a portion of onion chutney. The plate was sprinkled with dried cranberries and coarse sea salt. 'This is delicious,' said Christine. 'Foie gras has always been one of my favourites.'

'Mine too,' said Jed spreading a generous portion onto a crisp, sliver of toast. After that, slices of perfectly cooked goose were served with plum sauce, along with neat, artistic little stacks of vegetables. Roger raised his glass in a toast before they began.

'Thank you so much for inviting us Mum, and Jed. It is so nice to be together. Happy Christmas.' There were murmurs of happy Christmas around the table as they sipped their wine and began to eat.

'This is such a treat,' said Julie. 'For the last couple of weeks, I've been trying to cook on the little stove on the narrow boat. It's been a bit hit and miss,' she laughed.

'That's true,' said Roger, winking at her.

'I can't imagine living in such a narrow space,' said Christine.

'Oh, we love it,' said Julie. 'Every day is an adventure, and we've met some really interesting people on the river.'

When they had finished eating, Jed ordered some more wine to go with the cheese.

'Ooh, look at that cheese board,' said Roger, as a waiter approached with a trolley laden with cheese.

'Mont d'Or is my favourite,' said Christine. 'I wonder whether they have it.'

'I don't think I know that one,' said Juniper.

'Oh, you'll love it,' said Christine. 'It is like a tall camembert, served from a wooden box. They peel the rind back from the top, and scoop the cheese out with a spoon. It is so runny and creamy, absolutely delicious.'

After they had enjoyed their cheese, the traditional Bûche de Noël was brought out, and served with champagne.

'I don't think I can eat another thing,' said Julie, seriously.

'Are you OK, Ju?' asked Roger quietly.

She squeezed his hand as Jed said, 'Now, I think it's time for gifts. Have you all been good this year?' They all laughed, as Jed reached into the centre of the table. Seven small, beautifully wrapped presents, nestled among the holly and lights. The ladies received a small bottle of Chanel No5, and the men a bottle of Vetiver cologne.

'How lovely,' said Christine. 'Did you organise these, Jed?'

'You can thank Father Christmas,' he winked at her. Wafts of jasmine, rose and vanilla were released from the bottles, as Juniper and Christine splashed a little of the perfume on their wrists.

'This is heavenly,' said Juniper. 'Thank you, Jed.'

'On that note, shall we have that nightcap on the boat, Viddy?' said Roger. Julie looked pale, it was time to go.

'Yes, why not,' said Viddy. The three young people got up from the table to say their goodbyes. 'That was an absolute feast. Thank you so much, Jed,' said Viddy.

'It was,' said Julie. 'I don't think I'll be able to eat another thing for at least week.' They all hugged and wished each other a happy Christmas, before leaving the two older couples at the table.

As the men chatted, Christine leaned towards Juniper smiling. She glanced at Juniper's yellow diamond, and said quietly, 'I see you and Jed are engaged, congratulations! That makes two of us!'

She put her hand over the top of Juniper's to show her beautiful sapphire ring, surrounded by tiny diamonds.

'Congratulations!' said Juniper. 'I can't believe it!' The ladies stood to embrace one another.

'What's all this about?' said Jed.

Juniper turned to him and said, 'Christine and Alain are engaged as well, Jed. Isn't that marvellous news?'

'It certainly is,' said Jed, turning to shake Alain's hand. 'Congratulations to you both!' They raised their glasses once more, in a final toast, then sighed contentedly, comfortable in each other's company.

'What a lovely evening,' said Juniper. 'I think I would like to get some air, before we turn in.'

'Shall we all go out for a stroll?' suggested Alain.

'I'd love to,' said Christine. A few minutes later, wrapped in their coats, they stepped out onto the square, and walked towards the church. It was all lit up, and the Christmas Eve service was about to begin.

'Shall we go in?' asked Jed.

'Yes, let's,' said Christine.

As they walked towards the open door, Jed said, 'Apparently, this is the largest and oldest wooden church in the whole of France. It was built in the fifteenth century, by boat builders. If you look up, once we are inside, you'll see evidence of their skills, over our heads,' Jed finished quietly, as they slipped into a pew, towards the front.

Juniper's eyes were shining with the sheer joy of finding herself here, among friends, on Christmas Eve. How much her life had changed for the better this year, she reflected. She was truly blessed.

THE NARROW BOAT

As they made their way onto the stern of the narrow boat, Julie excused herself as soon as they were on board. 'I hope you boys won't mind if I head straight to bed. I'll leave you to set the world to rights.'

Roger squeezed her hand and kissed her lightly on the mouth, 'See you later,' he whispered. Roger poured a couple of tumblers of whisky, and put one in front of Viddy. 'So, welcome on board,' he said, raising his glass.

'Thank you,' said Viddy, taking a large gulp. He felt its warmth spreading through him, relaxing him. He was always a little awkward with new people, until he got to know them; but Roger didn't seem to notice.

'Our mothers get on well – they seem to have a lot in common, don't they?' Roger said.

'They have,' said Viddy. 'They're both pretty old school. Alain's not so bad, and Jed seems nice too.'

'This is the first time I've met him,' said Roger. 'I like him. It's a relief to see Mum happy at last. She and I haven't got on all that well over the last few years. It's a shame, I've hardly seen her.'

'Why not?' asked Viddy.

'Oh, it's a long story,' said Roger. 'There are things that happened, in the past I mean, that we've never really got over. I've made up my mind that next year will be different. I want Mum to be part of our lives.'

'Parents eh,' said Viddy. 'Can't live with them, and can't live without them.'

'I wouldn't go that far,' said Roger laughing. 'Top up?'

'Sure, why not?' said Viddy. Unguarded and tired, Viddy found himself saying more to Roger than he intended. 'I'm in a bit of a predicament,' he said. 'I seem to have backed myself into a corner, with nowhere to go.'

'What do you mean?' said Roger.

'It's complicated,' said Viddy. 'I'm heir to our family Château. I wasn't supposed to be, but that's another story. The trouble is, I love someone I'm not supposed to love, and without him, I don't think I can do it.'

'What's stopping you being together?' said Roger, swallowing another mouthful of whisky.

'Nobody is actually stopping me,' said Viddy. 'I've tried to be honest with Maman, about me and Jonny I mean, but she just pretends she hasn't understood me.' Roger thought of how formal and unbending his own mother had been, for most of his life, and he was full of sympathy.

'I think our mothers are from a generation where things were done differently,' said Roger. 'There was no room for anyone living an alternative lifestyle. At least there was, as long as everyone turned a blind eye. Where does Jonny live?' asked Roger.

'He lives in England,' said Viddy. 'We met in April, and then he came to France with me for the summer.' He sighed. 'I made such a mess of things. He's in Florida now, with friends.'

'In Florida?' said Roger. 'How funny, Ju and I are going over there in a few days, to my sister's New Year party.'

'Really?' said Viddy, remembering the party invitation he'd thrown away. 'What's your sister's name?'

'Lydia,' said Roger. 'Why?'

'I can't believe it,' said Viddy, amazed. 'I know Lydia! It was through her, that Jonny and I met!'

'That is a coincidence,' said Roger. 'Are you going to the party?'

'I wasn't planning to. I got an invitation, but it arrived on a particularly bad day. I'd just had an upsetting conversation with Maman, and I think I threw it away.'

'For God's sake man,' said Roger, standing up and slapping Viddy on his arm. 'This is your chance to put things right! Who cares what anybody else thinks. You need to come to the party, and make things right with Jonny! We could all travel out together.' Viddy's eyes lit up with hope. Maybe he could do this, after all. Then he remembered the way he and Jonny had parted, and his face fell.

'I think it might be too late for that,' said Viddy, crestfallen. 'Maman will never accept Jonny and me as a couple. If I want to be with Jonny, I must give up the Château, then what will become of it, and of me?' Viddy took another sip of his whisky. 'We were so happy in England; being with Jonny felt so uncomplicated.

'When I came home to France, everything changed. It was as if the Château was pulling me to her, from the very roots of my being – calling me to take my place in history. So although I thought I could turn my back on it, I know now, that I can't.'

'Nothing is without some form of complication,' said Roger. 'Isn't Jonny worth fighting for?'

'I've tried to fight, I really have. I'm just so weary of it. As far as I'm concerned, true love should be unconditional. If it was, Maman would accept me as I am, and give us her blessing, but she can't find it in her heart to do that.'

'I thought she seemed nice,' said Roger. 'Have you told her how you feel, in the way you have just told me?'

'I've told her in every way I can think of, but it falls on deaf ears. I am torn between love for my family heritage, and my love for Jonny. The trouble is, I want both, and that's something I can never have.' Viddy sighed.

Roger looked down into his whisky, tired now, trying to summon some words of comfort. Then Viddy said more quietly, 'The only place I have found unconditional love is with God. If I go into the church, I will be accepted and loved as I am. I will take my place at the Château, as I must, and it will have to be enough.'

'I admire your sense of duty,' said Roger. 'I don't think I could put duty before love. In my book, love is always worth fighting for.' Viddy didn't want to hear this. He was so tired of being pulled this way and that, bobbing about on the whims and opinions of others.

'Look, Roger, you've been so kind and I've already said more than I should have. I need to get to bed and leave you in peace.' Roger, remembering Julie alone in their bed, said nothing to dissuade him. 'Thanks for showing me the boat,' said Viddy, getting up to leave, 'and for the whisky,' he grinned.

Viddy raised his hand in a wave, as he walked back along the quayside. It was still lit up and festive, teeming with revellers. Some were still dining under the stars, and others were making their way home, laughing and chatting.

As Viddy walked slowly across the square, he heard singing coming from the Église St Catherine. He slipped inside and found a seat in the corner, at the back. The church was bathed in warm candle light, full of people celebrating the dawn of a new Christmas Day. The sound of carols rose up around him, swelling into the rafters of the lovely, wooden church. The ceilings look like the inside of two upturned boats, thought Viddy, fleetingly, as he gazed upwards. When he joined in the singing, a feeling of peace overcame him, as it always did when he was communing with God. On this special night, he knew that whatever the future held, he would meet it with love, grace and acceptance. God would guide him, as he always had.

The next morning, on his way out for a walk to clear his head, Viddy saw his mother wrapped in an elegant coat, enjoying coffee in the morning sunshine. 'Maman,' he said, walking towards her. 'Happy Christmas.' She stood up and held her arms out to him, and Viddy pulled her into an embrace. They held each other for a long time, a sense of love for one another, swelling their hearts.

'Happy Christmas darling,' said Christine smiling at him. 'Did you have a nice evening after you left?'

'I went to have a drink with Roger, on their narrow boat. He's really nice.' Viddy paused, and then asked her, 'Do you remember Lydia, the girl from the fashion show?'

'Yes, I do,' she said.

'It turns out she's Roger's sister,' said Viddy. 'He told me she's moved to Florida.'

'How lovely,' said Christine. 'I thought Lydia lived in England.'

'She did, up until a few months ago. Her grandmother died and left her everything, including her Florida home. By the sound of it, Lydia may be living there for the foreseeable future.'

Christine looked wistful, 'I would love to have travelled to the United States,' she said, 'but I never had the chance. My duty and family have always been here, in France.'

'I know Maman,' said Daveed. He looked at her sympathetically before saying, 'Have you decided when we'll be travelling home?'

'You're not in a hurry are you, Daveed? We are planning to stay on for another couple of days. In fact, I was thinking of inviting Juniper and Jed to come back to the Château with us, to celebrate

New Year.'

'I'm not in a hurry, but I do need to see the Curé again. I need a focus, Maman. Perhaps if I take the train back to the Château, there will be more room for you all in the car.'

'Darling, I thought you'd put this idea of the church behind you. What about the Château?'

'The Château doesn't need two of us Maman. You seem very comfortable remaining in control, and at the moment, I have no wish to be – not on my own, anyway.'

'Are you saying you want us to do this together?'

'Of course I'm not, Maman. I want to do it with someone I love, by my side. You have Alain; I will have God, whose love, unlike yours, is unconditional.' Christine sighed.

'Don't let's part on bad terms Daveed, please.'

'Maman, you need to let me be. I need to find a life for myself, a life that will make me happy. Château de Courcy means everything to me. I have no option but to do my best to take it forward into the future. You have made it clear to me, that to do that, I must forsake the man I love. It has all become so complicated; I am so tired of fighting.' He hung his head, exhausted, then said more quietly, 'I've decided to end it with Jonny and have further talks with the Curé about joining the church. I feel it is the only path open to me.'

'Oh Daveed, I can't bear this distance between us. I've tried, I really have.'

'Don't make this about you, Maman. This is my life, and only I can decide what is best for me.' As Daveed walked away from her towards the quayside, heart pounding, he silently cried out with grief, for Jonny. He sat down on the harbour wall and put his face in his hands in despair, screaming into them, in frustration. He was incongruous among the happy crowds, and heads turned towards him as people strolled by, giving him a wide berth on this glorious Christmas Day.

The words he had just spoken to his mother rang in his head, over and over again, relentlessly; until finally, he began to listen to them. He took some deep breaths, and then repeated the words to himself, slowly and deliberately, and with dawning clarity. 'This is my life, and only I can decide what is best for me.'

Viddy got up from the harbour wall, he needed some breakfast. He chose a table at a nearby café, and sat outside in the sunshine. He ordered a large café crème, a pain au chocolat and a croissant with some jam. By the time he got back to the hotel, there was no sign of his mother or the others. They had probably gone out for a walk.

Viddy went up to his room, to shower and change, then wrote a note to his mother. He pushed his belongings into his rucksack, left the note and his key at reception, and left.

WINDSONG

At Windsong, preparations were underway for Roger and Julie's arrival. Alberta had prepared the extra guest room, and was making some of the food in advance of New Year's Eve. 'I don't want you to have any trouble when your friends are here, Mizz Lydia. I'm makin' you some real good food. It's gonna be all ready for you to heat and serve. Nice and easy,' she finished.

'Jonny, why don't we go out and get some fireworks for the party?' said James. They were all lounging on the deck in sun chairs, reading and dozing.

'Why not,' he said. 'Do you want to go now?'

'Sure,' said James. 'It's off the island, so it could take us a while.'

'Come back and have lunch with us afterwards, James,' said Lydia. 'Alberta's making us some fried chicken and salad.'

'Sounds great,' said James.

Ten minutes later they were on the road in the yellow van. James was easy company. It had really lifted Jonny's spirits being around him and the others, over the last few weeks. He'd made up his mind to go back to France after New Year. He wanted to speak to Viddy in person; but for now he was going to relax and enjoy the rest of his time in the warm weather.

He told James about his plan on the way to the fireworks shop. 'I think it's a great idea,' said James. 'It's far better to talk to him face to face, than try and resolve it on the phone.'

'I'll fly to Paris and take the train out to the Loire Valley, instead of going back to London,' said Jonny. 'I want to surprise him; tell him I've been a fool.' He paused. 'I've got a lot of explaining and apologising to do. Not only have I misjudged Viddy, but, like an idiot, I spoke my mind to his mother, The Vicomtesse de Courcy, when she'd just offered me my dream job.'

'Oh,' said James. 'That's not good. Do you think they'll take you back into the fold?'

No idea,' he said. 'If it doesn't work out, I suppose I'll have to move on. At the moment, I don't want to think about that possibility. I have never felt more sure of anything in my life. I want to give this my best shot.'

They returned in time for lunch, the van filled with boxes of fireworks and crates of beer. They'd bought plenty of wine, some champagne for New Year, along with whisky, elderflower, lime and sodas.

'You are stars,' said Lydia, as they carried it all inside. 'Thank you. Your reward is lunch out on the deck, ready when you are.'

Over plates of Alberta's fried chicken and salad, they discussed the plans for the rest of the day. 'What time are they due to arrive?' asked Jonny.

'They land at 3 p.m.,' said Lydia. I've arranged for a car to pick them up, so they should be back here around four.'

'Berry and I are planning to make ourselves scarce this afternoon, so that you get some uninterrupted time with your brother and,' Jonny paused, 'Is it Julie?'

'Yes,' said Lydia. 'OK, that's thoughtful, thank you. James will be here when they arrive, to give me some moral support, won't you?' she asked him.

'Of course I will,' he said.

'You haven't actually fallen out with your brother, have you?' asked Berry.

'No,' said Lydia. 'Nothing like that. Roger just lives his own life. He's in his own world half the time. I haven't spoken to him for ages, and I hardly know Julie.'

'In that case, it's time you did,' said James. 'I'm glad you've invited them.'

'I honestly didn't think they'd come. Several people didn't even reply,' said Lydia. 'Or if they did, their replies were lost in the Christmas mail.'

'Who didn't reply?' asked Berry.

'Anya, my sewing teacher, Viddy, Jane, my therapist.' Her voice trailed off, and James put his arm round her.

'All the more for us,' he said, but Lydia continued.

'I suppose I wanted Anya and Jane to see that I'm starting to turn my life around,' she said. 'They've both been such a support to me this year.'

Jonny had gone quiet; it hadn't occurred to him that Lydia might have sent Viddy an invitation, but why wouldn't she? After all, she knew Viddy before he did. It was hard to realise that now, with so much history between them.

After lunch, Jonny and Berry borrowed the yellow van. With instructions from James, they made their way over to the far end of Sanibel Island, to see the old lighthouse and have a swim. It took them longer than they expected to get there, but eventually, they pulled into a sandy car park, in the shade of a mangrove tree. The ground was firm, made up of compacted sand, and patches of sea grass. They walked to the beach via the boardwalk through the mangroves. It was beautifully cool, shady and mysterious.

Unusual bird calls echoed around them, and suddenly, Berry saw a flash of red and stopped. 'Look Jonny,' she whispered, 'I think it's a red cardinal.' They stood still, and looked up into the trees. 'There it is,' said Berry, 'up there.' Jonny saw a beautiful, bright red bird, about the size of a blackbird. It had a tall scarlet crest on its head, and a short wide beak.

'It's beautiful,' Jonny whispered back, mesmerised.

'It's the first one I've ever seen,' Berry whispered. 'Listen, their song is so distinctive.'

A melodious, 'tweet tweet, chew chew chew chew', echoed around them and filled the air; 'tweet tweet, chew chew chew chew'. Jonny looked at his sister; her eyes were shining.

'I studied them once, for a painting,' she said. 'They are said to represent the people we love, and happy times; especially in winter when it can sometimes feel so bleak.' Jonny's heart surged with love for his sister. He'd never paid her much attention, and yet here she was comforting him with unexpectedly wise words. He'd been so self-absorbed over the past year, while she had become a thoughtful young woman.

'Thanks, Sis,' he said. 'I needed to hear that today.' He put his arm across her shoulders and they walked on, in companionable silence. As they continued on the sandy path to the beach, they became aware of the cardinal's song all around them. Every now and again, they caught flashes of red, high up in the trees.

Berry looked at Jonny and grinned, 'Now we know it's their song that gives them away, don't we?' She looked at Jonny, then took hold of his hand and said gently, 'I hope things work out with you and Viddy, I really do.'

The old iron lighthouse stood in a sandy clearing, among the trees. Its tall central pillar was supported by triangular, iron legs and a scaffold of metal struts, holding it all together. Just in front of it, at the edge of the beach, two white boarded houses stood on stilts. 'Isn't this lovely,' said Berry.

'Imagine living here,' said Jonny, 'Right on the beach.'

'Come on,' said Berry. 'Let's put our things down in the shade of these trees, and go for a swim.' They raced over the white, powdery sand towards a pale, turquoise sea. Shells lined the shore, glistening with sea water.

'I feel so lucky to be here,' said Jonny, standing in the sea, looking out towards the horizon. He took some long deep breaths, enjoying the moment. Then he pointed out to sea and said, 'Look Berry, I think those are dolphins.'

Berry saw them too, not too far out, so she walked into the water up to her waist. She opened her hands out flat, running them quickly over the surface of the water, creating lingering, light splashes to attract their attention. 'What are you doing?' asked Jonny, curious.

'Dolphins are very sociable creatures,' said Berry. 'If they see us, they might come closer.' Then she said, 'Look Jonny, they're coming towards me!'

Sure enough, three dolphins came within fifteen feet of them, giving a clear view of their slick, grey skin. The dolphins shone as their curved backs rose and fell, smoothly through the water, snouts appearing intermittently, as they swam parallel with the shore. 'I can hardly believe it!' said Berry. 'First the cardinals, and now these.' Her face was full of joy.

Later, as they lay on the beach, the sea took on a vast patina of silver, as the sun slowly began to move towards the horizon. 'I suppose we'd better make our way back,' said Jonny, reluctantly.

An hour later, they pulled up outside Windsong. Crickets were chirping in the trees and lights lit the front of the house. 'I feel so much better after doing that, thanks for a lovely afternoon,' said Jonny.

Lydia greeted them at the door, and as they stepped inside,

lively conversation drifted into the hall.

'What kinds of things do you sculpt, Julie?' asked James.

'Many different things, always for the garden. I've made small, Hepworth style seats, with oval holes through the middle, for example.'

'Why don't you come and see my studio, you'd be welcome to share it while you're here?' Julie looked across at Roger, delighted.

'I'd love to,' she said. They all looked round as Lydia led Jonny and Berry into the room, to introduce them. 'Jonny, Berry, this is my brother, Roger,' said Lydia, 'and his partner, Julie. You two, these are my friends Jonny, and his sister, Berry.'

'Hi,' said Jonny. 'Good to meet you both. How was your trip?'

'Long,' said Julie, smiling. 'I'm already overcome with jetlag and the need for an early night.' Berry went to sit down on the sofa next to her, smiling.

'I remember the feeling,' she said. 'You'll be fine in a couple of days.'

'Good to know,' said Julie.

'Jonny,' said Lydia. 'Come with me, I've got a surprise for you.' They all exchanged conspiratorial glances, and Berry was mystified. 'This way,' said Lydia, leading Jonny outside onto the deck. The palm trees, wrapped with fairy lights twinkled, throwing soft light over the table and chairs. The beach beyond, was in darkness. 'See you in a while,' she said. Then she turned to go back inside, leaving a mystified Jonny alone on the deck.

Jonny stepped out onto the beach, into the darkness. There was no sound but for the gentle ssschhhhh of the waves on the shore and the strange sigh of the breeze through the palms. It was almost like a song, he thought; a deep and visceral sigh of love and longing. Jonny was lost in thoughts of Viddy, when he suddenly became aware that he was not alone. He slowly turned, and there he was.

'Viddy!' he said, rushing towards his friend. 'Viddy, you're here!' He flung his arms around him and pulled him close, holding him as if he never wanted to let him go. Viddy wrapped his arms tightly around Jonny's back, his head resting in the side of his neck.

'Oh Jonny,' said Viddy, quietly. 'I wasn't sure you'd still be here.' His heart was ready to burst with happiness. They looked at each other for a long moment, eyes locked together, full of love and mutual joy.

'I was planning to come and find you,' said Jonny. 'I didn't want to be without you. I'm so sorry, Viddy.' They knelt down in the sand and their lips met in a long, slow kiss.

'There's so much we need to talk about,' said Viddy, gently pulling away from him and sitting down in the sand. 'My decision to come out to Captiva with Roger and Julie was impulsive, we met in Honfleur.'

'What were you all doing there?' asked Jonny.

'My mother and Alain were spending Christmas there with Roger and Lydia's mother. I couldn't believe it when I realised Lydia and Roger were siblings.' He paused, and then said more seriously, 'Jonny, I've come so close to giving up on us. Our relationship is fraught with problems, which at times have felt insurmountable. The final straw came yesterday, after another one-sided conversation with Maman.'

'What happened?' asked Jonny.

'Oh, it was the usual,' he said. 'Except that this time I told her I had no more fight left in me. I told her I was going to give you up and go into the church.'

'That's what I've been afraid of,' said Jonny, his face serious.

'It certainly took the wind out of her sails,' said Viddy. 'I would like to think she felt some sort of responsibility for my decision, but knowing Maman, I think it's unlikely.'

'I'm so sorry, Viddy,' said Jonny. They both sat in silence for a minute, the waves on the shore and the ringing of the crickets, the only sounds in the still of the evening.

'I've been so weak,' said Viddy.

'What do you mean?' said Jonny.

'The answer was within me all along. I have no idea why it has taken me as long as it has, to see it.' Jonny's attention was fully focused on his friend, as he continued. 'You see, the strangest thing happened as I walked away from Maman.' He paused. 'In my anger, I finally said something to her that I should have said months ago. It was only later, that I understood the clarity of my own words.'

'Viddy, you are speaking in riddles,' said Jonny. 'What did you say to her?'

Viddy continued, 'As I walked away from Maman, my parting words to her kept ringing in my head, over and over again. Finally, as I sat alone on the harbour wall at Honfleur, overcome with grief at the reality of losing you, I felt myself become calm.' He looked at Jonny. 'It was only then, in my stillness, that I finally began to listen and understand.'

Slowly and deliberately, Viddy said, 'This is my life, and only I can decide what is best for me.' He looked at Jonny for a long moment. 'So, you see, in spite of all the obstacles in our path, I want to make this work; if you can forgive me.'

'Forgive you?' said Jonny. 'There is nothing to forgive.' They sat on the beach together for a long time, talking quietly. Eventually, they walked back onto the deck, slid the glass doors back and stepped inside to join the others, hands held tightly, faces radiant with happiness.

THE MUCKY DUCK

'So, are you still at art college?' Roger asked Berry the next day. They were all at a pub on the beach, near Windsong.

'I'm in my final year,' she said. 'I want to be a portrait painter. Finishing the course is just a formality, really.'

'I might be able to help you get started,' said Roger. 'I already have many clients who ask me for portraits, but it isn't an area that interests me.'

'Do you mean in Paris?' asked Berry, hardly able to believe her luck.

'In Paris and London,' he said.

'Wow,' said Berry. 'How long have you been painting?' she asked.

'Most of my life,' said Roger. 'It all started during a summer holiday in Cornwall. A school-friend invited me to spend the holidays with him and his family. His mother was an artist. It was Caro who recognised and nurtured my talent. I would almost go as far as to say, that discovering art saved me.'

'Saved you from what?' asked Berry.

'From nonentity I suppose. You see, I was a very under-confident child. Up until then, I had no idea how to express the frustration I felt. It was all bottled up. Art gave me an outlet. I discovered freedom of expression and a pathway to my true self.'

'Lydia said you had an exhibition in Paris. That must have been amazing, what an incredible achievement.' Roger smiled at Berry.

'Well,' he said, 'When you paint under the name of Jacques d'iX, it does tend to open doors.' he said.

'What?' said Berry, incredulous. 'You are Jacques d'iX?'

'That's me,' said Roger.

'Oh my gosh,' said Berry. 'We've studied your work at college! I can't believe I've actually met you. Are you seriously offering to help me get started?' she asked.

'When the time is right,' said Roger. 'You'll want to finish your course first, I expect. Can you show me some of your work?' he asked. Roger's thoughts drifted off, reflecting on his own college days. It felt like yesterday. Those long afternoons, lazing on the river bank, wondering whether he had a chance with Julie. They were carefree days, he realised, quite suddenly.

'I've got a few photos, of my work,' said Berry, bringing him out of his reverie. 'I'll find them for you later.' Berry was overwhelmed. She couldn't wait to tell Jonny, they were in the company of greatness. Knowing Jonny, she thought, he would neither care, nor likely know, of Jacques d'iX's work. She sighed.

They were sitting at a wooden table, on the edge of a wide, sandy beach. The Mucky Duck, James explained, was almost an institution on Captiva, and very much the place to be, especially around Christmas time. A large, decorated Christmas tree stood in the sand, incongruous in the hot sunshine, but with a special atmosphere all of its own. One couple after another stood beside it, to have their picture taken, against a backdrop of turquoise sea.

The wafting strains of a live band drifted around them, as they relaxed in the sunshine. Julie and Viddy reclined in laid back wooden chairs on the sand, and Jonny lay at the water's edge, stretched out in the shallow water. James appeared at the table, carrying a tray of drinks for them all, and Lydia held a pile of menus. 'OK,' said Lydia, 'Here's the menu. There's quite a wait, so they've advised getting our order in soon.'

'Jonny, what do you want to eat?' called Viddy. Jonny got up and came over to the table.

'Steak if they have it,' he said. 'Medium rare with salad and fries. Thanks, guys.' He picked up a beer, and took it back to the water's edge.

'I'll have scampi, if they've got it,' said Viddy, 'thanks Lydia.' He winked at her, and then followed Jonny. 'Isn't this just perfect,' said Viddy, sitting down beside him.

'It is now you're here' said Jonny, smiling. 'Mind you, it was pretty perfect before,' he said grinning. 'You're just the icing on the cake!' They laughed, and then sat in companionable silence, watching the waves rising and falling around their legs.

'Jonny, I know you're worried about how things will be at the

Château for us,' said Viddy. 'But I'm determined to make it work. Alain spoke to me before Christmas. Apparently, he's trying to get Maman to back off and let me live my own life. He wants her all to himself, and that suits me fine.'

'Are they officially an item then?' asked Jonny.

'More than that, they're engaged,' said Viddy.

'That's great news,' said Jonny. 'I think it will make things easier, actually.'

After relaxing by the beach for several hours, the sun was low in the sky and they felt the need to move and walk off their lunch. 'There are some lovely little boutiques and galleries near here. Shall we go for a stroll?' asked Lydia.

By the time they gathered their belongings and set off along the lane, old fashioned street lamps were casting their glow over the ground. There was a festive atmosphere and the little boutiques thronged with people. White boarded buildings stood in jaunty rows, illuminated with fairy lights. Colourful canvases and pottery filled the windows, and these overflowed onto tables outside, where boutique owners sat with friends, enjoying festive drinks.

They ambled along the lane, the girls stopping now and again to look through rails of colourful clothes and admire unusual, hand-made jewellery. After a while, the boys left them to it and walked over to inspect a pair of Harley Davidson motorbikes, parked under some trees. 'They are cool!' said James.

'Have you ridden one?' asked Jonny.

'I wish,' he said. 'No, I haven't.'

'I have,' said Viddy. 'My brother had one. I think it's still in one of the garages,' he said. He was quiet after that, lost in his own reminiscences. After browsing a gallery of sculptures and paintings next door, the boys emerged into the warm evening air just as the girls came out of the boutique, carrying their purchases.

'I'm exhausted,' said Julie, smiling. 'I can't remember the last time I went shopping.'

'I don't have that problem,' said Berry, laughing. 'I can browse and shop for hours.'

'Come on, let's get back,' said James. 'I'm ready to put my feet up with a cold drink.'

Back at Windsong, Lydia brought out a jug of lime cordial and some glasses. 'This is such a beautiful place, Lydia,' said Viddy. 'I had no idea life had taken such an amazing turn for you.'

'I could say the same to you,' said Lydia, grinning. 'Friends, meet the honourable Viscount de Courcy, heir to a château in the Loire Valley.' Berry did a double take, suddenly seeing her brother's skinny friend with new eyes.

'Viddy, I had no idea,' said Berry, standing up and taking a solemn bow. They all laughed then. 'Jonny, you could have told me,' she said.

'Why?' said Jonny. 'I didn't think it was important,' he grinned at Viddy.

'So what you're saying,' said Berry, 'is that I'm about to spend New Year's Eve with the famous Jacques d'iX and a Viscount? Happy days,' she said. 'Shame you're both spoken for,' she laughed; but inwardly, she had to admit, she was more than a little bit jealous.

'On that note,' said James, doffing an imaginary cap, 'be it ever so humble, if anyone would like to visit my studio tomorrow, I'm heading over there at eleven.'

'Great,' said Julie, 'I'd love to.'

'Well, anyone else who wants to come, see you by the yellow peril at 11 a.m. sharp.'

After devouring large slices of take-out pizza, they were flagging. Lydia pulled herself up from the sofa and said, 'New Year's Eve tomorrow, I'm heading upstairs for an early night.' After the discussion about the studio, she couldn't stop thinking of James' hands, covered in clay, roaming over her body.

She took hold of James' hand, 'Looks like I'm heading to bed too,' he said, laughing. 'See you tomorrow.' They climbed the staircase at the far end of the room, and Lydia's door clicked closed behind them.

'Me too,' said Julie. 'Who would believe that lazing on a beach, doing nothing but eat and drink all day, could take so much out of you?'

NEW YEAR'S EVE

The next morning, Jonny pulled Viddy into his arms, 'Don't go to the studio,' he said. 'Let's stay behind.' When they eventually heard the van driving away, the house was quiet.

'Sounds like it's just us,' said Viddy, smiling. 'Do you think they've all gone?'

'I do,' said Jonny. 'I think Berry's got stars in her eyes. She's probably too young to be mixing with such a decadent and unscrupulous lot as us.'

'Who cares,' said Viddy. 'She'll be fine. She's got to grow up some time.' Little did either of them know just how soon that would be.

'For now,' said Jonny, 'I'm focusing entirely on you. I think we've got some catching up to do.'

Much later, they stood in the shower, soaping each other, rinsing and kissing, until finally Viddy got out. 'I've got no idea what I'm going to put on today. My entire holiday wardrobe is in that rucksack,' he said, grinning at Jonny.

Once he was dry, Viddy tipped the contents of his bag onto their bed, and pulled out a pair of clean boxer shorts. He hung up his dinner suit and only shirt, and then looked to see what was left. There were a couple of t-shirts and the swim shorts he'd bought at the airport and that was it. He was about to toss the bag aside, when he noticed an envelope tucked into the inside pocket. 'Mon Dieu!' said Viddy, pulling it out, and looking at the front.

'What is it?' said Jonny, coming out of the bathroom, with a towel round his waist. Viddy held up an envelope.

'It's a letter, from Maman,' he said, looking at Jonny. Viddy sat down on the edge of the bed and tore it open and then began to read it aloud.

Honfleur, 25ᵗʰ December 1986

Dear Daveed,

Happy Christmas, my darling. I pray that this New Year will herald a new beginning for us all.

I have a feeling you may decide to go back to the Château ahead of us, and so I wanted to make sure you have this letter. Daveed, it is what I should have said to you this morning.

Alain has made me see that things will move on in the world, with or without our blessing. We must adapt, or lose the people we love. I never want to lose you my darling boy; you are, and have always been, so very precious to me. I am only sorry my sense of duty has blinded me, to this most important of truths.

I'm so sorry we parted on bad terms this morning, on Christmas Day of all days. I wish I could have told you what you wanted to hear, but I was not prepared. I must admit, our conversation took me by surprise.

You have a beautiful heart, Daveed, and it has such a great capacity for love. I only have to think of all the birds and small animals you rescued as a boy, and the way you comforted me when I was sad, without even knowing you were doing it. There has always been a light within you darling, and that light must never be extinguished.

When you told me you wanted to go into the church, I was not altogether surprised. I know that God has, and always will, play an important role in your life; but please, Daveed, don't let it be at the expense of spending your life with someone you love.

You see, God will be with you always, through everything you choose to do. If being in the church is what you truly want, then I will support you with all my heart. What I fear, is that you are using it as an escape. Taking refuge there, to hide from the pain I have caused you. Can you ever forgive me, Daveed?

I'm sure you will be surprised to receive this letter, but it is important, because what I have to say concerns your future. I am addressing this to Jonathan as well, Daveed, because it also concerns him.

Jonny and Viddy looked at each other, apprehensive and yet hopeful, as Viddy continued reading.

I want you to know, Jonathan, that Alain and I are engaged to be married. Alain has finally made me see, that the time has come for me to step aside. He has asked me to live at Le Manoir with him, as we make our plans for a summer wedding.

It is time for new blood and new ideas at the Château de Courcy, and what better time than at the start of a New Year? Jonathan, you have proved yourself more than capable of helping Daveed take the Château forward, into a modern world. A world which – I acknowledge – has rather left me behind.

It is clear to me that my son loves you, Jonathan, and his happiness means everything to me. The two of you making a future together, is not a reality I could have contemplated, even a few weeks ago. You see, I convinced myself it was just a passing phase. I see now, that my failure to support you has cost you months of unhappiness. I hope you can find it in your hearts to forgive me.

So, I am writing to say this. If you both want to make a life together at the Château, I will not stand in your way. Alain and I have our own lives to lead now, and we give you our whole-hearted blessing. Le Manoir is not far away, and we will always be there with help and advice, if ever you need it; you only have to ask.

Happy New Year Jonathan and Daveed. The future of Château de Courcy is in your hands. I pass it on to you, Daveed, to share with the person you love.

I will be moving all my things from the Château, over to the Manoir, as soon as the New Year celebrations are behind us. I want to leave the way clear for you, Daveed. As you so rightly said, darling, this is your life, and you must live it, as you choose.

We look forward to seeing you back in France just as soon as you want to come. Dinner at Le Manoir awaits!

All my love
Maman/Christine xx

Viddy put the letter down on the bed and threw his arms around Jonny, with tears in his eyes. 'I'm so thankful,' he said.

On Sanibel Island, James unlocked the door to his studio, and went in, followed by Lydia and Julie. 'I'm surprised Berry didn't come,' said Lydia. 'I thought seeing the studio would be right up her street.'

'She's still fast asleep, I expect,' said Julie.

The smell of plaster and clay was strong, and Lydia was flooded with thoughts of James. She had spent so many afternoons here, posing for him while he made the sculpture of her. The smell alone was enough to transport her to the unexpected bliss of being loved, and so very much wanted, by James. As she lay there in his intense gaze, as he worked, he seemed to see into the very depths of her soul.

'Wow,' said Julie. 'This is incredible!' She walked towards a voluptuous, life-sized woman, made of clay. She was lying on her side, naked, eyes half-closed, languid and smiling. 'Lydia!' said Julie, suddenly recognising her. 'This is gorgeous.' Lydia's face flushed, as she smiled; shy, but delighted to be recognised. 'You are so talented, James,' said Julie.

At Windsong, Roger lay in their bed, barely awake. Getting up to go to the studio this morning seemed like too much effort. So, he'd turned over, pulled the sheet over his head, and gone back to sleep. He thought at some point, he'd heard the quiet click of his door, but assumed it was Jonny, in the next room.

A moment later, his bed creaked and he felt warm skin slide against his back. A moist little tongue began to flick over his bare skin, and he heard a purring sound; was he dreaming?

When he turned over, Berry was next to him, flat on her back, small breasts and pert nipples enticingly close. Her silky blonde hair was spread across the pillow, and she looked at him with pale, china blue eyes.

It seemed like forever since he'd had his way with Julie, she hadn't been herself lately. He felt himself growing hard, but he didn't speak, he just looked at the girl in his bed. His conscience held him back for the merest moment, before he leaned over to kiss her. She squirmed like a little cat, before lifting her slender leg to massage his balls. 'I'm your little pussy,' she whispered, clawing at Roger's back with her small nails, and purring. 'Your little pussy wants you,' she whispered.

Roger needed no more persuasion; he moved on top of her and slid into her wet, welcoming tightness. He closed his eyes in bliss. God, how he had missed this. Berry began to make soft, purring sounds, as she lifted her hips to him, a sly, triumphant smile on her face.

That evening, before darkness fell, Roger watched James and Jonny lining up the fireworks, ready for a spectacular finale to 1986. He reflected with growing remorse, on the events of the morning. He glanced up at Julie, but she was engrossed in her book. A vision of Berry, naked in his bed, came unbidden to his mind, and he felt himself growing hard again. Christ, what was wrong with him? It was Julie he loved. He went to get his swimming shorts, and headed down to the sea for a swim.

'Anything I can do to help, Lydia?' asked Julie, as Lydia carried plates through to the deck.

'No need,' she said. 'Alberta has prepared everything. All I have to do is serve it.'

'In that case,' said Julie, 'I'm going up to shower and change, ready for this evening.'

By the time they all gathered on the deck in their finery, there was a large jug of Lydia's cranberry and orange spritzer, as well as wine and beer set out on the wooden bar. The first canapés were in the oven, and Lydia had set out platters of fresh, raw vegetables with bowls of Alberta's blue cheese dip.

'This is amazing,' said Berry, walking towards them from inside the house. She was wearing a low-cut, pale blue jersey dress, decorated with sequins. 'Thank you so much for inviting us all, Lydia. I don't think I'll ever forget this holiday.' She paused to look meaningfully at Roger, but he was in another world. He was sitting on the edge of the deck, looking out to sea, a large tumbler of whisky in his hand. If Berry didn't know better, she'd say he looked sad.

'I think it's the sound of the crickets I'll miss most, when I go home,' said Julie.

'I know,' said Lydia, 'I've become so used to them singing me to sleep at night, along with the waves on the shore and the breeze through the palms.'

James smiled at her, 'You've all made me see my home through new eyes,' he said.

'I'm so glad you're all here,' said Lydia. 'You've made my Christmas and New Year. I finally feel I belong, and I can't tell you how good that feels.' She looked round at her friends with gratitude. Then she looked at Viddy and Jonny.

'What are you two planning in the New Year, or shouldn't I ask?' she said. They laughed, and then looked at each other.

'You tell them,' said Jonny.

'We're going to live in France together, at the Château de Courcy,' said Viddy, beaming.

'Wow,' said Lydia. 'That's amazing news! I'm so happy for you both. Roger, did you hear that? Viddy and Jonny are moving to France in the New Year.' Roger finally came over to join them all.

'Congratulations,' he said, shaking Viddy's hand, and then Jonny's. 'I'm so glad it's worked out for you both.'

'Now you're here,' said Julie, looking lovingly at Roger, 'I've got a little announcement of my own.' They all looked at her, expectantly. Then she smiled shyly, and said, 'I am delighted to tell you all, that I'm pregnant. Roger, you're going to be a father!' There were shrieks of delight, as Lydia rushed forward to hug her.

'That is wonderful news! Congratulations, both of you,' she said, moving on to hug her brother. 'I can't believe I'm going to be an auntie!' Roger looked at Julie with tears in his eyes.

'Why didn't you tell me, Ju?' he said, pulling her to him and holding her close. 'If only I'd known,' he said into her hair.

'I wanted it to be a surprise,' she said. 'I couldn't wait to tell you, but I've been saving it for New Year's Eve.'

Just then, the phone began to ring, and Lydia ran inside to pick it up. 'Mum!' she said. 'Happy New Year to you too! Yes, we're all here. Hold on, I'll put you on speakerphone. Roger, it's Mum,' she said beckoning him over.

The deck was open to the house, when the phone switched over to speaker, and Juniper's voice suddenly filled the room, 'Just a minute darling, Alain is trying to work out how to put you all on speakerphone, at this end.' There were clicks and crackles over the airwaves, as Alain tried different buttons.

'Where are you, Mum?' asked Lydia, as a disparate and slightly out of tune chorus, filled the room. 'Should auld acquaintance be forgot and never brought to mind.'

Junipers voice broke in over the top of it, 'We're at the Manoir darling, with Christine and Alain. Happy New Year to all of you!' The chorus continued, 'for the sake of auld lang syne. For auld lang syne my dear, for auld lang syne.' Then there was a crash, and the singing petered out. 'Hold on, Lydia. Are you alright, Alain?'

Then they heard Jed's voice, 'Come on Alain, let me help you up, old chap.'

'Is everything alright, Mum?' said Lydia. By now, the boys were crying with laughter.

'Don't worry,' said Juniper, the commotion still playing out in the background, 'Alain tripped over one of Christine's shoes, he's fine.'

'It must be after 2 a.m. over there,' said Roger, to the others, doubled over with laughter, 'sounds like they're all half-cut.'

Then they heard Juniper's voice again. 'Christine is asking if Daveed is with you, Lydia? She wants to speak to him.'

'He's here Mum, we all are and you're on speakerphone. First though, I think Julie and Roger have some news for you.'

'Hello Mum,' said Roger, still laughing. 'Mum, Ju and I have news. Guess what? You're going to be a grandma!'

'Oh, how wonderful darling! I'm so thrilled for you both.' Then they heard a slurred chorus of congratulations, coming down the line from France. Then Christine's voice came on, over an increasingly crackly line.

'Daveed, Happy New Year darling! Is Jonathan with you?'

'Yes, he's here Maman. We're so happy, thank you from the bottom of our hearts. We've just read your letter.' Viddy and Jonny's eyes were shining, 'We'll be home to France soon, I promise.'

'Thank you Christine, thank you for everything,' added Jonny, 'and happy New Year!' Then Lydia raised her arms and they all began to sing.

'Should auld acquaintance be forgot and never brought to mind, We'll drink a cup of kindness yet, for the sake of auld lang syne! For auld lang syne my dear, for auld lang syne, we'll drink a cup of kindness yet for the sake of auld lang syne! Happy New Year to you all,' they chorused.

In a flurry of New Year greetings, and promises to be together again soon, they finally put the phone down, and made their way onto the beach for the fireworks. Roger had his arm around Julie and Lydia held James' hand, as they walked slowly over the sand. Viddy and Jonny raced to the water's edge, whooping and laughing, as Berry followed behind, her mind full of the new world opening up before her.

'Gather round,' said James, 'but stay behind the line of palm leaves and shells over there, while I light the fireworks.' A sense of excitement filled the air as they stood together, looking up into the dark sky.

As the darkness suddenly burst into light, sprays of red and gold, showered sparkling plumes and swirls of scintillating colour over their heads. 'Happy New Year!' they chorused, taking turns to kiss one other. The girls kissed the French way, on both cheeks and the couples kissed lingeringly, while the boys exchanged backslaps and handshakes. As the last of the fireworks burst into the sky, seven illuminated faces gazed upwards; all but one, glowing with happiness and the joy of a New Year, full of hope and possibility.

A note from the author

I hope you have enjoyed Windsong as much as I have loved writing it. It has been a pleasure to share some of my favourite places with you. The characters I have created in Parisian Legacy and Windsong, have taken on lives of their own and I am not quite ready to let them go. The Portrait Painter will be the next in this series.

The Portrait Painter

by

Rosalie James

A talented young artist begins to forge a career for herself in London and Paris. Moving in privileged circles, she soon builds an exclusive clientele. It is during one of her sittings, that an unsettling and supernatural gift reveals itself.

The story will take you on a journey of discovery, among people and places that stay with you long after you have finished reading.

For the latest information on this and all other books by Rosalie James, please see www.rosaliejamesauthor.com

* * * * *

If you have enjoyed Windsong, please take a moment to review it on Amazon and/or Goodreads. Reviews make such a difference. Thank you!

For more updates and news, follow my pages on Facebook and Instagram and of course, my website.

www.rosaliejamesauthor.com
https://instagram.com/rosaliejamesauthor?utm_medium=copy_link
https://www.facebook.com/Rosalie-James-Author-110882358036939/

THE LOCATIONS IN WINDSONG

The Château de Courcy is based on the *Château de Chenonceau*, in the Loire Valley in France. For me, it has the intimacy of a home lacking in so many of the larger Châteaux.

I have spent a lot of time in the islands, off the coast of Florida, over many years. I am especially fond of *Sanibel and Captiva Islands*, where I have happy memories of sitting around a Christmas tree by the beach, at the Mucky Duck. Christmas carols at the Chapel by the Sea, and forays into little galleries and boutiques, surrounded by twinkling lights were all especially memorable.

As I write this, Hurricane Ian has recently devastated much of this beautiful area. The Ding Darling Wildlife Refuge is closed and many buildings have been razed to the ground. My thoughts are with everyone affected by this tragedy.

I have a passion for the preservation and enjoyment of the natural world. I find it inspiring and deeply connecting. If you would like to find out more about *Ding Darling Wildlife Refuge* or make a donation, you can do so here: www.dingdarlingsociety.org

Finally, my home in England is on the beautiful Sussex coast. *The Seven Sisters Country Park*, the setting for so many films, is my local beauty spot. I am blessed to live among unspoilt downland, white cliffs and spectacular coastal scenery. It is true that coastal erosion is an ongoing challenge. The cottages on the cliffs are under threat as a result. A charity has been set up to raise funds to shore up the sea defences and protect these iconic cottages and beautiful area. You can find out more, and see the cottages at www.cuckmerehavensos.org

Thank you for being part of this journey. It has been a joy to share some of my favourite places with you, in Windsong.

ACKNOWLEDGEMENTS

I would like to thank *Patricia and Jean-Claude* in whose lovely home in the south of France, I wrote much of this book, while house sitting for them.

Rosemary and Trevor and their dogs, Rico and Ronnie, in the Canary Islands. I was privileged to stay in their home whilst writing the final chapters of this book.

Cory and Debby and their dog, Patches, in Florida. I was fortunate to stay in their beautiful home while editing Windsong.

My sister *Karen* and her husband *Clive* for inviting me aboard their yacht in Greece. I learned enough about sailing on the trip, to write about it in Windsong. Thanks especially to *'Captain Clive'* for technical and practical advice regarding the channel crossing.

Finally, my husband, *Tim*, who has supported and encouraged me throughout my writing journey. He has been a great sounding board, proof reader and chef!

NOTES 1 & 2

1. The idea for the painting in *The Red Dress*, was inspired by a portrait entitled 'Pegeen' by American artist, Robert Henri. It was painted in 1926 and measures 24 x 20 inches. You can see it and find out more information here:

http://www.artnet.com/artists/robert-henri/pegeen-JGQH3cAL53-ca1ELnDSdbg2

2. I would like to thank Tracy Chevalier for her insights into the wall-hanging tapestries, in her book, *The Lady and the Unicorn*. She notes, and I quote, 'The tapestries were woven in c.1500, probably in Flanders. In 1841 they were rediscovered in very poor condition in Boussac. They were purchased and restored in 1882 by the French government for the Musée de Cluny in Paris (now the Musée National du Moyen Âge), where they still hang today.'

Contrary to my story in Windsong, the tapestries were never in possession of any Château in France. Nor has there been an agreement I am aware of, for them to be displayed anywhere other than at the Musée National du Moyen Âge in Paris.

About the Author

Rosalie has been telling stories since childhood, inspired by new places, new ideas and change. Her mother was brought up in India, and later began modelling for Dior. When she married, the family moved to the Bahamas, where Rosalie spent her childhood.

Rosalie raised her own family in Sussex, England and in Normandy, France. She is a regular house sitter in Paris, London and overseas, which inspires her writing. Her stories take readers on a journey that transcends everyday life, yet with themes we can all relate to; tragedy, hope, love, misplaced trust and new beginnings.

Windsong is the sequel to Rosalie's début novel, Parisian Legacy. For further details and the latest information, please visit her website at rosaliejamesauthor.com

Printed in Great Britain
by Amazon

24126781R00158